STRYKER

STRYKER

A NOVEL

CHUCK SCARBOROUGH

MACMILLAN PUBLISHING CO., INC.

NEW YORK

Macmillan Publishing Co., Inc.
866 Third Avenue, New York, N.Y.   10022
Collier Macmillan Canada, Ltd.

Library of Congress Cataloging in Publication Data
Scarborough, Chuck.
    Stryker.
    I. Title.
PZ4.S2847St [PS3569.C32] 813'.5'4   78-17284
ISBN 0-02-606920-2

First Printing 1978

Printed in the United States of America

To Linda and Chad

ACKNOWLEDGMENTS

There are three people who have my special gratitude:

Helen Brann for her enthusiasm and encouragement which helped me launch this book,

Bill Murray for his advice and guidance, and

Bob Levine for his editorial brilliance.

STRYKER

1

Benson Stryker stood in the entrance to the news room and waited for somebody—anybody—to notice him. Nobody did. It was no longer his fate to be immediately noticed and he knew it; but he still liked to play the game. It was one he had played successfully for several years and it had become a habit hard to give up.

After a moment, he forced a smile, took off his raincoat, and, holding it out in front of him, shook it dry. A light drizzle had begun to fall in midafternoon and had caught him on his way uptown. He usually walked to work these days, mainly because it gave him time to think, away from the claustrophobic stillness of his apartment, and he hadn't noticed the weather. Now, with his damp coat over his arm, the smile frozen to his face, he walked briskly through the room, skirting the central command post of cluttered desks, clattering typewriters, and jangling phones, where the six-o'clock news team worked in a buzz of feverish activity. Ben, hoping not to be seen, headed for the small, safe, neutral zone of his corner cubicle.

Mario Bellucci glanced up from the assignment desk and saw him. "Hey, Stryker," he called out, "we got a big one for you tonight."

Still smiling, Ben turned. "Yeah?"

Bellucci grinned at him, but there was no laughter in those dark, deep-set eyes. "Yeah," he said. "The Manhattan borough president is announcing another big porn crackdown in Times Square. That sounds like your kind of story, don't it?"

"Fuck you, Mario," Ben said pleasantly and turned, with murder in his heart, to continue back toward the haven of his desk.

"You *are* here now, among us mere mortals, aren't you?" Bellucci asked. "I mean, we can count on you, can't we?"

"Sure, Mario. You see me, don't you?"

"I see you; I see you," Bellucci echoed, his attention suddenly caught by the blinking lights of his board, the bright red lines of the scanners monitoring the police frequencies. He plugged in to listen. "Maybe this one's for you, Stryker," he said. "Maybe a good warehouse fire or some city councilman caught with his pants down on

Eighth Avenue. Stick around, Mr. Stryker, sir, and you'll learn the news business."

Ben fled. He turned the corner past the filing cabinets, away from the central maelstrom of the news room, went swiftly past the single row of private offices where the stars of local news worked, and came at last to his own cubicle, out of sight, and, he hoped, out of mind. He flung his coat into a corner and slumped into his chair. That bastard Bellucci. Every time Ben walked into the news room he felt like the carrier of some communicable disease, like a leper with a bell around his neck. OK—he could understand that no one liked being around a failure, perhaps because they were all afraid his bad luck would rub off on them. But Bellucci had to stick it to him, for no other reason but that Bellucci was a failure himself, a hack stuck in a hack routine, with a title and a little power and the worst job in the place; stuck there, plugged into his board like a telephone operator, his nerves open to every bit of filth surfacing through the muck of the city's night life. Bellucci couldn't forgive Ben his past glory; he had to rub Ben's face in it.

From the wall above Ben's desk a huge poster of John F. Kennedy, caught in a glowing moment of triumph, beamed down at him. The picture had been shot on the very day Ben had interviewed him in Pass Christian, on that first wild swing through the South when a whole world of possibilities had seemed to be opening up to Kennedy. And to Ben as well. A long time ago, Ben thought. Only a matter of a few years that could have been centuries, for all they meant to him now. And then there was Richard Nixon—Nixon, whose face haunted Ben's nights and left him weak with hatred.

5

"Hi! You all right?"

Ben looked up. Kathy was standing in the entrance to his cubicle, clutching a thick sheaf of copy torn from the UPI, AP, and Reuters wire machines that hammered away rhythmically in a little room behind the assignment desk. "I'm OK."

"You had such a funny expression on your face."

"I'm a little under the weather," Ben said. "Last night—"

Kathy blushed. "Hey, that was nice." She leaned over and gave him a quick kiss. "You bring me luck. I just got a raise."

"Yeah?"

"Big deal. I'm still a full-fledged desk assistant, but now I make a hundred and ten a week. How about that?" She laughed.

"And tomorrow the network," Ben said. "You'd better stay clear of me."

"Don't be silly. How could I manage that?"

"I'm contagious."

"Bull," Kathy said. She reached out to touch him.

"Don't," he said. "I'm a little edgy."

"Sorry—will I see you later?"

"I don't know. I'd better get to work."

"Yeah. So long." She dropped a stack of copy on his desk, grinned, waved, and disappeared down the corridor.

Ben shut his eyes and tried to concentrate on Kathy, tried to remember the look and the feel of her in his arms the night before. She had cried out to him there in the dark, her long-legged, silky body arched in sudden ecstasy beneath him; but he couldn't recollect now what his own feelings had been. Did he even have any feelings about her? He didn't know. He only knew the dull ache of his own frustration and his rage. His self-absorption enveloped him like a mist through which he found himself peering endlessly, never quite able to discern clearly exactly what it was he wanted so desperately to make out.

All around him—outside the private cocoon of his unsought, unwilled isolation—the routine work of the news room continued. Phones rang, Teletype machines and typewriters clacked, footsteps came and went, hurrying past on errands of assimilation and information, while overhead the clocks ate away the seconds and the minutes until air time. Only Ben Stryker sat alone, in silence, waiting.

An hour later, Ben was still sitting at his desk, his fingers drumming idly against the arms of his chair, when Cargill looked in on him. "Ben?"

"Hello, Derrick."

"I'm sorry about that wild goose chase last night." Cargill frowned; he was never comfortable with apologies. "The film you shot was good, but we just couldn't use it. We didn't even need to cover that kind of routine holdup at all."

"It's OK, Derrick. That's what I'm here for, isn't it?"

"Bellucci thought there might be a special angle. You know, that upper Park Avenue neighborhood. But then, well, shit—"

"That's what the nightside reporter eats a lot of, right?" Ben replied. "And I'm the only one you've got. Not the best one, maybe, but the only one."

Cargill smiled, but he looked ill at ease; he never quite knew how to act around Stryker these days. The man was a little edgy, which was only natural, but there was also this intensity about him that made Cargill uncomfortable.

7

"Listen," he said, "I just wanted you to know I don't like my reporters sent off on dumb assignments. It wastes everybody's time. Sometimes Bellucci gets too gung-ho."

"Yeah," Ben said.

"Anyway, I spoke to him about it."

"Good."

"Anything doing?"

"Not yet."

"It looks like a slow day," Cargill observed. "You heard about the indictment?"

"Indictment?"

"The guys they caught in the Watergate last June," Cargill said. "They indicted them today on federal charges. Some fun, huh?"

"I wouldn't know," Ben said.

"All the fun stories come out of Washington these days," Cargill said. And then he smiled again, because this was about as close as he could come to making a joke about what had happened to Ben.

"Yeah," Ben said, not smiling back. "Some fun."

After Cargill had gone, Ben retreated into himself again and waited. The first call from Bellucci on the assignment desk didn't come until after six, when the news room had about emptied and the monitor screens all over the floor gleamed with the brightly ordered patterns of the day's events filtered through the wholesome good looks of anchorman Bill James and the WACN six-o'clock news team.

By nightfall the stalker was hunting again, primordial stirrings moving him into the alley just beyond the subway entrance from which she would inevitably emerge. His blackness blended well with the darkness.

He could feel the rumble of the night trains beneath

8

him, hear the metallic howl of brakes and the footsteps of the homeward-bound on the littered concrete stairs. The footsteps always gave him the first thrill. Sometimes he could pick out the one it would be just by the sound of her footsteps. As this one passed, his nostrils flared for a moment, his breathing quickened, and tiny rivulets of sweat pricked his armpits. City-cautious and quick, the woman moved on; he waited, following her with his eyes.

A breeze stirred the heavy night air, swirling scraps of newspaper out of the gutter into minor whirlpools; scattering greasy McDonald's wrappers, blackened by the grime of tires and soot, across the sidewalks. The stalker shivered, cold in the heat of the June night, chilled by the message the breeze brought him. His hand tightened around the wooden handle of the foot-long kitchen knife tucked under his belt; he felt a movement in his groin.

He could see she was young, white, overweight, not too pretty. Yes. Now he stepped out of the shadows. Yes, she was the one. He was ten feet behind her now, keeping the distance between them, knowing that soon she would glance back, that what at first would be merely concern would become worry, which would then degenerate into naked fear; that that fear would make her walk faster, prompt her to take out her apartment key earlier, turn unease into longing to get home.

She glanced behind her, then scurried on, fumbling inside her purse.

He allowed the gap between them to widen to twenty feet, then matched her quickened pace. She had the key in her hand now as she turned left and ran up the steps of the paint-peeling brownstone. He could sense the terror in her now, the stomach-tightening panic, as she fought the lock frantically with the key, her arms and fingers seem-

ing to move in slow motion. Timing, he knew, was everything. He reached the bottom step just as the key turned
and the lock yielded.

He sprang, bounding up the steps in two leaps, and
shoved her through the door into the brown dimness of the
hallway, his left hand over her mouth, muffling her scream.

"Where do you live?"

She shook her head and gasped "Please!" through his
fingers.

His right hand grasped the familiar wooden handle at
his waist. Its brass rivets were cold, draining the heat from
his palm, channeling it into the steel blade. He always
marveled at the acuteness of his senses toward the end and
at the predictability of his victims. His right hand rose,
thumb toward the blade. With his left, he snapped her
head back, exposing her curved, white throat. The knife
sang through the air, followed by wild, horrified eyes, and
came to rest on her throat. Slowly he drew the blade along
her skin, inflicting a surgeon's cut that parted skin and
tissue but avoided arterial damage. He liked to taste his
woman's blood up there, too.

"Oh, no! Please! No—don't!" Her eyes were glassy with
fear and shock, her consciousness seemed focused only on
the long sting at her throat; the warm, sticky wetness of her
blood as it oozed down her neck.

"Which one you live in?"

Obviously consumed by a blind concern for survival, she
was more obedient to him now. She pointed.

"Open it."

She unlocked both the upper and lower locks, and then,
as she turned the doorknob, he rammed the blade into her
lower back. He pushed her through the open door,

watching her slide away from his knife, its eight inches of steel pulling bloodily out of her.

He closed the door and turned to see her staring at him, one hand on her back over the wound, jaw slack, mouth open, eyes pleading. Perfect. He put the knife down on a chair and became suddenly gentle, stroking her hair as he undressed her and pressed her back against the floor. Her head lolled slowly from side to side and she whispered, "Please don't kill me."

He kissed her softly, first on the forehead, then on her eyes, cheeks, and mouth. His lips wandered over her chin and parted, while his tongue explored the softness of her flesh. Slowly, slowly, his mouth moved down her neck, his tongue tasting, probing, exploring, finally finding what it sought—the thin cut halfway between her chin and breast-bone. He lingered there, running his tongue back and forth over the shallow wound, savoring the blood. His hands stroked her breasts and moved downward, across her heaving stomach, fondling at last her pubic mound. His lips followed.

She had closed her eyes to the horror above her, so she couldn't have seen him reach again for the knife.

He raised his head, opened his zipper, then slid into her and began pounding, grunting, his left hand buried in her hair. His right hand moved slowly toward her left breast, until the knife point was an inch from her side, then he plunged the blade between her ribs, and through the left ventricle and aorta. Once again the key was in the timing. After all, he wasn't a necrophiliac; he didn't like sex with the dead—only sex with the dying.

Her blood was spilling into her chest cavity and the pressure of her pulse was dropping steadily. She had about thirty seconds of consciousness left. Above her, thrusting into her, the stalker moved furiously.

"How much have we got on this?" Cargill asked.

"We shot about five hundred feet," Ben said, "but there wasn't a hell of a lot to it. Maybe you could use twenty feet of it."

"Yeah," Cargill said glumly, "a goddam traffic accident. Big deal—but it so happens I've got a spot for it."

Mapes grinned and looked up from his Moviola. "It's nice and gory," the film editor said happily. "Derrick, I'll have this in shape before you're off the air."

Cargill glanced up at the wall clock. "Too bad it didn't happen earlier," he observed. "I might have led with it."

"Yeah, tough," the editor said. "A slow night like this."

Feeling slightly sick, with the dull ache that had begun two hours earlier still pounding at the back of his head, Ben retreated to his cubicle. He glanced over his desk for messages, found only a note from Kathy, stuck it into his pocket, and grabbed his coat. Then he sat down and waited till just after eleven o'clock, when once more the face of Bill James loomed cheerfully into the monitors and Ben could be sure the news room would be empty. He reached the assignment desk just in time to hear Bellucci confirm an address with the police.

"Well?" Ben asked, after Bellucci had hung up. "You going to good-night me or not?"

The big man with the dark, unfriendly eyes rubbed a hand over his jowls, already blue-black with beard. "No, it looks like we got a good one at last. Just your kind of story, Mr. Stryker."

"Look, Mario, it's late, and I've eaten enough of your shit for the night. I'd like to go home."

Bellucci shook his head in mock sympathy. "You'll like this assignment, I promise you. We got a really good colorful killing up in the Bronx. Not presidential in scope, if you know what I mean, but full of vivid local color. I'm sorry to prolong your working day, Mr. Stryker, but it's just the sort of thing you do so well."

Ben jotted down the address; then, without another word to Bellucci, he took the elevator down to the street to wait for his crew. It was damp outside, with a threat of more rain in the air, and Ben leaned up against the side of the building, his coat draped over his shoulders like a cape. Above him soared the forty-four gleaming stories of the new ACN building, one of that forest of steel-and-glass skyscrapers that had sprouted along Sixth Avenue ever since the end of the Second World War. Like all the others, this one stood as a symbol of success, of corporate power and achievement, a vertical kingdom that Ben Stryker had dreamed of conquering and that had once seemed as accessible to him as Everest to Hillary. No longer. Ben Stryker now stood in the building's shadow, all but overwhelmed by its vast indifference to his fate.

Cameraman Jeff Campbell, leading the crew out the side door, strode toward the white Ford sedan parked on the corner. "Sonofabitch!" he was saying, "just once I'd like to get home on time—Ben?"

"Right here." Stryker stepped out of the shadows and headed for the car. "I'll drive."

Campbell nodded and shifted the weight of his 16-millimeter camera rig from his shoulder as he reached the car door. "It's like Bellucci plans these capers to keep us up half the night." Still grumbling, he piled into the back seat, followed by the audio man. "At least I wouldn't put it past him."

"Me neither," said the electrician, the third member of the crew, getting in the front beside Ben, who already had the two-way radio switched on.

"You OK, Ben?" Jeff asked, as they pulled away from the curb. "You look kind of funny."

"One of my headaches," Ben said. "I'll be all right."

"That fucking Bellucci," the audio man said, "he could give Mount Rushmore a headache."

"I don't know what that means, Ted," Jeff Campbell said. "Drive, Ben."

Stryker nosed the car through the late theater traffic along the West Side, then shot up Tenth Avenue past the first blocks of crumbling tenements. Within minutes they were speeding through block after block of the city's vast underside, through the blasted, seemingly bombed-out areas where every day small deadly wars were being fought and lost. The whole city, Ben thought, is dying—riddled with the corruption of its victims' rotting corpses.

2

"How'd you get here—Air Force One?" Chief of Detectives Richard Steinman asked.

"OK, Chief," Ben said, "you have a great sense of humor."

One of the homicide men shoved past Ben's mike hand. "You were right, Chief, it was under the chair."

Steinman bustled by Ben and four other reporters crowding about him to rejoin the homicide team now clustered around that piece of trivial evidence he'd expected all along to find.

Ben tagged after him. "Right about what, Chief?"

"Show him, Charlie."

The detective dangled a ziplock bag in front of Ben's face. "Get a good shot of this," he said, smirking. Steinman himself grinned at the reporter.

Ben studied the object for a second or two, shot Steinman a puzzled look, and lowered his mike. "What the hell—a used sanitary napkin?"

"Hey, Ben, you want a shot of it?" Jeff Campbell asked, focusing on the bag the detective still held up.

"Yeah, how about it, Ben?" Steinman asked sarcastically. "Take a good shot of it. Show them a bloody Kotex close up on the six-o'clock news tomorrow. Maybe it'll raise your Nielsen a point or two."

Everyone laughed—Steinman, Charlie, the forensics man, the police photographer, most of the other reporters and cameramen around them—but Ben ignored them. He turned to Campbell and waved him off. "No, Jeff, we have enough."

They had more than enough. They'd already filmed scenes that would never make the news at six o'clock or at any other time: shots of a bloody, spread-eagled, naked female corpse; limbs twisted crazily; throat cut; dozens of stab wounds in stomach and chest; fluids oozing from between its legs; the carpet beneath it soaked with browning blood. Feeling slightly sick, Ben pushed his way out of the group around the body and, followed by his crew, took temporary refuge in a corner of the room.

The police photographer's Nikon still popped and

whirred, while the other TV news crews pushed and elbowed each other out of the way to film the murder scene. They were all there, as usual: the crews from the other local O-and-O's—WABC, WNBC, WCBS; outfits from two of the independents, channels 11 and 5; the radio reporters with their tape recorders slung over their shoulders like handbags; the newspaper guys with their pads and pencils; the stringers and free-lancers armed with their silent 16-millimeter cameras.

These last were the real ghouls of the scene. They cruised the city at night in cars filled with police scanners, monitoring police, fire, and ambulance calls, beating everyone to everything that burned or bled in the dark and shooting pictures that they hoped to sell at a hundred dollars a pop. In this crowd of carrion-lovers, Ben could literally smell the bloodlust, and it did nothing for his own morale to know that he was one of them, just another member of the jackal pack. Worse, he was the only one in the room whose face might still have been instantly recognized by anybody outside of it. That made it all the harder for him, and everybody there knew it. Some, like Steinman, even took comfort in it; they would drag him down with them and make him sense every minute of it.

"Did we get enough on the neighbor lady?" the audio man asked.

"Yeah, I think so," Ben said. "She's the one who called the cops, isn't she?" He could see her still, just outside the door leading into the hallway, where he and Campbell had found her, dressed in her food-stained houserobe, her mouth full of platitudes about what a sweet girl the victim had been—so nice, so quiet, so religious, so loving to small children and stray dogs. Who could have done such a terrible thing to her? Why didn't the police do something? Why did they always come too late to the scene? She had cried real tears, which, as Ben knew only too well, would look fine on film and would almost certainly make the six-o'clock news.

"Ready to go, then?" Jeff asked.

Ben ignored him, pushed back into the middle of the room, from where the carrion-eaters had at last begun to disperse, and pulled Steinman aside. "Listen," he asked, "what's the big deal with the sanitary napkin?"

"No big deal, Ben," the chief answered. "I just like to keep score. Tell me, Ben, what are the odds? I mean, if you went out in the street right now and picked any woman at random, what are the odds she'd be menstruating?"

"Well, since most women menstruate approximately one week in four, I'd say I'd have a twenty-five percent chance of picking one who was having her period."

"Right! But about *fifty* percent of the victims of rape-murders are menstruating," Steinman said. "The sickos who kill them sniff them out. They can smell the blood, just like animals."

"I suppose that would be useful information for the ladies," Ben said.

"Yeah. If you could find a way to get the info across delicately, you could tell the broads out there to be careful when they're on the rag."

Ben signaled the camera crew to start filming Steinman.

"Helpful hints aside, Chief, who do you think did this and when are you going to catch him?"

Steinman stared at Ben out of cold, ironic eyes. "Well, Ben," he said at last, "we think it was a man."

Ben winced, but ever the pro, held his mike steady.

18

"About catching him—officially speaking, we are investigating every clue and we'll have the usual special telephone number for the public to call in case anyone saw anything that might help us solve this crime." Steinman waved the mike away and made sure Jeff had stopped shooting. "Off the record, Stryker, finding a witness is our only hope and the chances of that are slim to none. Even if anybody did see this guy, the description probably wouldn't be any good and the witness would probably be too scared to describe him anyway."

Steinman turned for one last look at all that was left of the young girl on the floor and gave a quick signal with his right hand; one of his detectives covered the corpse with a body bag. When the chief turned to Ben, he seemed oddly remote, like a man shielding himself from any possible personal involvement. "I've seen too many of these," he said softly, "and I can count the number of good collars in these random rape killings on one hand."

Ben studied the chief's leathery, seamed face, framed by large long-lobed ears. Steinman's sad brown eyes were all but hidden under bushy brows graying to the color of ashes, and he had a soggy cigar stub jammed between his thick, turned-down lips. It seemed to Ben that behind the cigar's fumes the detective was trying to screen out the worst of humanity's more desperate acts.

"Anything else, Ben?" the chief asked.

Ben shook his head helplessly, suddenly unable to speak. For one terrible moment he had the feeling that he'd been gazing into a mirror and that Steinman's sad, cynical face had become a reflection of his own inner turmoil and fears. He felt as though he couldn't breathe, as though an icy hand were toying with him, twisting him. . . .

19

"Ben? Ben?"

The alarm in Jeff's voice brought Ben back to reality.

"It's OK, Jeff," he said, trying to keep his voice steady. "Let's go."

Head down, he hurried away from the scene, trailing his crew after him. In the hallway the woman in the food-stained houserobe was still mouthing off to two pad-and-pencil men her summation of the victim's saintly character. Outside on the street, where a small knot of anxious neighbors and curious passersby had gathered, two of the TV crews were interviewing a man who was having a great deal to say about what crime was doing to the city and how something would have to be done to clean up the mess, especially by putting a stop to the coddling of perverts and criminals by the pinko authorities in the pay of the labor unions.

"Hey, Ben, where's your limousine?" someone from one of the camera crews called out as he passed.

Ben nearly fell into the front passenger seat of the Ford. "You drive," he gasped to Jeff.

Rage exploded and rose in him now, all but blinding him as the car eased away from the curb. *I'll kill the sonofabitch. I'll kill him. I will! I will! I will!*

"Ben? Ben, darling?"

The voice sounded distant, coming to him from a million miles away. And yet she was there, in the room with him. He could see and almost identify her in the dim pale-dawn light streaking through the venetian blinds. He did not get up to greet her.

"What do you want?" he asked.

"I've been calling and calling," she said. "You didn't answer. I was worried about you. I got the janitor to let me in."

"I didn't know he had a key," Ben said. "I'll get it back from him—go away, Kathy."

"Didn't you read my note? I said to call if you didn't want me to come over. Your phone's off the hook. I thought maybe something happened—"

"Nothing happened. One of my headaches."

"Can I do anything?"

"You can go away. Please."

"Darling, you're still dressed—"

"Kathy, I'll be all right," Ben said, not moving from the bed where he lay, fully dressed even to his shoes, his eyes fixed on the ceiling above him. "I can't talk to you now."

Evidently she didn't understand, but then how could she? She was only twenty-two—or was it twenty-three?—two years out of some fashionable Eastern girls' school, with her whole silly career ahead of her. To her, Benson Stryker still represented a worthy conquest, a possible partner, desirable and true, a portion of her small dream. She did not see the wreck there on the bed, only the glamorous figure of the media stud who had taken her so violently, so expertly, only hours before. Kathy nurtured her visions, too. Didn't everyone? She came over now and sat down beside him, reached out a hand to him. "Darling—"

Savagely, he shoved her arm aside and sat up. "Kathy, one good lay doesn't mean you can bust in here to play Florence Nightingale, for Christ's sake!" he shouted. "You don't know! You don't understand anything! Now get the hell out of here!"

Appalled, she rose and stared at him; she had never encountered such intense hatred before. "I'm sorry, I—"

"Go away," he said. He spoke very deliberately now, as if addressing a small, backward child. "Go away and leave me alone. Can you understand that?"

She ran out of the room, slamming the door behind her. Ben closed his eyes and sank back on the bed. He remained very wide awake, however, and soon his eyes were again open, fixed on the void above him.

3

How could it all have gone so terribly wrong so quickly? Ben wondered, turning the question over and over in his mind, as he had for weeks. My God, he was only thirty-four years old! Less than two months ago he'd been a network news correspondent covering the White House. He'd captured the fancy of the public with his probing, irreverent, but entirely proper questions at presidential news conferences. Not that he'd been popular with the Nixon administration. In fact, he knew that several times the Chairman himself had been called by one presidential aide or another. Nixon's men had never been shy about airing their grievances with the press and they had not taken kindly to young Ben Stryker. It had been suggested strongly to Ted Brennan, the head of the ACN news division, that perhaps Stryker could have done equally well elsewhere, made a big name for himself on some less demanding beat. When that had failed to elicit a response, the Chairman himself had been contacted. How about a quiet end to Benson Stryker's career?

"That's just about what the man said, Ben," the Chairman had told him at lunch that day. "Almost that crudely. I guess when you get that kind of attention, you *could* take it as a compliment, you know."

Yes, the Chairman himself had implied, Ben Stryker had become a true star in the TV news business.

But had there been something else, some other element in the way the Chairman had spoken to him that day? Some hint of disapproval or caution that Ben had missed or misinterpreted? He tried now to recall the exact words, the exact tone. "You're moving fast, Ben," the Chairman had said. "Very fast." Had he smiled? Ben couldn't remember. "You have a lot of ambition, I've always known that," the Chairman had continued. "I sensed it in you when I first saw you. I'd know that kind of ambition, that kind of drive, anywhere. You see, Ben, I had it myself. I'd have done anything, nearly anything, to get to where I am."

What had Ben himself done? Had the Chairman found him out, and if so, when, exactly? During that meteoric rise through the enormously competitive ranks of television news that had taken off back there in Mississippi and then gathered momentum in Texas? He'd been working in Dallas

24

when Kennedy was assassinated. Had the Chairman himself singled him out then, plucked him from the ranks? It was his local coverage of the tragedy that had first caught the eye of the network news brass, most of whom had rushed from New York to the scene of the shooting. But the Chairman himself had been above the action, as usual; he'd watched it all from afar and beckoned Ben to glory with a single telephone call. Could it have been ordained for Ben from the beginning?

"I like your style, Ben," the Chairman had said at their first meeting, many months after Ben had been brought to New York and then reassigned to Washington. "You come through the screen. People like you. It's the one great intangible asset in this business, and you either have it or you don't. You've got it. I think you're a natural. You've got a great future ahead of you with us."

Ben had never been hampered by a sense of false modesty. He'd always known his own assets and how to take advantage of them. Handsome, trim, clever, with quick blue eyes and sandy hair, he'd always seen himself as a newsman version of Robert Redford. He'd worked hard to shape that image, and he'd learned his business because he'd realized very early in the game that staying power took more than luck, a pretty face, and a deep baritone voice. He'd worked hard to perfect his craft during the nearly nine years since the Kennedy assassination—and it had paid off, just as the Chairman had predicted. Ben Stryker had become a hugely popular national figure, the obvious choice, along with Bill James in New York, to replace ACN's aging superstar, Harvey Grunwald, as anchorman of the evening news. The future had seemed absolutely unlimited.

What could have lulled him into such a false sense of security? How had he missed sensing his vulnerability? He'd gotten so used to being the star, so used to holding center stage at all kinds of glittering events. And the Chairman himself had fed his ego, especially during those periodic, intimate little lunches in the huge corner office at the top of ACN's new glass-and-steel tower. From up there, high above the dirty streets so far below, Ben had always had a special sense of his nearness to the throne, to that ultimate power which decided the destinies of men and of whole nations.

The Chairman had even begun to call him by his first name, though Ben could never have called the Chairman "Larry" or "Lawrence" or anything, in fact, but "Mr. Hoenig"; it would have been an act of lese majesty.

Until that memorable day when the Chairman himself said, "Ben, please call me Larry." It had startled Ben, but he had complied with a feeling of incredible elation. The Chairman had smiled broadly, Ben recalled, but there had been another element in the moment, some elusive purpose Ben had sensed faintly but had never been able to pin down. It was as if, in the granting of this final, small intimacy, the Chairman had bound Ben to him by bonds stronger than could be forged by any overt act of generosity. The Chairman had known something, had learned something about Ben that Ben himself had not yet grasped. . . .

Ben thought back again to that sultry day in late June when he and his crew had set up a watch on the White House grounds. They were guessing that Nixon would emerge from his long meeting with Haldeman and keep a scheduled rendezvous with his family on the *Sequoia*, the presidential yacht moored in the Potomac. The meeting stretched on and on; members of the various network crews had wandered off in search of refreshment, but Ben had kept his men on the alert. When at last the President had suddenly appeared and headed, scowling, for his limousine, it had been Ben who had spearheaded the charge of reporters and photographers surging forward, hounding Nixon for a statement.

No one had ever been able to reconstruct exactly what had happened, no matter how many times that bit of film had been run or the event recalled in detail by others, even by Ben himself. There seemed to be a gap, not as awesome as those that would later emerge in some of the president's own tapes, but nevertheless a genuine one. Or had Ben's own memory failed him now? He could not be sure anymore.

Anyway, one thing was certain. Nixon, in his flight from the press, had turned and used an aide as a shield, shoving him violently forward at the crush of newsmen. Ben, too, had recoiled. But something or someone had struck his arm a jarring blow, slamming his microphone into his chin. And Ben had reacted.

It had happened to him before, a long time ago, in some playground of his youth when a bully had cornered him, snatching at his toy radio and earphones. Ben, fighting back, had been struck hard on the chin, then forced to watch his precious toy fall and shatter at his feet. He had screamed his rage at this act of wanton violence that had robbed him, a small, lonely boy, of what he had loved most in all the world.

Now, again and again, Ben heard his own voice—as if from a great distance but with frightening clarity—as he stared wildly at Nixon. "All right, you idiot! Damn you, you see what you've done!" he had cried out in rage.

27

Who had glared at him with such malevolent hatred? The playground bully of so long ago, or the president of the United States? Ben could never be sure. He remembered only that the president had whirled about and gone, whisked away from the scene and out of the White House grounds by guards and retainers, temporarily safe from his tormentors.

It had been a rotten stroke of luck that Ben had been immortalized in that moment on film. There was a crush of shouting newsmen, all pushing, shoving, elbowing—that anyone had been able to film or record anything was extraordinary. And even then it was done, not by one of the competing network crews, but by the quick technical reflexes of a reporter-cameraman for a small independent station in Baltimore. It had been a terrific scoop, and the station had made the most of it, running it first as an exclusive, then hawking it at fancy prices to the other three networks. By eleven o'clock that night, the whole nation had been able to see the president of the United States push an aide and hear himself called an idiot by that rising, young ACN star, Benson Stryker. It was an astonishing incident, soon to become celebrated, confirmed in print the very next day by newspaper headlines all over the world.

Ben remembered now the way he'd felt as soon as the fatal words were out of his mouth. Stunned, instantly aware of the enormity of his offense, of his massive breach of protocol, he had stood there, mouth agape, ashen-faced, frozen to the spot. There had been a sudden hush, a quick parting of ranks, as if he'd been immediately isolated, physically as well as spiritually. He'd seen himself frozen in time, unmasked, stripped in a single blinding flash—his career, like the few desperately desired toys of his unhappy childhood, smashed in ruins around him. . . .

When had Ben first fully grasped the extent of his fall? During the month he'd spent twiddling his thumbs in Washington, after being pulled off the White House beat? Or during that summer night in New York, when, on his very first shift, he'd found himself assigned to cover a fire, a mugging, two rapes, and a murder? What a toboggan slide—from the heights of power to the depths of despair. Ben had told himself he was handling it well, but was he? Could he have done better if Bellucci, that bastard, wasn't all over him every goddam minute? It wasn't Ben's fault he'd been singled out, and Bellucci had no right to take out on Ben his own frustrations, jealousies, and rages. *No, goddammit, it wasn't fair!*

Fuck you, fuck you all! I've traveled the world in Air Force One, I've talked with presidents and kings, rubbed shoulders with the social elite of Washington, twirled the thin stems of champagne glasses and sipped the finest wines. I've luxuriated in limousines, been catered to, had my shoes shined expensively and my shirts hand-pressed. I've cracked jokes with the famous, swapped secrets with the mighty, been celebrated by celebrities and become one myself, an idol to a world of devout television viewers, and now—now—

Now Ben walked the night streets of New York, sidestepping broken bottles around sleazy tenements where humanity's most despicable creatures committed their vicious acts and lived out their vile lives. Now Ben moved among foul-breathed drunks and junkies, rude cops, dead bodies, through the alleys of the despairing. Now his senses were assaulted hour after hour by the rasping sound of handcuffs, the curses of the accused and the victimized, the fecal scent of corpses.

The first flooding realization of his fall had come soon after his arrival in New York, during a press conference called by a city official with an eye on next year's mayoral campaign. Ben had found himself with his crew on a Forty-second Street sidewalk, jostling with a crowd of reporters for space on a littered strip of cement lined by X-rated movie houses, massage parlors, and porn bookstores. Here, cloaked in virtue, the would-be candidate—a dumpy, middle-aged politico in a pinstriped suit and dark fedora—stood haranguing the forces of evil, which, he assured them all, had entrenched themselves in Fun City solely because of the incumbent administration's deplorable permissiveness. "I love this guy," Jeff Campbell had whispered as he aimed his camera. "He calls this press conference right where we can get some real good nookie shots. See him stand right in front of the displays?"

Sick with the realization that he was being had, that he and all these other alleged good citizens and seekers of truth were using and being used, Ben had turned away. His camera crew knew exactly what to shoot; they'd done it all a thousand times before—just good, clean, titillating stuff to hype the ratings a little and give the candidate a twenty- or thirty-second spot to plug himself and his virtue. Cute, very cute. And undeniably tawdry.

As Ben stood apart from the scene, a huge lavender-colored Cadillac Eldorado turned the corner and cruised past him. The machine gleamed with chrome; a white-vinyl top swooped down over the rear window, leaving only a small heart-shaped opening through which, as the car receded in the blinking night lights of the city, a grinning black face stared out at him. Sneering lips mouthed an obscenity, then the pimpmobile cruised on, impervious to the farce being played out on the sidewalk.

God, Ben had thought, is this all that's left of my life, my career? This vileness? In that moment, he knew that only one man had destroyed him, had been responsible for all that had happened to him. And that one man would pay for it with his life, if Ben had to carry out the deed with all the strength in his bare hands.

4

The call came two days after the shoving incident. Ben had been lying in bed after a sleepless night, and the ringing of the phone had shattered the morning stillness. Still groggy from the Valium which compounded his weariness, Ben picked up the receiver. He'd been waiting for a call about his future at the network, but he hadn't expected it this early in the day. He knew he'd have to put up a front, keep his head clear, play it cool. This was going to be Benson Stryker on the phone, not some desperate underling with his career in ruins.

"Hello?" Ben's voice had all its professional richness and depth. "Stryker here."

"Mr. Stryker, you don't know me. But please don't hang up. I have something important to say."

"Who are you?"

"I can't tell you that right now." It was a man's voice, but pitched very low and somewhat distorted. "You'll have to trust me."

"Trust you? What do you mean?"

"I work for the agency. I haven't much time."

"The agency?"

"CIA—look, I think what you did was terrific."

"Wait a minute—"

"Let me finish," the voice continued. "I want you to know that some of us are sick over what's been going on inside this administration. You have no idea what we're being asked to do. If you knew, if anybody knew, what this agency and others have been up to for the past few years—"

"Look," Ben said, "I don't see—"

"You will, you will. I'm—we're—looking for a reporter we can trust. I think you may be our man."

Ben's first instinct had been to hang up. He'd had several such calls from cranks and loonies, but something in this man's voice stopped him. Under the muffled tone Ben sensed urgency, a seriousness of purpose. This was no weirdo on the phone, but someone playing for big stakes. Over the years, Ben had learned to keep his prejudices at bay and not to make snap judgments. This was how "reliable sources" were developed, the way a reporter acquired eyes and ears inside the secret corridors of power.

"Ben—it's all right if I call you Ben?"

"Sure."

"Ben, I have secret information that could blow up this administration. Are you interested?"

"Maybe."

"I thought you might be."

The caller was right; Ben *was* interested. In the two days since the shoving incident he'd received no official word, not even a hint, from anyone at the network about what might be in store for him. He'd been shelved immediately, that was clear enough, but nobody had actually said the words. Even Sarah had kept her distance. His one attempt to reach Ted Brennan, the president of the news division in New York, had failed. Everybody was polite, but terribly busy or out whenever he approached them. Clearly his whole career dangled by a thread and he was in no position to be overly careful or choosy. During this conversation with his mysterious caller, Ben had suddenly glimpsed a way out. Maybe, just maybe, if what this man said was true, he could come up with a scoop sensational enough to save himself. God knew he had nothing to lose.

"Ben," the voice said, "I want you to listen carefully—"

"First, let me say that if you are who you say you are," Ben interrupted, "I can promise you complete confidentiality."

"I took that for granted, Ben. Absolutely essential."

"But I'm sure you understand that I get a lot of calls, and that before we develop any kind of relationship, I've got to be certain you are who you say you are, that you are inside the CIA."

"I understand."

"I can't accept anything this big on faith alone."

"Of course not. I realize that," the caller said. "This is a little one-sided right now, but I think you'll learn to trust me, despite the fact that I can't give you my name or any way to reach me."

Ben listened carefully to the voice at the other end of the wire. He was measuring not only what was said, but the whole tone of the conversation—the timbre and steadiness and intelligence behind the words—listening for any nuance that might discredit this new source. What he heard impressed him. "I'm listening."

"You were in Dallas during the Kennedy assassination," the voice continued.

"Yeah."

"Think back, Ben. You remember the name Jim Garrison?"

"Of course. He was the New Orleans D.A."

"Right. And you recall his conspiracy theory concerning the assassination?"

"That Cuban expatriates, who were being trained by the CIA to assassinate Castro, actually killed Kennedy?"

"Right. But why?"

"Because Kennedy called off Castro's assassination and because he reneged on providing U.S. air cover for the Bay of Pigs invasion."

"Correct."

"OK," Ben said, "but Garrison went down in flames with that theory."

"Of course. He was too close."

"Oh?" Ben was interested now, all right, but he wasn't ready to let the caller know he was hooked. Not yet.

"Well," the voice continued, "suppose I told you Kennedy had ordered us to kill Castro. It wasn't one of our more glorious efforts. We actually made more than a dozen attempts on that guy, with everything from exploding cigars to Mafia hit men. It all backfired on us pretty badly."

"Are you telling me that Castro found out about it and retaliated?"

"Let's put it this way: it wasn't Castro's enemies who shot John Kennedy."

Ben paused just long enough to absorb this piece of information, but he sparred for time. He wasn't buying this yarn, not quite yet. "Look," he said, "I find all this stuff about CIA ineptitude a little hard to swallow."

"Do you, Ben?"

"You're damn right I do," Ben said levelly. "I think that if the CIA really wanted to rub out a two-bit dictator confined to a small island, well, they'd probably get the job done cleanly and simply."

"Ben, I know it sounds unreal." The voice was confidential. "But Castro's security forces are topnotch, maybe the best in the world. And we aren't as good at pulling off these jobs as people think we are. We're good, but we make a lot of mistakes. In James Bond movies people don't make mistakes. In real life, they do."

"I'm sorry, I'm not convinced. Is that the best you can come up with?"

"OK, Ben, maybe this will do it." The voice was brisk now. "I'm going to send you a key to a locker in the downtown bus terminal. Inside, you'll find an official CIA dirty-tricks packet with a blueprint for one of the more imaginative plots against Castro, one that would have worked if Castro hadn't gone into hiding about then."

"All right," Ben said, "then if I want to get in touch with you—"

"Good-bye, Ben."

He was left holding a dead receiver. Slowly he replaced it, trying to stay calm, but he could feel excitement rising in him like a fever. All he could do now was wait.

5

Kathy did not get in to see Cargill until late that afternoon, about halfway through the six-o'clock news. She had
cried most of the morning after Ben had thrown her out,
and had tried several times to call him at home, but no
one had answered. When Ben failed to show up and Bellucci
told her he'd called in sick, she decided she had to talk
to someone. She was more than worried and upset; she was
frightened.

Something in the way Ben had looked at her hadn't seemed quite sane; it was as if he were in the grip of forces she couldn't comprehend or imagine. There was a distance between them—and so soon after that wonderful night, when they'd held each other and made love until dawn. Ben had aroused her in a way no other man had ever been able to before. He was a wonderful lover—violent, even cruel at times, but always masterful and somehow considerate of her needs, too. She had moaned with pleasure when she felt him enter her at last, holding her buttocks tightly in his strong hands and raising her powerfully against him as he thrust into her again and again. She loved him, Kathy had convinced herself, she loved him and she was going to be with him and help him. She knew she could, even though something terrible had happened to him. Perhaps Cargill could tell her what was really wrong.

She trusted Cargill and she respected him, too, as almost everyone did. Derrick Cargill had an innate sense of decency and a rock-hard core of integrity that commanded esteem. Most of his life had been spent in the United States, and all of his professional career as a working newsman—first in Canada, then later in the states, and for the past ten years with ACN News—but he still spoke with the soft inflections of his native Wales. His habitual manner was reserved, even courtly. He was in his early fifties, Kathy thought, but he looked older; his craggy features seemed carved out of rock and his thick hair was nearly snow-white and rumpled, unyielding to comb or brush. He had a fierce temper, but she had never seen it directed at anyone who didn't deserve his wrath. Unlike Bellucci and some others she could name, Cargill never bullied anyone under him. His worst outbursts always seemed to be directed at the network brass. He would brook no front-office meddling with the way he ran his show or his department, even if it meant risking demotion to a writer's desk and the loss of a sizeable portion of his income—to say nothing of his status as producer of the eleven-o'clock news.

That afternoon, in fact, when Kathy had first stopped by his office, she'd found him chewing out a white-faced network vice-president who had dared to intervene in the control room during the previous evening's broadcast. "Don't you ever go into that control room while I'm producing this program," she heard Cargill bite out. "You don't tell anyone who works for me what to do. You tell me. Is that clear?"

Kathy had backed away, but not before she'd caught a glimpse of the enraged face of the young executive, as he turned to flee. She herself had retreated, to give Cargill time to simmer down. She made herself wait until later in the day, when the news room had thinned out and she guessed Cargill would be relaxing a little, with only one eye on the six-o'clock show.

"Ah, Miss Lewis," he said, looking up from his desk when she tapped timidly on his open door, "come in."

"I—I wanted to talk to you about Ben. That is, Mr. Stryker," she said, suddenly feeling very foolish.

"Sure. Sit down." He got up and pulled a chair out for her. "He called in sick."

"I know. I—I saw him this morning."

"What's wrong with him? A touch of flu? Lot of it going around."

She shook her head, and then somehow it all came spilling out. She told Cargill she'd been dating Ben, but that he seemed so troubled, even irrational from time to time. "It worries me," she said mournfully. "You see, I really care about him."

39

Cargill didn't answer her immediately. He looked thoughtfully, appraisingly, at her as he rubbed his chin in a familiar nervous habit. "Miss Lewis," he said finally, "of course, what you and Stryker do outside of work hours is your own business—"

"I'm sorry. I didn't mean—"

"It's all right," he soothed her, "there's nothing wrong with you and Ben seeing each other. I don't mean to imply disapproval." He smiled. "I'm not that old-fashioned."

She blushed, but made herself go on. "He was acting so strangely," she insisted. "That's all I wanted to say. He seemed—I don't know—very removed. I couldn't reach him."

"Well, you know what he's been through."

She nodded miserably. "I just thought . . ."

He waited for her to finish the thought, but she didn't. He sighed. "It's no fun being in Ben's position," he said. "You know his recent history, I gather."

"Oh, yes."

"Well, that should explain a lot. It's tough to feel you're a has-been at thirty-four."

"But he's *not* a has-been," she protested. "I mean, he's young and he's talented and he could do anything he wanted to. I—I bring all this up because—well, because I thought maybe you'd known him a while and you could help me."

"In what way?"

"I want to reach him, don't you see? He doesn't have to give up, he doesn't have to feel he's through. He could start over somewhere else, he could write books, he could do so many things."

Cargill nodded. "What can I tell you, Miss Lewis? Did you want me to speak to Ben? I don't think I could do that right now. I'm in an awkward position here. The best thing any of us can do for Ben is to treat him professionally, handle him and talk to him as we would any other reporter or writer around here. I can't give him favored treatment. And surely he doesn't want our pity. He's going to have to work this out for himself."

"Yes, I know." Suddenly Kathy felt that she'd made a mistake in speaking to Cargill. She stood up abruptly. "Look, please don't tell him I talked to you."

"Of course not."

She tried to smile but couldn't, and turned to go. "Thank you."

"For what? Kathy—"

"Yes?"

"You're doing fine here, you know," Cargill said. "You're bright and hardworking and everyone likes you."

She stared wide-eyed at Cargill. "Please don't tell me I shouldn't see Ben. Please don't. I may be all he has."

"I wouldn't be too sure, Kathy," Cargill said. He got up and came around from behind his desk to put a fatherly arm around her shoulders. "Look," he said.

"What?"

Cargill pointed to the four TV monitors suspended from the ceiling over the assignment desk. Silently, in living color, each set projected over the temporarily empty news room the images of the shows the four networks were broadcasting to the nation's two hundred million potential viewers. "You see those pictures, Kathy? Do they seem complete to you?"

"What do you mean, Mr. Cargill?"

"Do you know what flyback is?"

She shook her head.

"You'd better learn these technical terms, Kathy." Cargill warmed to his subject. "When you're looking at a TV pic-

41

ture, you're looking at five hundred and twenty-five lines. The picture up there that seems so simple is really very complex. What's equally essential to every picture is, what we don't see, but it's just as necessary to that image as what your eye *does* see. Follow me?"

"I'm not sure. I think so."

"There's a process at work. It's the way the electronic beams go from the end of one line of information to the beginning of the next. That passage is called flyback. It's the invisible part of your TV picture, Kathy." Cargill paused and the girl turned to look at him. "You can't see it happen, but without it there'd be no picture at all. Do you understand? There's a lot of flyback in Ben Stryker, more perhaps than you know."

6

Ben could not stop thinking about that incredible sequence of events back in June, such a short time before, but such an eternity ago. Long after Kathy had gone, he continued to turn the events over and over in his head, reliving every strange, terrible moment.

He remembered now that he thought he had heard the doorbell ringing and that it had seemed very loud, as if it had happened inside his head. He'd been sleeping badly, he realized, and his nerves were on edge; that might account for it. In any case, it was very early, just after dawn, before the traffic became a noise factor and the harshness of the sound intruded on his thoughts. He went to the door, but no one answered his query, and a glance through his peephole revealed only an empty hallway. When he looked down at his feet, though, he saw a small white envelope addressed to him. It contained a key. The mysterious caller of the previous day had kept his word.

Still not sure whether or not this was an elaborate hoax, Ben reminded himself that he had little to lose. He took a taxi to the downtown bus terminal, located the locker, and turned the key. Inside lay a plain, bulky manila envelope that Ben stuffed quickly into his empty briefcase. He called the office to say that a doctor's appointment would make him late; then he went home, turned on the light in the small, windowless kitchen of his bachelor apartment, and opened the packet.

It took him a while to assimilate the full significance of the packet's contents, and at first he could hardly believe his eyes. He was staring at a kind of manual—printed on official CIA paper stamped "TOP SECRET"—listing specifications for making a deadly sophisticated weapon. The ingredients began with a tiny pellet, about the size of a grain of rice, made out of lethal poison distilled from clams. This "shellfish toxin," as it was defined, was so devastating that a single drop of it was enough to kill a good-sized infantry battalion. The instructions explained how the pellet could be coated with melted sugar that would harden into a brittle but soluble jacket. In from five to fifteen minutes, the pellet would dissolve in bodily fluids, thus, according to the comment, "giving the operative time to cover himself following introduction of the neutralizing substance."

This was to be accomplished by the use of an ingenious gadget, basically a modified 35mm single lens reflex camera. On the second page—also stamped "TOP SECRET"—was an engineering diagram, showing exactly how a small carbon dioxide cartridge, like the ones used in pellet guns, could be implanted inside the core of a standard 35mm roll of film, and how a puncturing pin could be recessed into the film crank spindle inside the camera. Powered by the shutter spring, the puncturing pin would strike every time a picture was taken. With a standard roll of film, the pin would hit nothing. But with the loaded film roll in place, the pin would strike a thin lead seal on top of the CO_2 cartridge, instantly releasing compressed gas into the airtight body of the camera.

Ben read on. A small hole would be drilled into the camera, beside the lens, and what looked like a harmless support rod would be threaded into the hole to protrude from the camera body to the front element in the lens structure. There it would connect to a false support ring encircling the housing of the lens, attached to the rod by a solid cap nut. This nut disguised the fact that the two-inch rod was actually a hollow tube. The nut removed, the tube would become the only avenue of escape for the compressed CO_2 gas that was released into the main body of the camera. The tube actually functioned as a gun barrel through which the deadly little pellet could be fired. With the lens serving as a sighting mechanism, the camera could thus be transformed into a lethal weapon, "accurate," the instructions noted, "up to a distance of 20 feet and capable, within that range, of penetrating four layers of

45

clothing and two inches of flesh." The operative was also advised that "for best results, the pellet should be injected into the fatty tissue of the buttocks."

Ben laughed. A nice touch, that "injected." *Shoot them in the ass*, it meant. How appropriate. The humorless euphemisms and bureaucratese could convince you to do almost anything, the way it removed you from the reality behind a barrier of clumsy syntax and official-sounding jargon.

He turned the page and read the section listing the advantages and disadvantages of the weapon. Under "Advantages," Ben's eyes were caught by the words "Field Preparation," printed in bold type. "This weapon," the text proclaimed, "can be constructed by operatives in the field using tools and materials easily obtained in most nations, thus obviating the need to smuggle anything past security checkpoints."

Ben also found instructions on exactly how long to let the clams spoil under specific conditions, in order to produce the toxin. A CO_2 cartridge could, if necessary, be made by using metal tubing of various kinds, dry ice, and lead. Nothing had been ignored or overlooked, Ben thought.

Under "Disadvantages," he found the word "Noise," also printed in bold type. "The weapon makes an explosive 'pop' when fired," the instructions warned, "which could attract attention unless muffled by crowd noises or highway and airport sounds. In any such areas and under such conditions, the weapon can be fired almost with impunity and with no danger that the sound can be detected."

Below this section, again in bold type, Ben came across the word "Smoke." "The weapon does not produce smoke, as from a firearm," he read, "but a momentary cloud of condensation is produced upon firing. When the compressed CO_2 gas is released, it expands rapidly, becoming very cold. As it emerges from the firing tube, it will cause moisture in the surrounding air to condense into a faint, white vapor cloud that will vanish in a few seconds. It is unlikely that, under normal circumstances, such a phenomenon would be detected."

Ben was stunned. He found himself staring blankly at the gleaming white surface of his refrigerator; he shook his head and shuffled through the papers once more. "Good God," he muttered, "this is the real thing."

He stood up, went to the sink, and splashed water on his face. He couldn't quite comprehend the total significance of what his CIA contact had given him. He was appalled, but also—what?—elated? Yes! He dried his face and went back to the material lying so innocently on his kitchen table. He tried to analyze exactly how he felt about what he'd just read, but for some reason it wasn't easy. The surface emotions were clear enough, but there were darker, less rational forces working within him.

First of all, he was shocked by the cold, clinical efficiency with which an official government agency could approach the possible elimination of human life—as if human beings were no more than troublesome insects to be wiped out of existence by pressing a tiny lever in a mechanism no more complicated than an aerosol can.

Secondly, he was swept by euphoria. He'd stumbled onto something that could develop into a sensational story. At the very least, the CIA assassination attempts against Castro would make headlines for weeks. Ultimately, Ben might even be able to prove that John F. Kennedy had been the victim of an international conspiracy, exactly as so many people believed but had never been able to substantiate. Ben was on the track of the greatest story of his career.

His career? Again he experienced those strange, fleeting moods he could not quite identify, though he *could* sense violence in them. He tried to consider the implications rationally. All right, he thought, if I can break this story, whatever damage I've done to myself will be undone. *I can get out of this mess!*

Something blind and murderous moved in the room. As if from a great distance, Ben heard the sound of a blow. He staggered and almost fell, then braced himself on the table. What had happened? He looked around dazedly. Nothing. Nothing had happened. His hand throbbed. With a start, Ben realized that he had struck the surface of the table so hard that his whole hand ached from the force of the blow.

Puzzled, he straightened up. Then he heard the phone ringing. Trembling, he walked into the living room and picked up the receiver.

"Ben?"

"Yes."

"Oh. I rang and rang. I thought you might still be at the doctor's. Your office said—"

"I just got back. Who is this?"

"It's Barbara, Ben. In Mr. Brennan's office in New York. Are you ill?"

"No. I'm OK."

"Good. Mr. Brennan would like to see you this afternoon some time. Can you catch the shuttle?"

"Yes. Certainly." Ben's head began to spin and he sat down quickly. "What's this about, Barbara?" He knew the question was stupid. Already he could hear the swish of the ax blade through the air, feel its cold, sharp edge on his

48

neck. This summons from the president of the news division could mean only one thing and he knew it.

"I'm sorry, Ben," she said cheerfully, "but Mr. Brennan didn't say."

"I see. OK. I'll be there."

Sarah Anderson was never to forget the look on Ben Stryker's face when he'd stopped by her office that morning in Washington, before he left for the airport. His eyes had been strange, almost wild, although she could tell that he was making an enormous effort to appear unruffled, cool. He'd stood just inside her door, the hint of a smile on his face.

"Come in, Ben," she said.

"I'm going to New York," he said, not moving from the door. "I imagine you've spoken to Brennan about me."

"Yes, I have, of course. After all, I am the bureau chief here."

"He's going to fire me."

"I don't know, Ben," she said kindly. "He didn't tell me that."

"What *did* he tell you?"

"Only that you were to be kept off the White House beat; but then you knew that."

"Nothing else?"

"No. I imagine he's going to discuss everything with you today."

"What did you tell him about me?"

"That you're the best reporter I've ever worked with," she said seriously. "And I mean that, Ben."

"Thanks." He sat down opposite her now, absently drumming the fingers of one hand against the arm of his chair. "I *was*."

She shook her head. "No, you still are. Ben, I don't think they're going to let you go. You're too valuable. You've made a bad mistake, sure, but you'll come back, I know you will. You'll be reassigned, probably, as soon as there's an opening for you. Maybe some foreign bureau. Eventually this will all blow over."

He looked at her gratefully; he really liked this woman. She was about ten years older than he, but she still drew long second looks. Tall, and strikingly handsome, she had a mane of soft, reddish-brown hair streaked with gray that she made no effort to hide. Despite lines at the corners of her eyes, her skin glowed with health and vitality, imparting a luminous quality to her classic features, and she had the firm body of a much younger woman. Her eyes were compelling—wide-set, dazzlingly clear, with vivid green irises the color of new leaves flecked with golden-brown. Often, in elevators, strange men were transfixed by her glance. She radiated confidence and concern, intelligence and femininity, as well as a distant promise of mature passion.

Ben had been drawn to her from their first meeting, and though they had a running flirtation, he'd never pursued her actively. He knew she was married—that the marriage was little more than a habit—but he had known better than to romance his boss. And he knew, instinctively, that a man did not trifle with Sarah Anderson. She was at least as ambitious as he, with a steely purpose beneath her soft surface that compelled respect—and caution.

"I hope you're right, Sarah," he said, standing up to leave. "And I'm glad you're on my side. I appreciate it."

"Why wouldn't I be, Ben? I'm sick at losing you."

He shrugged ruefully. "I don't know what got into me. I

still can't believe I said what I did. It was as if somebody else said those words."

"Maybe it's just our esteemed president." Sarah said lightly. "He seems to bring out the worst in nearly everyone. The other day, I heard a columnist who's supposed to be one of his chief supporters refer to him as 'the armpit of the nation.' Compared to that, what you called him was pretty mild."

"Yeah," Ben said, "only I did it on film, for at least fifty million viewers."

Sarah didn't answer. She came out from behind her desk, put her arms around him, and kissed him on the cheek. "Good luck, Ben," she said gently. "I'm in your corner, you know that."

7

"I don't have to tell you what a stupid thing you did,"
Ted Brennan had said before Ben had even been invited
to sit down. "You can't imagine the kind of flack we've
been catching ever since that film went on the air. What
the fuck happened to you?"

"I don't know, Ted."

"I couldn't believe it, even after I saw it."

"Ted, honest to God, I don't know what got into me."

"Well, goddammit, come in and sit down," Brennan snapped. "And shut the goddam door."

Whenever Ben recalled the scene later, it always seemed to be happening in slow motion. Brennan's office became huge, dark, menacing—the solid oak furniture in the room distorted grotesquely to resemble the illustrations in a collection of *Grimm's Fairy Tales* he'd owned as a boy. Brennan himself, in this fantasy, came to resemble one of the evil gnomes that had pranced across those pages. He perched behind his looming desk like an underground king punishing a terrified subject. In the vision, Ben always wilted and sank to the floor. The scene had become as real to him as the one that had actually taken place, and sometimes he had to fight to clear his head, to recall the exact circumstances, the simple words spoken.

"Ben, you're off the White House beat," Brennan had told him immediately. "But then, that shouldn't surprise you."

"No."

Brennan had hesitated before going on, distaste for this meeting evident on his ruddy, soft Irish features.

Everything about Brennan was a little soft, Ben thought. He was a "newsie," who'd begun on newspapers and clawed his way up through the ranks, making the jump into TV at the right time. He had the professional newspaperman's hard-shell, cynical exterior and an instinct for the jugular, Ben surmised, to rise this high in the executive hierarchy. But he'd never impressed Ben as really tough; there was this strange quality of softness. In his mid-fifties, Brennan looked every day of his age—a little stooped, a little blurred around the edges, a little overweight. Almost automatically, he chain-smoked unfiltered cigarettes and his hacking cough jolted his rimless glasses. From their first meeting, he had struck Ben as bright and capable, but somehow always a little insecure. Brennan seemed to fade into the background whenever the Chairman was in the room, but then, didn't everyone? Ben had never taken Brennan too seriously, especially during these past few months when his own star had seemed so securely on the ascendant. Maybe he'd misjudged Brennan, underrated him.

"You're going back to Washington, though," Brennan resumed. "For a few weeks, anyway."

"Oh?"

"You'll write for the morning news."

Ben stared at him, but Brennan swiveled away to avoid his gaze. Groping in a lower drawer for a Kleenex, he blew his nose and reached for another cigarette. Ben waited. He knew as well as Brennan exactly what this assignment implied: the performance of a menial, humiliating task that would be made more unendurable by turning out to be no task at all; they'd stick him at a desk and give him nothing to do.

"You said a few weeks," Ben prodded.

"Yeah," Brennan said, inhaling deeply. "As soon as we have an opening here, we'll bring you into New York."

Ben's spirits rose, but only fleetingly. "Here?"

"Not network," Brennan explained. "You'll be covering the nightside beat for local news. We have a man retiring."

"You're kidding, Ted."

Brennan looked hard at him. "That's it, Ben."

"That's it?"

Brennan nodded. He kept his cold gaze on Ben and it was at this very moment, Ben thought, that the fantasy scene which would haunt him later began to take shape in his subconscious. He'd just been crushed, as finally as if sentenced for some unspeakable crime against humanity. Brennan, the gnome, blandly gazed back at him and kept silent.

"Ted, just tell me this," Ben said. "Was this your idea?"

Still Brennan didn't answer.

"One mistake and you throw me on the shit heap? Did Mr. Hoenig—"

"Mr. Hoenig does not run this division," Brennan said without emotion. "You're off the White House beat and you're—"

Stunned, Ben did not hear Brennan repeat himself. In a matter of a few minutes, he'd lost everything he'd worked for during his whole life. All he had left was the rubble of a career; the door he was entering led out and away from everything he'd always dreamed of. It was over, finished. *He* was over, finished.

He did not remember leaving Ted Brennan's office. His surroundings seemed surrealistic, dreamlike, as though he had detached himself from the man who walked like an automaton along the thickly carpeted halls of the executive floor at network headquarters in New York. Somehow, he could stare down at himself with objectivity. That wasn't Ben Stryker, not the real Ben Stryker. That was a creature he didn't know, a lost creature, abandoned to the surge of so many conflicting emotions that he risked being torn apart by them as by so many animals. *Poor bastard. Look, he's almost crying.*

In the elevator and on his way out of the building, he was recognized and people spoke to him. He couldn't hear what they were saying, but he answered them, nodding, smiling, keeping up the façade so that no one would perceive that he wasn't a man at all, only the shell of one, the semblance of a reality, a shadow of what had once been Ben Stryker.

In the taxi, on his way back to the airport, he leaned back in a corner and closed his eyes. *You'll never amount to anything, Ben,* he heard the man's voice say. *You're nothing, boy. . . .*

"I am, too," he heard the boy's voice reply, and knew it was his own.

The man laughed. "Shit, boy, you're nothing but a liar and that's what you've always been." He was a brute of a man, with the beefy, red neck of a retired athlete. He stood in the middle of the living room and mocked the boy. "You're always telling everybody that black is white and white is black, that your father is some kind of goddam war hero—"

"He was! He is!" the boy shouted.

"He's a bum and a liar, just like you, boy."

"He isn't, damn you! You're the liar!"

The big man reached out and cuffed him, and sent him staggering back onto the sofa. "Harry, don't!" His mother's voice.

"Listen, Ellen," the big man said to her, "it's about time he faced up to what he is. He's a goddam liar, aren't you, boy?" Ben did not answer. "Aren't you?"

"I don't know."

"Well, I do. Hell, you're always telling everybody how your family's so much better than theirs, so much richer, so much happier, and that you're so high and mighty over all of them. My God, they're laughing at you, Ben. Your father was a bum and a drunk who left your mother in the lurch without a dime. If it hadn't been for me—"

"Don't, Harry, please." Her voice again, but for some reason Ben could only hear her in this recollection, never see her. Was she hiding from him? Was she too afraid to let him see her?

"When I married your mother I gave her a home and security." The big man stood over Ben now, rocking on the balls of his feet. "And I want some respect from you, boy. I don't want any more of your damn lies, you hear me?"

How he hated that man, hated him so much he still couldn't bring himself to call him by name. Why had his mother ever married him? Could she have been that desperate? Why didn't his father ever come to see him anymore?

I ran. It seemed to me I was always running. We moved four times more after my mother remarried and I just couldn't seem to crack the cliques at every new school. I didn't go on joyrides or to ball games or to parties. No, I ran, I kept on running. . . .

Maybe that was why he'd joined the Air Force in 1957, immediately after getting out of high school. *Yeah, I was still running.* The Air Force had structure and a disdain for emotion which comforted him. And he liked, actually enjoyed, the physical rigors of basic training. He'd felt consumed, and used in a positive way.

But at night, before he fell asleep, he'd think about his classmates, how most of them were spending a leisurely summer vacation and how, in the fall, they'd be heading off to college, to join fraternities and sororities, their lives rich with friendship and acceptance. It was during those long, lonely times that Ben began to nurture his dream.

I swear, I swear to God that someday, somehow, I'm going to be somebody important. . . .

In the airplane, all the way back to Washington that day, Ben fought hard to put the pieces of his life back together in his mind. He began to nurture one tiny flicker of hope—the CIA contact. All his thoughts and energies focused on it. Over and over he recalled every word of the conversation with his mysterious caller, and he realized how important to him that dialogue had become. He had to hang on, wait for the man to call again, and begin—bit by bit, one small piece at a time—to weave a lifeline to haul himself out of the pit into which Brennan and the network had hurled him. Slowly, carefully, he would put together the story of the century—authenticated, backed by solid evidence, with facts, names, dates, places. And he'd explode it in their faces. Ben Stryker would come back.

As the wheels of the DC-9 smoked onto the runway at Washington National Airport and the plane shuddered to a stop, Ben stared through the Plexiglas window beside his seat. Somewhere out there, he thought, somewhere in that city is a man who is going to pick up a telephone anytime now and dial my number. *I'll wait. I'll hang on and wait, no matter what happens. It can't be long.*

The weeks passed and Ben moved through them as if in a dream. Hour after hour, day after day, he sat at a desk in the morning news offices of the ACN Washington complex, pretending he was busy. Occasionally, he'd pay a visit to the bureau premises down the hall. He smiled a lot. He traded jokes with the other staffers. He maintained a resolutely cheerful front and even put off Sarah each time she hinted she was still on his side, that she was available for counsel, if he so desired.

Ben didn't so desire. He had built a wall around himself

and he kept his distance, impregnable behind his one defense; he would work out his own salvation. All he had to do was wait it out, hang tough.

His only moment of real panic came when Sarah informed him one morning that he was being transferred to New York the following week. Ben realized he had only five more days. *Five more days.* And he'd been waiting three weeks now for the man to call. What in God's name was delaying him?

"Ben, are you all right?" Sarah asked him. "You look terrible."

"I'm OK," Ben said. "I'm fine."

He managed to control himself for the rest of the day, but he wasn't sure he could get through the night. He went home, panic weighing heavily in his gut. As his key turned in the lock, he heard the phone ring.

Sweating slightly, Ben picked up the receiver. "Hello?"

"Ben?"

"Yes. It's about time."

"I'm sorry about what happened."

"Yeah, well, those things—"

"I mean, about your new job in New York."

"How'd you find that out?"

"I'm in the business of finding things out."

Ben chuckled. What did it matter, after all? The important thing was that the contact had been reestablished. "Since you know," he said, "you can see that you've become pretty important to me. I intend to do your story and do it right. It'll serve your purposes and it'll save my ass."

"I understand your thinking perfectly, Ben," the voice replied smoothly, "and I have a certain amount of sympathy. But if you think about it a little, you'll see that what I'm doing is far too important and far too risky to involve someone who's trying to save his own ass, as you put it. You have serious problems, Ben. I can't use you."

Ben flushed and tried to control his rising fear. "Wait, you don't understand."

"No. *You* don't understand. Good-bye, Ben."

"You waited all this time to tell me—"

The click at the other end of the line severed the connection. Ben held the receiver to his ear for what seemed like hours. "No," he muttered over and over, "no." The pain and desolation that had swept over him periodically during these past weeks were nothing to the horror that gripped him now. He had prevented himself from cracking up by focusing all of his hopes on this one way out, and now it had vanished, turned to dust in his hands, and blown away.

For the first time in his life, Ben felt himself slip out of control. He staggered and almost fell; then he leaned over the table and threw up.

8

"How's Stryker coming along?" the Chairman asked, swiveling away from the smoke-gray, twelve-feet-high Thermopane windows on the forty-fourth floor. "I'm worried about him."

"No need to be," the younger man replied. "He's doing very nicely, I think. All that's required is another couple of months, I think."

"Good. I believe we have the time."

"I'm sure of it."

"You're keeping an eye on him, I take it?"

"An eye *and* an ear, Larry."

"Fine. I don't want any mistakes."

"There won't be any. It's all going to work out very well. You can count on it."

"It had better work out." The Chairman drummed the tips of his expensively manicured fingers together, rocking back into the depths of his oak-and-leather chair. It was a sound program they'd worked out—he was certain of that—but still there were risks. He knew he could trust Crawford to give it his full attention and that was reassuring, though no one could guarantee success in these matters. The Chairman had been around long enough never to take anything for granted.

"We do have a couple of other alternatives," Crawford reminded him, "just in case."

"I'm not interested," the Chairman snapped. "I'm interested in one thing—success."

"Right."

"There's a lot on the line here."

"I know that, sir."

The Chairman's silver hair, parted perfectly on the left side and brushed smoothly backward, glowed in the filtered rays of the late-afternoon sun. He rocked slowly back and forth behind the vast expanse of the uncluttered burled-walnut desk and gazed with studied calm at his visitor. The Chairman wore the look of success, his face deeply tanned and etched with the lines of seventy years and decades of command. Above the strong, aquiline nose, emotionless blue-gray eyes looked coldly at the world. Even at first sight, it was easy to believe the stories about Lawrence Hoenig, the ruthless climber who had started from nothing so many years before and built himself a monolithic communications and entertainment empire. Now his eyes locked with those of the younger man sitting opposite, seeming to pierce the guarded nonchalance the visitor affected. "Nothing must be left to chance, Crawford. We must overlook nothing."

Crawford nodded. Casually elegant in his gray pinstriped suit, club tie, and neat button-down collar, slouching in the smaller chair opposite the Chairman, at first glance Crawford seemed overmatched. But the latent power of the man—the bulk, the weight of toned muscle—was not completely disguised by the Madison Avenue costume. Suddenly he seemed as formidable as the Chairman. This was clearly a partnership, a relationship between equals. The tension in the room had nothing to do with fear; it was the lust of combat, of the impending kill, that permeated this rarefied air.

"I'm paid not to overlook things," Crawford said, the hint of a smile on his lips.

"Exactly."

The Chairman swiveled away from the younger man again and resumed his contemplation of the skyline, his gaze sweeping the battlements of the skyscrapers lining the Avenue of the Americas. His mouth tightened slightly and his fingers drummed idly on the arms of his chair. "And how soon," he asked quietly, "before we pull the plug on Agnew?"

"Very soon."

"Can you be more specific?"

"No, I can't. But it shouldn't be too much longer."

"I'm hearing rumors. Actually, they're more than just rumors."

"About Nixon wanting to dump him?"

The Chairman nodded. "Right."

"Forget it," Crawford said. "He has the nomination locked up. They want him."

"Good."

"No doubt about it, Larry."

The Chairman spun slowly around and, almost idly, fingered the remote-control panel just below the surface of his desk. The wall behind Crawford parted noiselessly to reveal four large screens, each one silently alive with the afternoon news programs. On one screen, the sincere, smiling face of Bill James addressed WACN viewers; on two of the other channels, as if by command, loomed the slick, smoothly ingratiating features of Spiro T. Agnew. The vice president of the United States was answering reporters' questions, prior to his departure for Miami. Even without audio, he seemed supremely confident.

"Look at the creature," the Chairman said, with no hint of anger in his voice. "You'd think he didn't have a worry in the world."

"He doesn't even look like a good con man," Crawford said, turning to watch the screens without real interest. "He fooled a lot of people, didn't he?"

The Chairman nodded grimly. He remembered sitting in this very room when the news of Agnew's first attack on the networks was broadcast. He remembered the exact date and place, too—November 13, 1969, Des Moines, Iowa. The man had touched a nerve in the national consciousness with those first well-turned, inflammatory phrases. "Media excesses," he had said, and hundreds of thousands of Americans—perhaps millions—had responded immediately, almost all favorably. TV news commentators, Agnew had implied, could, "by the expression on their faces, the tone of their questions, and the sarcasm of their responses . . . make or break by their coverage and commentary." The networks themselves, Agnew had continued, were clearly to blame. They represented "a concentration of power over American public opinion unknown in history," administered by a small group of privileged men "elected by no one and enjoying a monopoly sanctioned and licensed by government." What the country faced, he clearly implied, was a conspiracy by these privileged few, who talked only to one another and were responsible to no one but themselves. Pressed some time later to justify his attacks on the networks, Agnew had said, "As with other American institutions, perhaps it is time that the networks were made more responsive to the views of the nation."

The Chairman could recall that speech almost word for word, as well as all those that had followed it. He had recognized the danger before any of his colleagues, seen it spelled out on the faces of the enraptured believers, who cheered and laughed and rose as one in the tens of thousands to pay homage to their new champion. The Chairman could smell death in the air. An emperor, he felt his empire totter. To him, the Spiro T. Agnews were not gadflies; they had too much power and were not averse to wielding it ruthlessly, and in their own interests.

"Do you remember what I told you at the time?"

Crawford nodded. "Sure. I was sitting right here. You sniffed it out before any of us."

"That crowd reaction," the Chairman said thoughtfully. "I knew then—immediately. They were going to blame us for everything—the protests, the campus burnings, the agonies of Vietnam."

"It was dynamite, all right." Crawford shook his head. "I always thought the guy was a clown."

65

"He knew what he was doing." The Chairman's eyes were still fixed unwaveringly on the images of Agnew mouthing silently on the wall screens. "He tapped into a wellspring of public discontent that he knew—that they *all* knew—they could focus on us. You were here."

"We had advance word on what Agnew would say in Des Moines," Crawford said. "I remember I called you about it."

"Right. And nobody understood it fully but me."

"Correct, Larry."

"You even thought we'd have to wait a bit. And Frank Stanton at CBS—calling the speech an unprecedented attempt to intimidate us. As if we didn't know. We didn't need any damned rebuttal. We needed action."

"You called it, Larry."

The vice president's features faded from the screens and were replaced by commercials. On the ACN monitor, Bill James was into a human-interest story about a boy in Queens and his tree-climbing dog. The Chairman switched off the sets and pushed himself away from the desk, his cold gaze riveted on Crawford. "I was the only one who realized Agnew was the perfect tool for the administration at that particular moment," he said. "His very ineptitude worked to Nixon's advantage."

Crawford nodded and waited, knowing that, by this confirmation of his own wisdom, the Chairman was leading up to the final endorsement of the campaign they had mapped out, the two of them, here in this very room. They'd come a long way together, he and this powerful man, and he knew he could neither rush nor alter the Chairman's calculated strategy. Crawford's tactic was born of years of experience. He let the Chairman outline all the reasons for an action, weigh all the options, and formulate the outlines of a plan. The details and the implementation were Crawford's specialties. He sat back until the Chairman could pick his way through every possible pitfall and trap, every confusing diversion, to where they now stood, almost ready to move at last.

"Of course, I was never fooled by Agnew," the Chairman said reflectively. "I knew who he was, what he was doing, and who was behind it."

"You certainly did, Larry."

"The only thing we had to be sure of was his renomination," the Chairman continued. "That seems assured, if your estimates are accurate, and I've no reason to think they aren't."

"I don't make that kind of mistake."

"No."

"Anyway, Larry, let me fill you in a little."

"Good."

"We're digging up all kinds of interesting items in the financial records of the Republican Party in Baltimore County. It looks as if Agnew's been taking payoffs for years, about a thousand a week from construction interests while he was county executive and then governor. We think he may still be taking bribes. Anyway, we should have it pretty solidly nailed down and ready to feed to Justice right after the election."

The Chairman's gaze strayed back to the view from his window, as if deriving added reassurance of his power and impregnability from the splendor of the sight. "That thieving clown," he mused contentedly. "And we thought he'd be the difficult one."

"It's pretty clumsy," Crawford agreed. "I mean, if you're going to steal, you might as well steal big. This hack got bought for little more than a song."

Again the Chairman swung away from the window, and this time he smiled. "You were telling me earlier about those two young reporters . . ."

Crawford nodded. "It looks promising. They're pretty low down in the pecking order over there at the *Post*, but they're ambitious and dedicated. We've been feeding them some pretty good stuff. Carefully, of course."

"That's essential."

"Yes. We drop hints, provide clues. When they go shooting off on tangents or make dumb guesses, we make it pretty clear they're fucking up. We've dropped a nice trail of crumbs for them to follow and so far they've been pretty bright and inventive."

"Any major problems?"

"Not so far. The main one, as I told you, is to see that the higher-ups on the masthead don't kill the story."

"You make certain they don't."

"I'm working very hard on it, Larry."

"What is it they're calling you guys now?"

"Deep Throat. Cute, huh?"

The Chairman smiled again; then he leaned back in his chair and began to chuckle. When Crawford rose to go, the Chairman turned back to his window, waiting for the sound of the closing door before he reached for the phone.

"Shirley, get me Washington," he said.

For two months, Lisa Parks had been working in the secretarial pool on the executive floors, but she had never seen the man before. After she passed him in the hallway beyond the elevators—feeling herself blush under the appraising stare of those clear hazel eyes—she stopped at Shirley Boyd's desk. The older woman had just hung up;

she raised an eyebrow at the girl's obvious excitement. "Miss Boyd," Lisa asked, "who *was* that?"

Shirley looked her over. Pretty, she thought, but a dimwit. After two months, she still didn't know enough not to ask too many questions. Shirley smiled her cool, professional smile and said very sweetly, "Whom do you mean, Lisa?"

"That gorgeous hunk of man by the elevators." The girl looked longingly down the corridor. "My God, he looks like an ad or something. I mean, he's beautiful."

"That's Mr. Crawford, I believe," Shirley said. "And he is *not* beautiful, Lisa. Women are beautiful, men are handsome."

"Oh, not to me, Miss Boyd," the girl enthused. "I think he's super looking."

"Yes," Shirley said, "now, if you'll get on with your work, Lisa—"

"But who *is* he?"

"Mr. Crawford is vice president in charge of Special Projects here."

"I've never seen him before."

"He rarely comes into the office," Shirley said patiently. "Mr. Crawford travels a lot and works mainly on his own." She picked up the phone and again smiled brightly at the girl. "Go back to work, Lisa," she said. "This is not *Cosmopolitan* Magazine."

Outside the ACN building, settled comfortably in the back seat of the taxi pulling away from the curb, Crawford reached into his breast pocket and produced what seemed to be a gold cigarette lighter. Holding it below the driver's rearview line of vision, he opened it and withdrew a miniature cassette. Scribbling a date on the label, he slipped the packet into an inside pocket and returned the recorder to his breast pocket. How much easier it was these days to tape conversations than it had been back in 1954, when he had first met Lawrence Hoenig. Then he'd had to carry his equipment around in a briefcase and find excuses to leave it behind. So many things had changed for the better.

9

The Chairman's call had come toward the end of a slow day. Sarah had been expecting it, but even so she still couldn't quite believe it. Brennan had telephoned her, too, a few minutes later, ostensibly to congratulate her, but she couldn't remember exactly what she'd said to him. His florid good wishes had seemed genuine, even though he must have recognized the threat posed by her promotion and her rapid rise in the news division. Perhaps Ted

71

didn't care anymore. His career, after all, was behind him. Anyway, she wasn't going to worry about that now; tonight she was going to make the most of her good news and tell Farwell. It wouldn't matter to him, of course, but he'd have to know just the same, and the sooner the better.

The news had leaked out before she left the premises. Fred Skinner, one of her reporters, caught her in her office. Grinning with open admiration and genuine pleasure, his blue eyes snapping with excitement, he sauntered into the room. "Did I hear right, Sarah? You're going to New York?"

She nodded and smiled back at him. "Yes. Mr. Hoenig called me this afternoon."

Fred pursed his lips and whistled. "I'm properly impressed. Straight from old Genghis Khan himself, eh?" He beamed at her. "I think it's terrific, Sarah. No kidding."

"It's nice of you to say so, Fred."

"You deserve it, lady. You're the best."

"You're prejudiced."

"Maybe. I might just inherit your job."

Sarah's smile faded. "They're bringing Dalton in from London—"

Skinner grinned and waved a deprecating hand. "I know, I know. Old Fred always gets passed over."

"Come on, you didn't want it. You told me so."

"Right!" He laughed. "Just wanted to see if you still loved me. They'll bury me with a camera strapped to my shoulder, a tape recorder glued to my ass, and a microphone nailed to each hand. You know me, kid. I'm not bureau chief material. You are."

"I hope that's a compliment."

"It is, lady, it is." Suddenly he dropped the pose, came close to her, and took her hand. "Sarah," he said seriously, "it's been great working for you. I wish you all the best.

I know Ned Dalton. He's a good man. I worked for him in the Middle East during the late fifties and again in Paris. But you're the best. Good luck."

She hoped he wouldn't kiss her and he didn't. Poor Fred perspired a lot and it made him a little clammy to the touch. Besides, Sarah was wary of sentiment right now. Two drinks and Freddy would cry on your shoulder at parties. He cried in movies, he'd told her. He was a good man and first-rate on stories in which his emotions didn't get in the way; but he was limited, definitely limited. He was the sort of reporter every bureau needed—solid, committed, dependable, a real pro—but a routine talent. There was nothing inspired or unusual about him. He wasn't a golden boy like Ben Stryker, just a good company man. Some epitaph that would make, Sarah thought. She would miss his wide grin and his relentless cheerfulness, but not that badly. She'd become too much of a pro herself, too good for the Fred Skinners now, though she'd never have said so out loud, and she was ashamed of herself for even thinking that way.

"Freddy," she said, "I've got to get out of here. Does everybody know?"

"It's no secret, is it? I was on the phone to New York and Bellucci told me. He overheard somebody talking to Cargill about it."

"No, it's no secret. It's just that I want to get out of here tonight without any big farewells."

"No problem. I won't tell a soul till after you've gone."

"We have a dinner to go to and Farwell hasn't heard—"

"I understand. When are you leaving, by the way?"

"I'm going to New York tomorrow, then I'll come back to clean things up and get out in about a week, I guess. I'm going to Miami, of course."

"Well, OK, that's great," Fred said. "But by tomorrow it'll be all over town, you know. I think you're the first woman ever to be put in charge of presidential coverage during an election, aren't you?"

"The first one at ACN, certainly."

"Or any network. It's swell, really."

"You're a nice guy, Fred. Thanks. I appreciate it."

She managed to make her escape without any other encounters with the staff, at least with anyone who might know. Weaving expertly out of the bureau complex, she eased the big Lincoln Continental into the rush-hour traffic that moved away from the hub.

A storm hovered to the west of the city and a few big raindrops spattered her windshield, but outside she could tell it was still hot and unbearably muggy. Even within the air-conditioned comfort of the car, she could feel her skirt sticking to the leather seat, and the backs of her bare legs felt sweaty. She was eager to get home and plunge into a cool tub before confronting Farwell, but there was no way she was going to beat this traffic. All the roads over the Potomac bridges were clogged by now; there was nothing to do but to wait it out.

She turned on the radio and picked up the news. Agnew, the commentator was saying, would almost certainly make the nominating speech at the convention in Miami, even though it was by no means certain that he himself would be asked by President Nixon to run again. The vice president's attacks on the war protesters, the young, and especially the media had made him extremely popular within the party, but perhaps somewhat too controversial.

Sarah smiled, turned the dial, and found some soothing music—a lush Cole Porter medley with lots of strings and a delicate, understated beat. She began to hum as the car

74

inched toward the Virginia hills. She'd made it, made it in a big way, and no one, certainly not Farwell, was going to block her career any longer. He'd see it her way or she'd leave him. That was something, she reflected, she might have done a long time ago. . . .

She had married well, just as her mother had taught her. Farwell Anderson had all the qualifications. He was a good deal older than she, he came from a good Eastern family that had figured prominently in the Social Register for generations, and, most important, he was wealthy. "It's just as easy to fall in love with a rich man as a poor one," her mother used to say.

Sarah owed a lot to her mother, a strong-minded woman born into an Irish family of modest means, a woman who had known hard times. Young Mary Murphy had scrubbed floors to work her way through school and become a nurse, first in a small rural hospital back home in Indiana, then for a group of doctors who set up a private clinic in Milwaukee. She'd married one of them, the ultimate ambition of most nurses of her day. Prosperity and two daughters had followed, before her husband, overworked and under too much pressure at home, had keeled over dead early one morning in the bathroom. He'd left some property and enough insurance money for Mary to raise their two girls properly.

Mary had never forgotten her early years of struggle; Sarah and her younger sister Lee had had the best of everything. And from the moment they could think, it had been drummed into them that a successful woman was a woman who caught a successful man.

"We were brought up to think of ourselves as ornaments, the sort of possessions prosperous men acquired," Sarah had once told an interviewer in a careless moment. "We were taught how to dress, we were taught manners, we learned to disguise our real emotions and to be properly refined and submissive, eager to bow to masculine superiority."

Why else had she suffered through all those goddam piano lessons, for instance? Today, Sarah thought, smiling inwardly, about all she could play were seven bars of a Chopin prelude.

Lee had cracked under this regime. She'd run off and married a trombone-player, and she'd paid the price for it. Divorced three times, she was an alcoholic now, a lonely, embittered middle-aged woman living off her alimony checks. But Sarah had learned her lessons well. At the age of twenty-one, during one of those terrific football weekends at Princeton, she'd met Farwell Anderson.

He was perfect in every way. The thirty-five-year-old scion of a wealthy Washington family, Farwell was good-looking, lazy, and weak. He made few sexual demands on her, even at first, but then Sarah had never enjoyed sex much. She'd always had some vaguely formed ambitions, but had never been able to focus them on anything. She'd been taught by Mary that it was a man's world, and you lived with that reality and made the best of it. First you achieved security through a man, then you could fulfill your real self in other ways, preferably through your children. She'd submitted to Farwell's clumsy, brief love-making, but he'd made it clear very early that all he really expected of her was to manage his social obligations. For his family's sake, of course, they'd have to produce some heirs. It was unthinkable that the Andersons, with all their grace and power, could simply be allowed to fade away.

The heirs never came and the social obligations had soon

begun to wear thin. By the time Sarah had turned thirty, her relationship with her husband had become chilly, even, on occasion, openly hostile. Luckily, Farwell was weak and she'd been able to avoid an open split. She had Lee's example to warn her of the pitfalls of divorce, and she needed Farwell's social connections to build a life for herself. He'd blamed her, of course, for the absence of children, but she'd tried very hard. It wasn't her fault that she could get him into bed with her only rarely, even to go through the obligatory motions. At best, his performance was unsatisfactory and fleeting, and she had considered having an affair simply to conceive. But she was afraid Farwell might guess the truth and his misplaced pride would make him divorce her. No, she'd played the game with him strictly by the rules; she was safe, as long as she didn't bend or break them. But, as the years passed, more and more she'd resented this role as social director and brood mare.

At thirty-five, over Farwell's objections, she'd begun her pursuit of freedom. By then, she knew enough about his secret vices to force him to let her do what she wanted. She used her social leverage to land a job as a researcher for the Washington bureau of ACN.

It could have led nowhere. The job itself was of no consequence, and from the beginning she'd had to buck the resentment of the staff. She'd earned their respect by her sheer hard work and her quick mind, and she'd used the job and her connections to create a new and independent future for herself. She hadn't had to use her body either, and that, too, had earned her the respect of the men for whom she worked. Like Ben Stryker, she'd been drawn irresistibly to the power and privilege of television news. Instead of gossiping with the wives of important men,

Sarah had found herself talking to the high and mighty themselves, prying out information for nationwide telecasts. It was a heady feeling, being at the center of things, and she loved it.

Within two years, she'd been promoted to news writer. This corporate recognition of her worthiness had aroused in her feelings of warmth and pride that she hadn't suspected were there. Above everything now, she lusted for success—and mostly for power that satisfied her deepest needs and fulfilled her as her marriage never had. She'd married the corporation, she realized. She had become its willing instrument and it suited her perfectly.

At thirty-eight, Sarah had been promoted from writer to field producer, and two years later she'd become the Washington bureau chief. Now a whole new vista was opening up to her. She would make the most of it. The Chairman himself had called to tell her the good news. What better confirmation of her talent and worthiness could she have had?

Despite the heavy traffic, Sarah arrived home earlier than usual that afternoon. She saw the little Fiat sports car parked in the circular driveway, but she didn't immediately make the connection. She and Farwell had always played by unwritten rules that banned their secret lives from their picture-book home. It was a rule that applied mainly to Farwell; Sarah had nothing to hide. She was as faithful to her career as she had been to Farwell.

She parked the big Lincoln under the porte cochere over the side entrance and let herself into the house. Evidently, they hadn't heard her drive up. They came walking hand in hand toward the front door. The boy was fully dressed, but Farwell was in shirtsleeves, his collar was open, and his bare feet were thrust into bedroom slippers. He colored deeply when he saw her, but the boy smiled and held out a hand to her.

"Hi!" he said, unruffled. "You must be Sarah. Farwell's told me so much about you. I'm Eric."

"He just came by to return a book," Farwell mumbled. "I was napping."

"Nice to meet you, Eric," Sarah said pleasantly, allowing him to shake her hand. "I'm sorry you can't stay."

"Oh, no. I'm so late now. Good-bye. I'll call you, Farwell." With another dazzling smile, he bounced out, shutting the door behind him.

"He's a nice kid," Farwell said after a moment. "I met him at the Johnsons'."

"He's darling," Sarah purred. "You bastard, Farwell."

He tried to make his escape into the living room, but she followed him inside, closing the double doors behind her. He headed for the bar, but she caught him by the arm. "I want to talk to you," she said. "Please don't get drunk."

"I'm sorry, Sarah," he said, avoiding her eyes. "I didn't invite him here. He just showed up."

"And so all you could do was make him feel at home. Anyway, I don't want to see him here again, or anywhere, for that matter."

"You won't, I promise. I tried to make him go, but he thinks he can charm his way out of anything."

"I don't care what you do, Farwell, you know that," she said with steel in her voice. "But we do have servants and in this town—"

"I know, I know. I said I'm sorry."

"It won't do. Even when I'm not here, this is our home. Find some other place to play in."

"I've never—you know I haven't—"

"Yes, all right, I know. I believe you about Eric. Let's not belabor it."

He stood there facing her, his small, pudgy hands fiddling nervously with the seams of his trousers, while his eyes implored her not to punish him further. She couldn't feel sorry for him anymore; he didn't even disgust her as he had years ago when she'd first found out about him and his dismal young men. None of that mattered to her, but she had her own life to think about now, and she wasn't going to have her reputation ruined, not as long as she and Farwell lived under the same roof.

She turned away from him and gazed out the picture window, her eyes sweeping over the long, gradual slope of manicured lawn leading down to the stables, and beyond them the wooded ridge that marked the western boundary of their property. From this window she could not, in fact, see a foot of land that didn't belong to them. Twelve years before, when she and Farwell had bought this Virginia estate, she'd been charmed by that realization; today it held no meaning for her.

"I'm going to New York," she said quietly.

"Oh? When?" He rustled around for ice cubes at the bar and dropped several into a silver shaker. "Want a drink?"

"No, thanks," she said, without turning around. "I'm going tomorrow, for a day or two. Then I'm coming back here to pack up."

"Pack up? What do you mean?"

She sat down then and told him about the job and what it meant to her. He heard her out in silence, sipping steadily at his drink. "I'll be here from time to time," she said, "but most of the time I'll be living in New York."

"You expect me to come with you?"

"No, I don't, Farwell. If you want to come occasionally, of course you'll be welcome. We'll rent a big enough place, though eventually we should buy, I suppose. It depends on how the job works out."

"That's what you want?"

"Yes."

"I'll have to think about it."

She smiled. "Farwell, there's nothing to think about. I've already accepted."

"Do you want a divorce, Sarah?"

"No. Do you?"

He didn't answer; he sat slumped in his chair. He looked even more vulnerable now than when she'd surprised him with Eric. "I—I'll have to think—"

"I'll do whatever you want, Farwell," she said. "I've been a good wife to you and you have no reason to complain. I don't mind what you do and whom you see, so long as we try to be kind to each other. Maybe it's better this way. Anyway, it's what I want."

She got up and went over to him. Leaning down, she kissed him on the cheek. He looked up at her helplessly. "I'm sorry," he said. "I'm sorry it all came out this way."

"Don't be sorry for me, Farwell," she said brightly. "I'm grateful for everything, really I am. And I'm very happy with my life right now. I wish you were."

She left him alone then, in the darkened room, his empty glass in his hand, and she went upstairs to begin packing.

10

"Ben, darling, you don't have to explain anything to me."
"But I wanted to, Kathy. I don't know what got into me."
"It's OK. I understand."
"Do you?"
"Yes, I know what you've been through. I spoke to Mr. Cargill about it."

"You spoke to Derrick about me?"

"Oh, God, don't be angry. I was so darn worried about you. Listen, he's really on your side."

"I'll bet."

"He has so much respect for you. He thinks you're really good."

"Yeah, that's nice."

They were sitting in a dark corner of Kathy's favorite little French bistro, a hole in the wall somewhere in the east seventies. It had little checkered tablecloths, big, dripping candles in wax-encrusted bottles, and an indifferent menu that was healthily overpriced. There was no wine drinkable under ten dollars a bottle. Still, Ben reflected, it had been sweet of her to ask him and to insist on paying the check. He wasn't going to let her do that, but he appreciated the gesture. He'd been feeling rotten about the way he treated her that morning. A nice kid, Kathy, and she really did care about him. The day he came back to the office, she was the first one to pop in and say hello. A nice kid, with a wonderful body.

"I'm sure everything's going to work out for you," she said. "I just know it is."

"Let's forget all that tonight."

"Darling, don't you want to talk about it?"

"Not much."

"It might help, if we could talk."

"I don't think so. Let's not."

"You heard about Sarah Anderson?"

"Oh, sure. That's great for her."

"You told me she likes you a lot. I just know she'll help."

He was tired, he told himself. Mainly, he was tired of her chatter. If only she wouldn't try so hard, wouldn't keep pushing all the time. He was going to put it all together in the end, he knew that. He was going to make it all come out fine. He'd made some adjustments in his thinking these past two days and he had a good grip on the whole situation. He had a job to do now, but he wasn't about to discuss it with Kathy Lewis. Or with anybody, for that matter.

She leaned across the table and reached out for his hand. She loved the way the candlelight flickered over his face; it made him more handsome than ever. It deepened and emphasized his character lines, even as it made him seem more vulnerable than perhaps he was. She remembered what Derrick Cargill had said, that there was this mysterious element in Ben. It was one of the things that attracted her to him. She wanted to solve the mystery in Ben; she felt it would bring him closer to her, within reach of her love and everything she could give him and bring to their relationship.

"You're right," she said. "We shouldn't talk about it anymore tonight. I just want you to know I care about you, that's all."

"I like you, too, Kathy."

She took his hand and held it tightly. "I love your hands. They're so strong. You must have been a wonderful little boy."

He winced slightly. "What do you mean by that?"

"Well, you built things, I bet. Or you were terrifically good at sports, maybe. I'll bet you were a neat kid. Where'd you grow up?"

"Here and there. I was alone a lot."

"Ah," she exclaimed, smiling, "and you were an only child, I'll bet."

He nodded. "Why?"

"I knew it," she said triumphantly. "I just knew it. *That's* your problem. . . ."

"The boy's alone all the time, Burton," his mother used to say. "Why don't you spend more time with him?"

"How the hell can I do that?" his father would shout at her. "Who's going to earn the money around here?"

"Don't you care about your son?"

His father had never answered that question; at least Ben couldn't remember him answering it. He'd storm out of the room and sometimes he wouldn't come home for days. During those periods, his mother would move around the house like a zombie, going through the motions but hardly alive, emotionally unconnected from everything and everyone, including Ben.

The outside world was no release, either. I couldn't make friends, I don't know why. I tried. Maybe it was because we were always moving. I always knew, wherever we went, that someday soon we'd be moving again and I became wary of the pain of all these separations. I was always the outsider, and after a while I didn't care about making friends. And they didn't want me either. I was the stranger in town, the new kid shut out from everything, from everyone.

"Damn you, Burton Stryker!" his mother had screamed late one afternoon at the drunken, swaying figure in the doorway, the wreckage of a man standing there, a briefcase of samples dangling from one hand. "Damn you to hell for what you're doing to us!"

I always thought they could hear them screaming at each other. Maybe that was why I had such a hard time.

I mean, nobody who heard those fights would want their own kids to have anything to do with such a family.

Ben remembered how his parents embarrassed him. Other kids' folks didn't behave that way. Other kids' houses looked lived in, but neat and comfortable just the same, not empty of warmth and forever in disarray. He remembered clearly how it pained him to see other kids' parents kissing and touching every time they said hello or good-bye; his own parents never kissed, never touched. The houses they lived in during those years of his childhood, all of them, were wastelands, empty of love but cluttered, like rubbish-strewn lots, with the litter of their living. *All those dishes stacked for days in sinks, ashtrays full of stubs, overflowing trash baskets, unmade beds . . .*

During the worst times, Ben subsisted on cold cereal and canned soup, and he learned to wear his pullovers inside out when they became too dirty. He adapted—and retreated into himself.

"He lies about you, Burton," his mother shouted at his father late one night. They didn't know he could hear them arguing. He'd crept down the stairs and hidden in the hall closet. He couldn't see them from there, but he could hear them, all right. "He lies about you. He lies about everything."

His father mumbled something in reply that Ben couldn't make out, but he heard his mother's answer clearly. "It's because he's alone all the time," she said. "You're never here and I've got to work. He lies about you, about us, because he wants to believe we're normal parents, like everybody else. Don't you see that? Can't you see anything?"

Ben heard the door slam and he knew that his father had stormed out of the house again, and out of his life. Huddling there in the closet, his arms around his knees, he had cried himself to sleep.

I was so alone, always so alone. . . .

Kathy's apartment was a perfect expression of her personality. She lived on the fifth floor of a brownstone between Fifth and Madison, and from her tiny rooftop terrace she had a good view of the elegant bulk of the Metropolitan Museum. The apartment was small, consisting basically of the back half of a floor-through—two rooms, a kitchenette, and a large bathroom with a deep, old-fashioned tub in which she soaked for hours while leafing through *The New Yorker* and *Vogue*. She didn't read much of either, but she enjoyed the cartoons and ads in the former and the knockout fashion layouts in the latter. She liked to stretch out on the couch in the living room and listen to her stereo; she played a lot of Puccini, and her taste in pop music ranged from the old standards to the quietest of the soft-rock groups. There was always music in the background while she made love or just dreamed there alone, her gaze roving tranquilly over the posters and lithographs—Klee, Steinberg, Matisse—with which she had decorated her walls.

The bedroom was small, almost filled by the double brass bed she'd picked up at an auction. It was the only piece she'd had to buy; the rest of the furniture, comfortable and undistinguished, had come from her family's summer place back in Michigan. Kathy loved her apartment. It was the first time in her life she had ever lived alone, and she was thrilled by the feeling that she was on her own—a young career girl in New York—and that she could bring this complicated older man back to her place. It fulfilled the fantasies she'd always had about the glamorous life that some day she would lead in New York, absolutely the only in place in America to be for a person, like herself, of sophistication and taste.

"It's nice," Ben said, looking around.

"You've never been here before," Kathy said. "I wanted you to see it. It's kind of cute, don't you think?"

"Very nice."

She turned on the radio and the soft, warm tones of Dionne Warwick—singing a medley of Bacharach tunes—filled the room. Ben sighed and sat down. Kathy, who knew his late-night tastes by now, poured him a brandy and an *amaretto* for herself. She came back to the couch, sat down beside him, and kissed him. "I think I'm in love with you," she whispered.

"Kathy, let's not make a huge event out of this."

"I don't care how you feel about me," she said. "I don't care if you just want to make love to me. But I can't help how *I* feel."

"You don't really know me."

"No, but I'm finding out." She giggled. "Please undress me."

She stood up and let him take her clothes off. She did have a miraculous body, he thought, as he removed her blouse and ran his hands over her large, firm breasts. Caressing her, he unzipped her skirt and tugged her panties down to her ankles. Warm to the touch, her long, bronzed legs straddled him as he sat back on the couch and she thrust her mouth hungrily down to kiss him. "Take me now," she murmured. "Right here. Now. Don't undress . . ."

He bit at her uptilted breasts as he thrust himself into her. With a moan of pleasure, she impaled herself upon him, moving violently to his rhythms as his hands clasped her buttocks and opened her up to receive him more fully.

88

They came together quickly, and her cry of pleasure wafted into the hot summer night through the open windows.

Moments later, he felt her shuddering in anticipation as he picked her up and carried her into the bedroom. Naked, she lay on her back against the sheets, watching him strip, marveling at the well-muscled proportions of his body. He was so tall. He came around the bed now to take her a second time, just as the music stopped and the news came on.

". . . the only issue seems to be, aside from the Agnew question, whether, in fact, there will be anything to occupy our interest at this convention," the commentator was saying. "What begins to appear certain is that the Republican party is facing the prospect of a convention devoid of inherent drama. According to the best-informed inside sources, what we are likely to get, two weeks from now in Miami, is the spectacle of a group of professional actors reading polished lines on cue, while President Nixon and his men accept the homage of the delegates and bask in the orchestrated, 'spontaneous' demonstrations that will acknowledge his renomination. However contrived and unspontaneous this spectacle may seem, there is no question that it will express the genuine affection the delegates feel for this man, who will have every right to derive the maximum pleasure from what is sure to be his most enjoyable and well-merited hour of triumph. For a week, now, the party faithful have been at work here preparing for the great event. . . ."

"What's wrong?" she asked.

He did not answer. Above her, as she lay on her back, her legs open to receive him, something calculated and savage moved within him. She felt herself pinioned; his hands twisted her flesh, his teeth sank into her. Before she could scream, he had thrust himself violently away from her. He sat, huddled in misery now, at the foot of the bed.

Her shoulder throbbed where his teeth had torn her skin, but she ignored the pain. She pulled herself up, feeling the cold brass tubing of the headboard against her back. He was crying, she was sure of it.

"Ben, are you all right?"

"I'm—fine."

It was a voice she had never heard before. "You sound strange."

"Do I?"

"And you hurt me."

"I'm sorry. I've got to go, Kathy."

She knew better than to question him. She stayed where she was, watching him fumble on the floor for his clothes. Before he left, he spoke to her only once more. "It's my nerves," he said. "They're really shot. I'll be OK."

"I understand," she said. "And I do love you."

Without touching her again, he walked out of her apartment, closing the door quietly behind him.

11

Most of the way home, Crawford thought about that sexy ACN secretary who had given him the eye. He knew exactly what he'd do to that luscious young thing within the walls of his own place. His small, elegant co-op was just off Park Avenue, in the East Sixties. He had chosen the building ten years before because it contained only twelve apartments and had no doorman; he could come and go at any time without arousing the slightest curiosity.

He carefully avoided any intimacies with his neighbors, most of whom were rich, middle-aged, and traveled a good deal. Encounters in elevators and hallways were casual and distant; he kept his professional life well hidden and he entertained no visitors.

He let himself in and double-bolted the door. In the bedroom, he took off his jacket and tie, kicked off his shoes, and slipped his feet into a pair of thong sandals. He reached into the drawer of his night table; from under the loaded .38 he kept there, he took a small, brown loose-leaf notebook. He flipped through several pages until he found the number he wanted. Then he reached for the phone.

"Reynolds here. One-one-two-seven-viceroy-three-double-a-ziggy."

"Yes, sir."

He waited, humming softly and tunelessly to himself. The blank, curtained walls of his bedroom enclosed him in a comforting embrace. Through the open door leading back to the living room, he could see the floor-to-ceiling bookcases and the stereo, with its expensive taping apparatus, in the far corner. He waited, desire rising in him, as the silence at the other end of the line lengthened.

"OK," the female voice said at last. "What time?"

Crawford glanced at his watch. "Eight-thirty sharp."

"Same address?"

"Yes."

"Would you repeat the specifications, please?"

Crawford spoke, and hung up. He went into the kitchen, took a bottle of beer out of the refrigerator, flipped off the top, and carried it back into the living room. When he pressed a hidden panel behind the stereo, the bookcases swung open soundlessly. Behind them, packed solidly from end to end and reaching nearly to the ceiling, were shelves of tapes, all neatly—and cryptically—catalogued. Crawford slipped the new cassette into a slot prepared for it; he was about to walk away when a thought struck him. Expressionlessly, he reached down to a lower shelf and removed a larger cassette from a slot.

He had a couple of hours, he told himself, time enough to reminisce. Besides, as he'd learned over the years, it sharpened his reactions to review old events and conversations from time to time. Small nuggets of valuable information, forgotten tidbits that might have seemed insignificant, sometimes took on new weight. Meaningless when first recorded, they could yield heavy dividends in light of later developments. To Crawford, the accurate recreation of past incidents provided not only aesthetic pleasure in remembered success but potential for manipulation of the present and future.

He slipped the cassette into the playback slot on the machine. Fitting earphones to his head, he adjusted the volume and tone controls, and then sat down with his beer to listen. The first voice he heard was his own. How much younger he seemed. Perhaps it was the age of the tape but, after all, the meeting had taken place nearly twenty years before.

"I don't mind," said Crawford's voice. "I'll go downstairs for a cup of coffee."

The Chairman's voice: "Fine. I'll have Shirley call you."

There was the sound of a door opening and closing. The briefcase, Crawford remembered clearly, was left beside his chair. He'd have it all on tape, unless they moved over to the window and whispered, which hardly seemed likely. How naive everyone was in those days about eavesdropping devices. Even the Chairman hadn't suspected.

"I don't like it, Larry."

That was Ted Brennan's voice. He'd changed more than any of them. He'd been a forceful, dynamic personality when Crawford had first met him—probably thought of himself as a young Ed Murrow. Crawford smiled and turned up the volume.

"We're not the only network to be approached": the Chairman. "This is a very big operation. They're exploring the possibility of actually establishing bureaus in foreign capitals—the works. They've contacted the news agencies, some of the news magazines, newspaper correspondents, free-lance people abroad. It'll be a worldwide setup."

"Have any of the other networks agreed?"

"We have reason to think so, Ted. I'm pretty certain that CBS is going along. And why shouldn't we? Isn't it also our patriotic duty?"

"CBS? I can't believe it. Journalists are supposed to be a burr under the saddle of government, to tell the people everything the government is doing, good or bad. We simply can't get in bed with an agency of the government we're supposed to monitor objectively." Brennan paused a moment, obviously collecting his thoughts. "Look, you're telling me we should become an arm of the Central Intelligence Agency—that we should provide cover for their spying operations overseas, let them look over the film we shoot, give them our information. If we do this, and it ever gets out, *ever gets out*, our credibility is shot. The news division, maybe the whole network, will be ruined."

"Calm down, Ted. Nobody's going to find out about anything. It's a very informal arrangement. I don't think there will be anything in writing. They just want to know whether we'll cooperate or not."

"Whether we'll be 'friendly assets,' isn't that the term?" A little misplaced sarcasm there, Crawford thought, but then the younger Brennan was more outspoken.

"Listen, Ted, you're not working for newspapers anymore."

Ah, now he was getting to it, the nitty-gritty. Crawford chuckled and sipped his beer.

"You hired me to run a news operation, Larry. I don't think of myself as a quote friendly asset unquote."

A pause now. Crawford imagined the Chairman leaning back in his seat and eyeing Ted Brennan, gallant young newsman, with the cold calculation of a boa constrictor sizing up a plump frog. The image made Crawford smile. He waited and heard a drumming sound—the Chairman's fingers at work on his desk top. Then silence.

Ted Brennan's voice: "Is that it, Larry?"

"No. Sit down."

Another pause, the clearing of a throat, probably Ted's.

"I think you must have a pretty naive idea of our situation": the Chairman, ready for the kill.

"I hope not, Larry. I like this job."

"Sure you do. And I like you in it. But let me explain some facts of life to you."

"Shoot."

"We're the youngest and most vulnerable of the four networks. You do understand that?"

Silence, and no doubt an understanding nod from old Ted. Yielding ground, perhaps, but ever ready to battle for his integrity.

"But essentially our position is no different from the others. We can't run this operation, any part of it, like a newspaper or a magazine."

"Why not?"

"Because newspapers and magazines don't depend on the government for their survival. I'll spell it out for you, Ted. Every one of the five stations we own and operate has to be licensed every three years by the federal government to stay on the air, and every single one of our eighty-nine affiliates has to have its license to broadcast renewed every three years."

"I realize that, but—"

"Let me finish, Ted. I know you know most of this, but I want to make sure there's no misunderstanding between us about our exact position. OK, now the Federal Communications Commission is made up of seven guys appointed by the president. If we're going to survive and become a preeminent power in broadcasting, then we've got to start right now building up some credits. They have to owe us something."

"But is this the right way—"

"It may be the *only* way. Not only does the government have this life-and-death power over our stations, it dictates to us how much time out of every broadcast day we, as a network, can have, and it indirectly determines the nature and the quality of our programing. Is that clear?"

"Yes, Larry, but the news division is different."

"How?"

"Because we're supposed to be impartial and objective."

Was there a quiver in Brennan's voice, the hint of a tremor? Crawford thought he'd caught the first audible crack in the verbal façade, though Ted would go on playing angel's advocate for a while. And the Chairman would let him.

"As far as my division is concerned"—Brennan again—"I can't buy it. I don't see how we can agree to it."

"If you want to cling to your newspaper ethics"—the Chairman—"then perhaps you ought to look for a newspaper job again."

A long pause after that one. Crawford closed his eyes and the vision of the boa reappeared. The big snake took its time and enjoyed the kill.

"Ted, I don't want you to leave." The Chairman at last. "You're the right man for the news operation here, the best I know. But I have no choice in this matter."

That was Brennan's last chance, wasn't it? Yes, Crawford told himself, that was the moment of truth. He should have resigned or made the integrity of his department his only condition for remaining. But he didn't. The seconds passed and he didn't. Amazing, how few people did have the integrity and the capacity to resist. That single factor, more than any other, never failed to delight Crawford.

He heard sounds of movement on the tape now. He guessed that the Chairman had come around from behind his desk and maybe put an arm around Brennan's shoulders. Through the rest of the dialogue, he could hear footsteps, a rhythmic pacing that punctuated the Chairman's affable sales pitch.

The Chairman's voice in a key statement: "Yes, Ted, we help them and they help us. Let them think of us as a friendly asset, the way they put it. We can use them, too. They can feed us information. We can break stories before anyone else. It'll be the price of our cooperation, don't you see? We can use them as an extension of the news division. In fact, if not officially."

Brennan's voice, very low now, barely audible: "I want a little time, Larry. I want to think about it."

"Sure, Ted. Of course. But I have to have a decision by

Monday. I want you to stay. I want you to consider it very carefully. Take the weekend and think about it."

A little chitchat now, and Brennan was gone. The decision had been made, of course, and Brennan knew it. The Chairman knew it. But the string had to be played out and appearances maintained. Ted Brennan had never thought of himself as anything but an incorruptible newsman, a Pulitzer Prize reporter from the Midwest who rose to become managing editor of the second-best newspaper in Illinois. The Chairman had personally plucked him from obscurity to head the news division of a major network at four times the salary Brennan could ever hope to earn in the newspaper business. That was what Brennan had thought over that weekend, or gone through the motions of thinking over. The decision, the Chairman and he both knew, had already been made. Crawford laughed and turned off the machine.

Had Brennan ever fully understood what the Chairman really expected to gain, Crawford wondered. It seemed so obvious now, but perhaps, in those less troubled days, that more naive era, it had not seemed so obvious. Crawford had grasped it right away, but he'd been trained to analyze such problems. What the Chairman expected to gain was insurance. Not only would the government—through one of its agencies—be deeply indebted to him, but it would never be able to reveal or admit the connection. The networks that cooperated with the CIA could make their own quiet demands and feel assured they could never be refused. Furthermore, the government would never be able to settle that debt; each successive administration would find itself paying off interest on the original loan forever.

Soon after that, the Chairman had begun to keep his

own dossiers on everybody. Crawford wondered where these were kept and what, if anything, the Chairman had on him. The hazards of his career, Crawford reminded himself constantly, were that no one could be fully trusted —ever.

He replaced the cassette and shut the bookcase. Glancing at his watch, he saw it was time and went into the bathroom to prepare himself for his eight-thirty appointment.

Penny knew the guy was weird, but she had been assured that he was absolutely safe. She suspected he was a politician or a high official of some sort, but she never asked questions about identities. This was the third time in the last eight months that "Reynolds" had asked specifically for her, which was flattering, in a way. And he paid well, no trouble on that account. Still, the trick made her uncomfortable; it was humiliating to be treated that way. She had a good opinion of herself, even though she was a hooker, and it bothered her to be handled so impersonally, exactly like a piece of meat.

Still, it was a job. If the john didn't want to make small talk and got his rocks off in this off-the-wall way, that was his business. Hers was to get paid for it, which she always did, and promptly, through the Service.

She arrived at the apartment at exactly eight-thirty, as she had been instructed. The guy had moved since the last time, but this place was much like the other one. It was a basement flat on West 81st Street, about a block and a half from the river—one large room empty of everything except a narrow army cot with a hard, bare mattress and an armchair facing the foot of the bed.

"Hi," she said.

He did not answer. Fully dressed, as usual, he sat down

in the chair and waited for her to get ready. She shrugged, stripped quickly, and hung her clothes on two wire hangers in the empty closet. Then she walked over to the cot and lay down on her stomach.

She guessed that he preferred her in this position because he didn't want her to look at him too closely. She knew, of course, that he was wearing a wig and that the blond mustache was probably false, but she would never have hinted as much to him. Would it matter? She didn't know, but she'd survived this long by keeping her mouth shut. And by being well-protected, through the Service, of course.

He produced the broad leather straps he'd used before, and tied her by the ankles and wrists to the four corners of the bed. She went into her act right away, straining against the bonds and moaning. For a while, as usual, he sat and watched her, shifting in his chair, sometimes walking around the bed to get a better look at her.

She tried to think of other times and other places, just to keep herself from going mad with boredom. She knew precisely what would happen next and she was determined not to let it get to her. All these perverts had their own precise routines, unvarying and equally uninteresting to her. After a while, he would produce the dildo and insert it, relieving himself with his other hand and she would moan, writhe, and pretend to climax in rhythm to his fantasy. *What a freak . . .*

12

"Sarah, I know how busy you must be," Ben said, "and I'm damn grateful you wanted to see me."

"Don't be silly, Ben," she told him. "I'd have called you yesterday, but the minute I got in Mr. Hoenig wanted to talk to me and Ted, and then there was a series of meetings."

"I can imagine."

"Anyway, we were going till nearly midnight. I've got so much to do. The convention is practically on top of us and I've got to set up things here and go back home and settle things there and—oh, God." She laughed. "You know, I feel like a kid with some great big toy I always wanted and never expected to get."

"I know the feeling," Ben said.

"I guess you do." Briefly, she looked away from him. "I'm sorry to run off at the mouth. It's just that I still can't quite believe it."

"I think it's wonderful."

"You're sweet to say so."

"I mean it."

"I know you do, Ben."

She looked better than he had ever seen her. They were sitting alone in a corner of the St. Regis bar. Across the room a piano tinkled, and waiters flitted like amiable ghosts from table to table. Ben sipped his Scotch and water and tried to recall exactly how it had felt when he'd received his major promotion. He and Sarah had had drinks together then, too, right in this very room, and he remembered again how gracious she had been, how kind, how genuinely pleased that he was coming to work for her in Washington. She had asked for him, she told him, though she realized later there had been no need to; the Chairman had had plans for Ben all along and Ted Brennan had always been high on him, too. Still, Ben had known from the start that he'd had a real ally in Sarah. And, more important, a friend. They'd been good for and to each other during his time in Washington. Now here they were again —having drinks at the St. Regis, where Sarah always stayed when she came to town—but so much had changed. Sarah was going into a big, new job, one of the most exciting assignments available to a news exec, and he was an outcast, wandering through the alleys of the New York slums.

"How did Farwell take it?" he asked, making small talk.

He was hoping she'd have a fragment of information for him from the corridors of power, that he could catch a glimpse, at least, of a possible future, but he was too proud to ask.

She laughed again. "Oh, Farwell. You know, Ben, it's been over between us for a long time."

"So I gathered."

"We stay together, I suppose, because it's easier than *not* staying together. He putters around the house and the stables and I have my career now."

Ben had met Farwell Anderson casually and seen him around at social gatherings, but the man had never made much of an impression on him. Now Ben found himself beginning to wonder about Sarah. He tried to envision her in bed with Farwell Anderson, but he couldn't. He'd never heard any rumors about her or seen her with another man. What *did* she do about her sex life? She was a very attractive woman and she had to have needs, desires like anyone else. Could her career be all she cared about?

"What about you, Ben?" she asked abruptly. "How's it going?"

"Some days aren't as bad as other days," he answered, trying to keep his voice casual, underplaying his despair. "I'm—I'm trying to figure out, actually, where I go from here."

She nodded sympathetically. "I can imagine." She sighed and put down her drink. "It's a rotten shame. I wonder if there's anything I *can* do."

"Does my name ever come up? With Brennan or the Chairman, I mean?" He tried not to seem too eager.

103

"Ben, I asked about you."

He looked startled. "Me? When?"

"When the Chairman called me about this job."

"You're kidding."

"No." She clasped her hands together tightly, like a child anticipating pain. "I mean, not right away. But after the Chairman called me last week, I talked to Ted. I asked him whether he thought I could talk to the Chairman about you."

"And?"

She shook her head. "No good, Ben. Ted said the Chairman couldn't do anything."

"But then—I mean, why did you—"

"Because I thought I could at least remind them what a hell of a good reporter you were," she explained. "Lord, I knew I couldn't get you to work with me again, but there ought to be something they could do for you. You're totally wasted as a nightside local reporter. This network has five stations and a hundred and forty affiliates now. Surely somewhere, maybe abroad, they could use you better than this way."

Ben smiled bitterly. "I'm being punished, Sarah. Like a naughty boy caught sassing the teacher."

"In a way," she said. "I guess I knew it. We all knew it. But we all figured it wouldn't last, didn't we? I know I did. You must have, too."

"I was hoping. That's why I've been trying to hang on and make the best of it."

"It's no good, Ben." She paused and took a deep breath. "It's tough to have to tell you this, but I want to be fair. I want you to know I didn't take Ted's answer as final. I spoke to Mr. Hoenig directly about you."

"When?"

"This morning."

If Ben had been standing, he might have fallen. His head felt light and the room seemed to be slowly spinning around and around. He shut his eyes, so that he could concentrate on Sarah's soft, sympathetic voice over the hum of conversation and the distant notes of piano music.

"And?" he heard himself ask.

"He said there was nothing he could do about it," she told him. "He likes you, Ben. He really feels like a father to you. But he can't do more than he's doing. Just keeping you on has been a problem."

"How?"

"You can't imagine what happened. I told you the White House called me that night."

"Yes."

"Well, they also called Ted in New York, of course. And they wrote us letters. It was unbelievable—Ben, are you OK?"

He must have gone white, he realized. *I've got to get control of myself.* He dug his hands into the sides of his chair below the level of the table. He was barely holding on, but he wanted to know everything now, absolutely everything. "I'm all right," he made himself say calmly. "I'm fine, Sarah."

"We had calls two and three times a day from various people," Sarah continued. "They wanted you fired, Ben."

"I—I figured."

"Pretty high-level pressure, even for the Chairman himself."

"How high up did it go? Ziegler, of course. And Jerry Warren. I guessed that. Who else?"

"Higher than that."

"Who? Colson? Haldeman?"

"I'm not sure. But Mr. Hoenig told me this morning, Ben, that he had one late-night call from the president himself."

"From Nixon directly? Jesus!"

"Yes. It was incredible." Sarah shook her head. "I mean, the pettiness of it. My God, he's the president of the United States!"

"And—and he asked Larry to—fire me?"

"Oh, no. Nothing like that. That came in the other calls. No. Nixon just wanted the Chairman to know that he had an eye on us, that he was taking a personal interest in ACN, because he'd always considered us less biased in our coverage. He was disappointed and regretful, he told the Chairman. And he hoped we'd get back to the kind of unbiased, objective coverage he'd learned to expect from us."

"Oh, my God," Ben whispered.

"The s.o.b.," she said. "And he's almost certainly going to be reelected."

"Oh, Christ . . ."

"I'm sorry, Ben." Sarah leaned closer to him. "I hate to have to tell you all this. But what could the Chairman do? He does feel like a father to you and he's not punishing you. He's gone as far as he can by just keeping you on at all."

She waited for some response from him, some sort of outburst. She'd have understood that. In fact, she expected it.

"Ben?"

But he said nothing. He only stared at her, ashenfaced. Then he heaved himself to his feet. "I'm—I've got to go," he said tonelessly and fled from the room.

Outside the air-cooled lobby of the hotel, the sidewalk sweltered in summer heat. Homegoing traffic packed the

106

narrow crosstown streets and the broad avenues; pedestrians jostled each other toward subway entrances, from which blasts of oven-hot air exploded like escaping gas, or swarmed around bus stops to stand in sweating, irritable knots.

Ben pushed his way through the crowded sidewalks, weaved across the car-choked streets. Eventually, he found himself farther uptown, in the quieter residential areas, wandering erratically through building-shadowed streets, then up along the cobbled sidewalk of Fifth Avenue that skirted the park. He must have walked for hours. He had no idea where he was going or why; he just needed to be alone, to work it out in his own head. Because he knew by now what he had to do. *Yes, and I'll do it, too, no matter what the cost or what the consequences....*

"Where did Daddy go?" he remembered asking his mother.

"I don't know," she'd say.

"Is he coming home?"

"I don't know."

"Why did Daddy go?"

"Your daddy doesn't want us anymore, that's why," his mother would say. Later he would hear her crying in her room and, alone in the darkness, he'd cry, too.

Tears and loneliness and the sounds of sobbing were what he remembered best from his childhood.

Ben remembered dimly that once they'd all been together and happy. He'd been so proud of his father, who looked really terrific in his Air Force uniform, with all those ribbons and decorations. His daddy had been among the first to go and fight Adolf Hitler and all those wicked Nazis. He'd been a real hero.

107

Ben had pieced it together later, long after his father had vanished from his life. Burton and Ellen Stryker had been a glamorous young couple. She was so pretty and he was a swell guy, everybody said. They'd met in college—he couldn't remember which one but it was somewhere in the Midwest—gotten married, and pretty soon Ellen found herself pregnant.

His daddy had gone to war by then. In 1939, at the age of twenty, he'd left his pregnant nineteen-year-old wife and joined the Royal Canadian Air Force; a year later he was flying Spitfires out of England. By 1941, when the United States got into "the big one," Burton Stryker was a war hero, a combat ace with five confirmed kills.

"What did Daddy do *then*?" young Ben would ask his mother.

"He shot people," she'd say bitterly. "Your daddy loved to shoot people."

That wasn't fair; Ben knew his father was a hero. His daddy had joined the U.S. Army Air Corps and switched to flying B-17 bombers—Flying Fortresses, they called them. He'd had a lot of experience in the air by then, and it wasn't long before he won the Distinguished Flying Cross. He was a *real* hero.

"Weren't you proud of Daddy?" he'd asked his mother.

She hadn't answered. She'd always walk out of the room when he asked that question. He remembered doors slamming all over the house and more tears, always the tears.

Ben remembered his daddy coming home. Ben was six years old then and he couldn't quite remember what his daddy looked like, apart from the lifeless, tinted photographs he pored over. Those weren't pictures of a living man; they were snapshots of a war hero, somebody Ben idealized, but didn't know at all.

108

Often, Ben tried to think back, to recall whether his father had ever hugged him or kissed him or even taken him anywhere. He couldn't, though there must have been some good times.

"Your daddy couldn't get the war out of his system," his mother said once, after he'd gone. "He couldn't live at home and be just a daddy, don't you see?"

Ben remembered best the six years he spent shuttling between his maternal and paternal grandparents' houses, at opposite ends of Pennsylvania. How many times did they move him? He could count at least eight, and remember living in five different states. . . .

And the fights.

The shouting.

The tears . . .

"Your daddy's gone," his mother told him one day. "Your daddy's gone, Ben, and we're getting a divorce. You know what that is?"

"I want my daddy."

"Oh, Ben . . ."

"I hate you. And I hate Harry. He's mean . . ."

I want my daddy. I'm so lonely. I'm so terribly lonely. . . .

Not even the Chairman, with all of his power, could save him now. At first, Ben had not been able to imagine the full extent of the Nixon administration's paranoia about the media, nor its true vindictiveness. He was to be sacrificed on that altar, his whole career destroyed because of one man. Well, two men, really. First, of course, there had been Spiro Agnew, with his vicious attacks on the press and the networks. But who had put him up to it? Who else but Richard Nixon . . .

Ben found himself in front of the monkey house in the

Central Park Zoo. He didn't know how he had ended up here, but it seemed oddly important to him, fitting in somehow with what he had to do. He leaned against the metal railing and stared into the cage. The two huge apes sat placidly, backs against the wall, and stared back at him. A small boy scrambled up beside him, his voice shrill with excitement. "Mom! Mom! It's the gorillas! Come and look!" Unmoved, the big apes and Ben eyed each other.

At last, Ben was able to tear himself away. It was beginning to get dark now. He turned south and walked rapidly, purposefully, toward the long row of hotels and apartment houses lining Fifty-ninth Street along the edge of the park. He knew exactly where he was headed. There was a large camera store on West Forty-sixth Street that had a sale in progress, and Ben felt sure it would still be open. Until nine o'clock, the ad had said.

13

"Are you all right, Lawrence?" Louise asked.

The Chairman stopped drumming his fingers on the glass top of the long dining table. Through the flickering candlelight, he gazed at his wife. "Of course. Why do you ask?"

"You seem unusually distracted tonight."

"Not at all," the Chairman said mildly. "I do have a lot on my mind."

"I see. The office, dear?"

"Of course."

"Then you'll be working after dinner, won't you?"

"Yes, I will, Louise. Crawford and I have some matters to discuss."

"Such a strange man," Louise said. "I can't say I care much for him."

"A very good man, Louise, very good." The Chairman resumed his restless finger-drumming. "You don't have to see him socially."

"No, of course not." She smiled patiently. "Shall we have coffee now?"

"Yes."

"Let's go in the living room, then." She rang to inform the servants, then rose regally from her chair.

"I haven't much time, Louise. He'll be here soon."

"I know, dear," she said tolerantly. "And I have the mayor's committee to contact and some invitations to send out for the big do at the museum."

"What's that?" he asked, following her out of the room.

"The garden party for the Matisse retrospective," she explained. "You *are* planning to show up?"

"I don't know."

"But I told them you'd be there."

"I'll try, Louise. This is a busy time, you know."

She smiled sweetly. "It always is, isn't it, dear?" She patted his cheek as they sank together into the living-room sofa and the butler appeared with a silver coffee tray. "Over here, Henry." She indicated the coffee table in front of them.

For the next ten minutes, while he sipped his *espresso*, the Chairman managed to relax. It had been many years since he'd shared everything with his wife, but she could always calm him, get him to unwind, even when the complexities of his affairs exerted the greatest pressures on him. That was her chief service to him, that and the fact that she was a Philadelphia blue blood, a perfect hostess who could handle their many social obligations with all the aplomb of a seasoned diplomat.

It was what she lived for, he had realized soon after their marriage some thirty years before, and what gave her the most satisfaction. As a public figure, she was perfectly cast, every socially ambitious woman's dream of what a great lady should be. As a private person, the intimate partner of his dreams, she was nonexistent. It was what he wanted, of course; he had never shared his secrets. He encouraged her role and her view of him. Louise had always seen Lawrence Hoenig as a means to her own ends, never as a living, breathing man; that, too, had always suited the Chairman perfectly. His self-absorption was total, his passion the accumulation of power and prestige. His life was the network and the network was his life; that was all he lived for. They were perfectly matched, he and Louise; she provided him the cover for his real ambitions, and he repaid her by providing an impeccable position in a brilliant social world.

To some, it was like a stage set, their town house on East Seventieth Street, between Park and Lexington avenues. He'd bought it back in the early fifties and they'd spent a fortune redesigning and furnishing it. Louise had flawless taste, and under her direction a team of architects, interior decorators, and workmen had labored for months over every detail. She had created for them both a supremely functional home and the private palace of an enlightened despot. The paintings on the walls were masterpieces, from the small Rembrandt over the living-room mantel to the Renoirs and Degas that splashed the background of their dining room. A Manzù horseman graced the front hall, and all through the house each precious piece glowed against its surroundings, but never denied the comfort of the home. In Louise Hoenig's house lived an emperor and his consort; power and wealth were on display. The illusion created was one of exquisite taste humanized by a zest for living. No mean achievement, the Chairman often reflected. What else could he want of her, or she of him? They lived together as loving strangers.

"More coffee, dear?"

"No, thanks. I must go." He rose to his feet. "Crawford's always very punctual and I have to organize my papers."

"Of course, dear," she said, offering her cheek.

By the time he had climbed the stairs to his apartment, she was already at her own desk, busily scanning the invitation list for the Matisse opening. In her own way and at her own deliberate pace, Louise Hoenig worked as hard as her husband.

From his study on the third floor, the Chairman could look down into an elaborate garden, almost unique in this part of the city. A small forest of exotic plants grew inside a greenhouse; around and beyond it, a graveled walk meandered through thick hedges and rose bushes to an Italian marble fountain and sun dial, the focus of the entire garden. Visitors always found the prospect enchanting, another manifestation of Mr. and Mrs. Lawrence Hoenig's flawless taste.

Crawford seemed out of place in this setting. The Chairman always received him in the study, a functional room equipped with TV monitors, a film projector, two electric typewriters, filing cabinets, and antique furniture converted to office use. Even here, Crawford seemed incongruous, physically too large for the room. It was in here, the Chairman now recalled, that Crawford had first offered his services, nearly ten years after the initial CIA contact with the network.

They'd been through a lot together since then, he and Crawford. Crawford had made the first approach, but both men had profited hugely. Crawford now earned ten times what he'd made as a CIA agent, and been worth every penny. Through his agency contacts, he'd kept abreast of every development in government affecting the fortunes of ACN. And he'd organized a private intelligence operation that provided the Chairman with the clout to defend and greatly increase his power.

The only risk, of course, was that Crawford could become indispensable; he knew everything and ultimately that could become dangerous. That was a hazard to be dealt with later, much later. The network had to face the government's challenge head-on, and only Crawford could serve as the instrument of the Chairman's power. Once the threat had been met—his enemies finally and totally crushed—then the Chairman would deal with Crawford himself.

The former agent knew far too much, the Chairman realized, and already he anticipated having to dispose of him. It would not be easy, but there would be a way. The Chairman believed in careful forethought; he was always several moves ahead of his friends, and his enemies.

The telephone buzzed, the Chairman picked up the receiver. "Yes?"

"Mr. Crawford is here," the butler said.

"Please send him up, Henry."

The Chairman sat behind his desk, calm and relaxed, his

eyes watchful, his hands placidly folded in his lap. He waited for the massive former agent to lumber softly into the room. They had much to discuss.

"I've weighed all the options," Crawford said, after a brief survey of the most recent developments, "and I think the plan is not only workable but sure to succeed. I can't see how we can miss."

"We can always miss," the Chairman said. "Nothing is foolproof. We have to minimize any chance of a failure. What about this girl?"

"Kathy Lewis?"

"Yes."

"Apparently she cares about him."

"Could that be a problem?"

Crawford nodded. "Possibly. I'm keeping a very close watch on that relationship."

"They see a lot of each other?"

"Quite a bit."

"That could be dangerous."

"Yes. On the other hand, she could be a help."

"How?"

"She doesn't seem to suspect the real dimensions of the problem," Crawford explained. "She's very happy he wants to develop a new facet of his talent. She's been hoping he'd break out of his depression and work toward his own re-habilitation, if that's the word."

"I'm counting on you, Crawford," the Chairman said. "I think you know how much is at stake here."

"Have I ever let you down, Larry?"

"Not yet," the Chairman said. "Now bring me up-to-date on the Agnew situation."

"We've had two men on this full time, as you know,"

116

Crawford said. "We've gone right back to the beginning, to his early days in Maryland politics. We've got the bribery business thoroughly documented and we have a direct pipeline into the Justice Department. The trick here, as in everything, is the timing. We don't want Justice to move against Agnew until after the election, right?"

"Correct."

Crawford smiled grimly. "It's quite a delicate juggling act. I mean, this guy was so naked about taking money it could be pretty hard to keep the lid on long enough."

"I want him driven out of office, Crawford," the Chairman said firmly, "not dumped before the voters go to the polls, and certainly not before the convention."

"I know that."

"I want the man disgraced and driven from office."

"I'm pretty sure we can sit on the information for a while, but it doesn't make me happy."

The Chairman snorted. "I'm not peddling happiness, Crawford."

The big man laughed, and began going through some isometric exercises. The Chairman, watching the play of muscles along the powerful arms, found himself wondering how easily a man like Crawford could break someone's neck with his bare hands. As if reading the Chairman's thoughts, the agent grinned. "There are easier ways, of course."

"So you told me. What's our back-up, in case Justice won't play?"

"We can feed it to the *Washington Post*."

"That could be tricky, too. Better a different newspaper. We've got the *Post* heavily involved in the Watergate investigation."

"The *New York Times*?"

The Chairman shook his head violently. "No, not those bastards," he said. "I wouldn't do Sulzberger that big a favor. That liberal monkey's been knocking our shows for two years, as if we invented the goddam ratings system. No, not the *Times*."

"Then I'd say our best bet is the *Wall Street Journal*. They should jump at this story without any encouragement. But if we need it, I have an arm over there that can be twisted—a contact."

"On the payroll?"

Crawford laughed. "Not exactly. I have a little wedge."

"What kind of wedge?"

"A very interesting tape, actually." Crawford smiled. "He has some pretty odd sexual preferences, likes to be tied up and humiliated by either sex."

The Chairman looked dubious. "These days who cares?"

"His wife and kids might. It's a videotape, by the way."

The Chairman nodded. "You seem to have a very fine collection of tapes, Crawford. I'm always astonished by their variety."

"I began early, Larry. You never know when they could come in handy." He gazed blandly at the Chairman. "After all, Larry, what other insurance can I carry?"

The Chairman did not answer, but began that restless drumming of fingers that always gave away his tension. Crawford saw it; he knew he had gotten the message across. They were playing this game for the highest stakes in the world—the lives and careers of influential politicians—and, once the game was won, who would stand between Crawford and the Chairman? What better insurance could Crawford carry through life than his library of tapes? How else could he deal with the Chairman as an equal?

Satisfied the Chairman understood him, Crawford returned to business. "I won't have any trouble with the *Journal*. They know a good story when they see one."

"Perhaps it won't be necessary," the Chairman said softly.

Crawford nodded. "Lot of gung-ho lawyers in Justice," he said. "They won't cover up for Agnew. For Nixon, maybe. But not for Agnew."

The Chairman paused again. His fingers stopped moving, as they always did whenever he had determined on a course of action or was confident of his ability to deal with a problem. "I think we can expect Nixon to begin moving against the networks right after the election."

"Not before?"

The Chairman shook his head. "Not out in the open," he said. "Of course, they've been laying the groundwork for action for months. I knew that from the beginning."

"We gave them every out," Crawford said. "They wouldn't make a deal."

"No, they wouldn't accommodate us," the Chairman agreed. "Strange, isn't it? Here's an administration committed heart and soul to giving big business everything it wants—the oil companies, big steel, the automakers—and we couldn't reach any kind of understanding."

"Nixon's always been paranoid about the press. Remember that famous speech of his after he lost the governor's race in California?"

The Chairman permitted himself a slight smile. "Yes, he assured us he wouldn't be available for kicking around anymore. Too bad he didn't stick to that resolve."

"Well, Larry, you were right," Crawford observed. "You called it from the start."

The Chairman sighed. "It's been said that successful men make their own opportunities," he pointed out.

Crawford nodded, knowing what came next, but making

no move to anticipate it or let the Chairman know how familiar it was. He always enjoyed the Chairman's aphorisms and great thoughts. Crawford began working on his leg muscles.

"Of course, that's not true," the Chairman mused. "We are all surrounded by opportunities every day. Successful men recognize them."

14

"Just one more," she said, waving him back toward the cluster of boulders at the edge of the meadow. "By those rocks. They'll make a perfect background."

"Kathy, the idea is to try for a variety of shots," he explained. "I'm figuring out how this machine works and what I can do with it, not working up a family scrapbook."

"You don't have a real family, you already told me that,"

she argued, lining him up in her sights as she waved him back into a recess between the rocks. "There, like that." She snapped his picture again.

He went to her and took the camera away. "How many we got left?"

"Four on this roll."

"Good," he said. "We can shoot a few in the zoo."

"Let's eat," she begged. "I'm starved."

"We'll finish this roll and then eat."

"Where?"

"They have an outdoor cafeteria in the zoo," he said. "The food's lousy, but we can eat on the terrace and watch the sea lions."

She began to run across the dusty meadow, her arms outflung and her hair tangled by a stiff breeze that whipped bits of paper over the green like scattered snowflakes before a winter wind. It was a perfect summer day. The long heat wave had finally broken and the wind had cooled the city off. The park was full of Sunday strollers, joggers, picnickers, kids kicking soccer balls, couples hand in hand, old people dozing on benches. The rest of the city seemed to have emptied out. Only a few cars rattled along the avenues and streets; the tall, silent blocks of apartment houses and the glass-and-steel towers of industry clustered over empty canyons. By nightfall, the residential part of the city would come to life again, filling up with returning weekenders, but now Ben was able to imagine himself and Kathy completely alone on civilization's last island—this soiled piece of meadow within an empty, stone sea. For some reason, the image comforted him. He patted his pocket, where the other roll of film lay, and walked briskly after Kathy, who stopped running and, panting, waited for him to catch up.

"God, I'm so out of shape," she said. "I could just die."

"You don't look out of shape."

"How do I look?"

"Terrific."

She did, too. In fact, he had never seen her look better. She had been so excited when he first told her he was thinking of getting into photography. She had stopped by his desk early Wednesday afternoon. He had been studying the books on photography he'd bought the night before, and she had lit up when he told her his plans. They'd made a date to spend Sunday together, taking pictures, and she had talked about nothing else since. First, she'd bombarded him with questions, then spread the word around the office, so that Bellucci, who needed no excuse, had found a rich, new lode to mine. He'd begun referring to Ben immediately as "the poor man's Capa."

For once, Ben hadn't minded. He'd grinned at his tormentor and given him the finger. If the poor bastard only knew, Ben had told himself. If Bellucci had only had the wit to imagine what that harmless-looking little Minolta represented, the jokes and quips would have frozen in his throat. From the moment he'd bought the camera, on his way home from the zoo that night, Ben had felt himself in control of his own destiny, full of power and a sense of his own worth. *I am the avenger. I am the light that kills. I am the enforcer of the rules. . . .*

"Sweetheart?"

"Hmm—what?"

"You looked so funny."

"Funny how?"

"I don't know," she said, coming up to him again and staring into his eyes. "Like—like somebody enjoying a secret."

"Yeah," he told her, "something like that."

123

"Kiss me."

He touched her mouth with his, then firmly but gently pushed her away from him. "Let's get to the zoo, Kathy."

"Then promise me we'll go home."

"Sure," he said, striking out at a brisk pace, his mind made up and hardened with resolve.

She skipped along beside him. "You promise?"

"I promise."

"I have evil designs on you."

Ben smiled and took her hand. The camera bounced on his chest as they walked toward the zoo; it hung there in its leather case, as comforting to him as a talisman that would unlock all the secrets of the universe. In a way, it was. Funny how much simpler and easier everything seemed since he'd made his crucial decision. He was excited, yes, but calm, too, and supremely confident. Machines, technology in general, had always fascinated him. And guns. As a boy, he had loved guns. The loss of the .22, the confiscation, was still a bitter memory. He realized now that his stepfather had been afraid of him. He laughed.

"What is it, darling?"

"Nothing," Ben said. "Maybe I should have been a cop."

"You *are* strange today," she answered with a giggle.

Poor Kathy, he thought, *you really don't know anything about anything, do you? All last night, while I was making love to you and you lay there in my arms, moaning with pleasure, you couldn't imagine I wasn't thinking only of you. I was remembering, Kathy, remembering. And putting all the complicated pieces of my life together, so I can be sure now that what I'm doing is right, because it's important to be sure. So much is at stake. . . .*

The Air Force had sent Ben to an electronic training

124

school where he excelled. He had been chosen to become an instructor, and had completed an advanced course at another school, again finishing near the top of his class. He'd always had this aptitude, this gift for technology, but the real revelation was still to come. After he graduated and began teaching, the experience proved to be astonishing. Young Benson Stryker, the shy, insecure boy who had spent his adolescence withdrawing from contact with the world and its capacity to inflict pain upon him, suddenly found himself entrusted with the lives and careers of others. He had the undivided attention of a room full of students —adult human beings less advanced, less well-equipped than himself—who depended upon his ability and kindness.

He'd seen the moment for what it was—that these students paid him their respect because they were caught up, as he was, in the military system, at the mercy of the military pecking order. It had been a valuable lesson. He had learned that a semblance, at least, of social success depended upon achieving a professional one, and the knowledge filled him with new confidence, with a determination to succeed at all costs.

During the last two years of his four-year stint in the Air Force, Ben managed to cram in two years of college. He taught electronics on the evening shift at the base, and commuted a hundred miles a day to the nearest junior college.

As his discharge date approached, Ben had begun to think hard about a civilian career. He knew electronics, he enjoyed talking to people from a position of superiority, and he was driven by his need to be demonstrably successful. Above all else, Ben wanted to be important. Clearly, he had become a candidate for a career in television.

So he'd found himself drawn toward broadcasting. As the idea matured, he eliminated radio in favor of television, the medium that would best fulfill his needs. In the secrecy of his room, Ben still felt inadequate; in a studio, before an audience of millions, he would feel complete—a real man, an object of worth desired by all.

His teaching years had given him an artificial self-assurance. His nearly straight A's in college had confirmed his intelligence. The conditions under which he'd attained those grades testified to his energy and ambition. It had been easy for Ben to convince the general manager of the little ACN affiliate in Pass Christian to hire him on as an all-purpose hand. Unlike most candidates for a job in TV, Ben understood the technicalities of the medium. And what he didn't know he quickly set about learning.

His rise through the ranks had been meteoric. Within a year, while still picking up college credits on his own time, Ben had found himself virtually running the station.

He enjoyed his authority. He enjoyed making money for the company. Most of all, he enjoyed doing the local newscasts, at 5:00 and 10:00 P.M. every weekday evening. Ben's difficulties with personal relationships vanished the minute he stepped in front of that live Dumont Image Orthicon camera. He had an almost frightening rapport with the thing that could only be described as symbiotic. The moment the camera's red tally light winked on, Ben Stryker ceased to be a shy, ill-at-ease country boy; he became a man—gregarious, assured, magnetic. During those very first broadcasts, Ben had established himself as an on-the-air presence to be reckoned with. And he'd also begun to reap some interesting social dividends.

Women found the television Ben extraordinarily attractive. Even though the real Ben didn't have the luster or magnetism of the TV image, they hardly seemed to notice. They offered up their hearts and bodies to him, or at least to that image of Ben that had stirred them on the screen.

Ben had never been much aroused by women; his deeper feelings centered on himself and his career. His tenderness and capacity to love lay buried under thick layers of emotional scar tissue. But he did have sexual needs, and now he fulfilled these at will. Technically, he became a proficient and skillful lover. He studied sexual intercourse with the same overachieving intensity he'd learned to apply to all his other pursuits; he developed into an adept sexual athlete whose considerable charm and seductive powers concealed an inability to be touched. What turned Ben on, the only thing that had ever turned him on, was his own image on a TV screen.

In July of 1962, on the first anniversary of Ben's new career, the news director of the Dallas ACN affiliate had called to offer him a job as a reporter. He had caught Ben in a local newscast out of Pass Christian and, like everyone, had been impressed. "You've got a nice quality," the man had said on the phone. "I think you have a future in this business."

In Dallas, Ben had begun to win the hearts and minds of his Texas viewers from the day he had loomed into view on screen. By November of 1963, Ben's popularity had eclipsed even that of the station's well-established anchorman.

Strangely, since then his whole career had been tied to the fates of presidents. Ben's network ascent had been launched by a rifle bullet, the one that had cut down John Kennedy that fatal November day in Dallas, and it had been aborted by the incident with Nixon nine years later in Washington.

Or had it?

"Darling?"

"Yes."

"Hello!"

"What is it, Kathy?"

"You're so funny today."

"Funny? How do you mean?"

"You're kind of—well, abstracted."

"Yeah, I know. I've got a lot on my mind."

"Can we eat now?"

"One more shot."

"Isn't that the end of the roll?"

"I have another one."

Kathy groaned and slumped in mock exhaustion against Ben's shoulder as he changed the film. They were sitting on a bench, facing a long row of outdoor cages full of aloof-looking deer. This was a less crowded area of the zoo and he'd been able to shoot in relative peace. But now, with the new roll in place, he needed a noisy crowd around him. Abruptly, he stood up. "Come on," he said, and began walking briskly toward the monkey house.

The big apes basked lethargically in the midday warmth. As usual, the largest knot of viewers clustered in front of the main cage, in which two full-grown mountain gorillas sat side by side, staring disinterestedly out at the world. Ben maneuvered himself toward a corner of the cage. By leaning over the railing, he could get a clear line through the bars at the nearest beast. As Kathy gazed in fascination at the animals, Ben deftly unscrewed the cap nut over the miniature gun barrel beside the lens and slipped it into his pocket. He leaned further over the railing and sighted between the bars.

"Hey," Kathy called out above the noise, "wait till he turns toward you."

Ben didn't answer. He focused through the lens as a plane passed overhead, the sound of its engines blending with the crowd noises around him. The nearest of the apes turned reproachful eyes on Ben, and he fired.

Ben heard the pop; it sounded like an explosion to his ears and he experienced a second of total panic. A thin puff of condensed vapor floated past his horrified gaze, then vanished in the warm air. The animal scratched itself through the fur on its thigh.

"Ben, what's the matter?" Kathy asked.

"What?"

"You look like death."

"I—I must be hungry," Ben said. He turned and pushed his way out past the throngs around the cages.

The cafeteria was crowded. By the time they found a table on the terrace overlooking the sea lions, nearly twenty minutes had gone by. Ben hung the Minolta over the back of his chair.

Kathy smiled. "Feeling better?"

"Oh, sure."

Over her shoulder, Ben could see the beginnings of a commotion around the gorilla cage. People stirred restlessly, a father hoisted his small boy to his shoulders and the child pointed excitedly at the cage.

"What's going on?" Kathy craned her neck.

"I don't know."

"There's a lot of excitement over there."

Ben didn't answer. He ate slowly, oddly calm now and very sure of himself. He glanced over at the monkey house

129

from time to time, watching the crowd grow and hearing a murmur rise. Kathy wanted to investigate on their way out of the zoo, but Ben was indifferent. He felt wonderful, powerful, on top of the world.

"Come on," he said, "let's go home."

As Ben and Kathy left the park, strolling hand in hand toward Fifth Avenue, the big man looked up from his newspaper. He had been sitting there for some time, on a bench from which he could watch both the monkey cages and the cafeteria terrace. He stood up now, stretched, and glanced back toward the cage where the crowd, subdued now, still pressed forward. Then, with a quick look at his watch, he began to walk south toward Sherman Square.

While he waited for Kathy to come out of the bathroom, Ben switched on the news. He knew what had happened, but he wanted it confirmed on the screen, where all reality, all truth, could be established daily.

"And that's the weather," the male image declared. "Back to you, Bill."

"This final note," Bill James told ACN viewers. "The Central Park Zoo is short one gorilla tonight. One of the senior citizens of the gorilla colony died suddenly today. His name is being withheld pending notification of the next of kin."

Ben heard the laughter off-camera and watched James struggle to keep a straight face. He sat up now to turn off the set.

"Oh, that's what it was all about," Kathy exclaimed from the doorway, her astonished gaze focused on the screen where a huge, furry shape lay motionless on the floor of a cage. "The poor thing. It must have happened right after we were there. Do gorillas have heart attacks?"

130

Ben stared at Kathy and felt a desire for her rise within him. Grinning, he reached out and took her by the waist. Her naked body, just out of the shower, felt cool and fresh to his touch. He kissed her breasts. "I want you, Kathy," he murmured.

"Oh, God—"

He pulled her down to him and opened her up to receive him again. He felt wonderful, all-conquering, immortal. As he rose above her to thrust himself into her, the flickering images on the silent TV screen continued to roll mindlessly on.

15

At precisely 9:50 P.M. on the night of August 23, Senator Robert Griffin, right on cue, stepped to the rostrum of the convention hall to introduce Spiro T. Agnew to the 1,348 voting delegates, mostly white, mostly middle-aged, all true keepers of the Republican faith. "The magic hour is at hand," Griffin proclaimed.

Outside, in the streets of Miami Beach, dubbed by one

newsman as "Babylon on Biscayne Bay," police battled thousands of roaming anti-war protesters and eventually arrested 900 of them. As the senator spoke, fifty-two persons were in the process of being injured, twelve of them policemen. Except for unpleasant whiffs of stinging CS—"pepper" gas—that brought tears to the eyes of delegates entering the hall and invaded some of the press trailers, no echo of these disturbances was permitted to mar the orderly, perfectly scripted procedure by which the Republican party went about nominating and enshrining its candidates. By ten o'clock, Vice President Agnew had the microphone. "It is our mission to create a climate of dignity and security and peace and honor," he said.

In New York, alone with his wife in their huge living room, the Chairman watched his veteran anchorman, Harvey Grunwald, supervise the ACN coverage from a booth high above the convention floor. Louise had been watching, too. She knew Harvey and liked him, but she also worried about him. "God, Larry, he looks old, doesn't he?" she observed.

The Chairman didn't answer. He sat slumped into the sofa and stared at the screen. He was worrying not only about the millions of dollars the network was blowing on this boring, totally predictable political fiasco from Miami, but he was also unhappy over the fact that two of the three other networks were obviously doing a better job. NBC, for instance, had thirty-two tractor trailers on hand and was spending even more money than ACN, but with better, sharper, tighter coverage. And the commentary from NBC's anchormen was more amusing and more calculated to hold whatever viewer interest there might be. The ratings had already confirmed the Chairman's feelings, and he was

133

angry. Goddammit, he told himself, he'd let Grunwald stay on too long. He looked like a goddam Methuselah up there, pontificating and analyzing as if there were a serious contest, for Christ's sake. Didn't he realize the convention was a farce, that the real story was out in the streets and not inside the hall where nothing unpredictable or even faintly interesting had happened since the opening gavel? Eighteen million dollars they were spending, and for what?

The Chairman got up to freshen his drink and turned just as Agnew launched into another round of platitudes. "Want a drink?" he asked his wife.

"No, thank you, dear." She looked up briefly from her needlepoint. "You seem annoyed. Are you all right?"

"Yes, Louise."

"Is there anything—"

"No, there isn't," the Chairman said. "I'm angry, my dear, because we blew our goddam budget on this thing and we're doing a lousy job of it."

"I'm so sorry."

"So am I." The Chairman swirled his drink. "I should have fired Grunwald two years ago and come down harder on Brennan. We lost out four years ago."

"That's too bad, dear," Louise said placidly.

The Chairman sat down again and resumed his irritated viewing. Could anything have been more boring than this convention, with all these idiot professional actors reading their lines on cue, all the phony "spontaneous" demonstrations by the assembled thirty-two hundred Young Voters for the President; the taped, teary encomiums from Mamie Eisenhower; those ghastly filmed tributes to Pat and Dick; the precisely timed "unplanned" events—no, why go on? Surely the country had never had to sit through two more boring political events than the 1972 conventions, but the

134

Democratic circus, with all its mismanagement and endless catalogue of stupefying failures, had been slightly preferable to this one, symbolized for the Chairman by the spectacle of Sammy Davis, Jr. clasped in Nixon's arms. *Good God . . .*

"Good night, Lawrence." Louise rose. "I'm going to bed." She patted him on the shoulder and started out of the room. "Shall I turn the light off?"

The Chairman nodded.

On screen, Spiro T. Agnew was well into his acceptance speech. "The basic issue of 1972 comes down to this. Do we turn our country over to the piecemeal, inconsistent, and illusory policies of George McGovern? Or do we entrust the future of this nation to the sound, tested leadership of Richard Nixon?"

At 10:26 P.M., as the band struck up "The Stars and Stripes Forever," President Nixon arrived on the podium. He waved and smiled and nodded. "Four years ago, standing in this very place," he said, "I proudly accepted the nomination . . ."

Alone in his apartment, Crawford was enjoying himself. He had the picture on and he kept the sound just loud enough to make out most of what Nixon was saying, but not so loud that it would interfere with his pleasing train of thought. Or with his conditioning program. Dressed only in boxer shorts, the big man was quietly, with awesome efficiency, fully testing and extending every muscle in his body. In the quiet of this room, so effectively sealed against any possibility of outside intrusion, Crawford was maintaining the machinery in perfect working order, part of the contract for which he was being paid so handsomely.

"The choice in this election is not between radical change

and no change," Nixon continued. "The choice is between . . ."

No, it wasn't going to be easy, Crawford knew. Everything had to go precisely according to plan and there could be no major mistakes or miscalculations. It would have to be, in the Chairman's phrase, a strictly manageable crisis for the country. The success of the plan depended upon Agnew's going first. He'd been the front man for the administration's whole operation against the networks, and now he'd pay the price for having allowed himself to be so used. When he fell, the public disgrace would come as a shock to the whole nation. It would not only startle the public but might even force Nixon and his men to pause, to rethink their entire strategy. This would mean that he and the Chairman would gain some time. Because to make the Chairman's grand strategy pay off, time was needed. Nothing could be rushed. Crawford would have preferred a more direct solution but the final decision was certainly not up to him. He would execute what the Chairman ordered; that was his job.

"I ask everyone listening to me tonight—Democrats, Republicans, and independents—to join our new majority," Nixon urged his listeners, "not on the basis of the party label you wear on your lapel but what you believe in your hearts."

What did he believe? Crawford asked himself. *I believe in the success of missions, that's all.* It was a simple doctrine, uncluttered by metaphysics. It worked. Then what did the Chairman believe? Crawford smiled. The Chairman believed in opportunities and making the most of them. What the Chairman and he now saw on their TV screens would not have seemed an opportunity to most people. The unimaginative would see in the outcome of this convention merely the triumph of two men, viewed here at the height of their power. Neither Nixon nor Agnew had ever looked better. More confident. More serene. And why shouldn't they? They expected to carry at least forty-eight or forty-nine of the fifty states in an election landslide that would surely make history. They could not have conceived of themselves as anything but impregnable.

"Come home," Nixon trumpeted from the rostrum, "come home to the great principles we Americans believe in together."

Crawford had to admit to himself that there were elements of genius in the Chairman's tactics. What subtler, more masterful way could have been devised to counter this Nixon scheme than by discrediting it completely and so defusing the public rage at the media in general? The Chairman had constructed his plan, found his tool, and molded it to use in the most effective way possible. Genius, Crawford reflected, true genius. All they needed now was time. That and the other delicately balanced elements and events that only he, Crawford, could guarantee . . .

At 11:05 P.M., President Nixon concluded his acceptance speech. "Let us build a peace," he said, "that our children and all the children of the world can enjoy for generations to come."

Sarah had never been so physically tired in her whole life, but still she found the experience exhilarating. Probably the most difficult part had been the long commute from her dingy room in downtown Miami to the convention hall. CBS, in another of those small but telling competitive maneuvers calculated to make life difficult, had snapped up all the good hotel space months ago, leaving ACN, ABC, and NBC to scramble frantically for quarters. Sarah and the rest of the ACN brass had wound up with the worst accommodations in town, a good half hour's drive away, and it had been small consolation to know that the incompetent responsible for the goof-up had already been fired.

But what did it matter, really? Here she was, on the scene at her first major convention, and having the time of her life. She'd enjoyed every single minute of it, even the uncomfortable few hours when the gas used by the cops to break up the demonstrations outside the hall penetrated the air-conditioning systems of the trailers and the power had been turned off. It had gotten suffocatingly hot, but she'd hardly noticed, what with supervising the coverage from the floor, checking the film processing, monitoring the on-the-spot editing of incoming reams of film and video-tape, and learning as she went along exactly what it meant to function as an executive producer at one of these spectacles. What it meant most of all, she realized, was a frenzied coming and going and talking and shouting and sometimes screaming, checking every single detail of every single operation to make sure no one screwed up, and catching only two or three hours of sleep at a time. It also meant having fun, just in the heady knowledge that she had the power to shape events by deciding how to cover them, how to present them to the public. Power and the ability to use it, Sarah had discovered, was adrenalin; it could substitute for sleep. It could substitute, in fact, for almost everything.

She even loved the claustrophobic feeling of being cooped up, hidden away inside the windowless tractor trailers the network had hired and that were drawn up into a cluster outside the hall, in much the same way, Sarah reflected, that the pioneers had sheltered within and behind their covered wagons. But who were the Indians here? The public? That huge, blind, dangerous enemy they all served? Or the politicians inside?

"How you doing, Sarah?" Brennan asked. Coatless, shirt unbuttoned, he had a glass of Scotch in his hand, as usual. He sat down beside her, where she lay stretched out to snatch a five-minute breather on the daybed just beyond the control room. From here she could keep an eye on things, make sure nobody goofed. If only Ted would leave her alone.

"I'm fine, Ted."

"You've done a terrific job." He smiled at her and rattled the ice in his glass. "Sure you don't want a little drink?"

"No, thanks, Ted."

"I had the Chairman on the phone just now. He told me to tell you. I would have, anyway."

"Thanks. I appreciate it."

She hated the look in his eyes. She knew what it meant. He'd begun drinking really heavily about three days before, and with the drink had come the look in his eyes and the occasional groping hand. She hadn't realized how far gone he was and she'd begun to wonder how much longer he would last. Surely the Chairman had to know about him. Was she the one who would succeed Brennan? In these past few days, she'd begun to think she might and that thought had buoyed her and cushioned her physical fatigue. If only he hadn't decided to push his luck with her; she hadn't perceived this aspect of Ted Brennan before. Maybe the view came with the territory.

"Terrific job," he said again. "Sarah—"

The hand again, this time on her thigh just above her knee. She sat up. "Ted—"

He smiled crookedly at her. "You're a beautiful woman, Sarah."

"Ted, please stop this."

"It's not that I want to get laid, Sarah," he continued plaintively. "Shit, the hotels down here are crammed with hookers. Ever notice all the fucking that goes on at these conventions? My God, if you could just harness all the sexual energy a political convention generates you could run the whole country on it without actually having to elect anybody to anything. Know what I mean?"

"I'm not certain I do, Ted."

"Anyway, I'm sorry if I bothered you."

"It's all right, Ted."

"It's just that you're a very beautiful woman. Sure you won't have a drink?"

"I'm sure, Ted. Thanks."

She could look beyond him now and follow the play of images on the monitors in the control room. On the ACN screen, Bill James was maneuvering his minicam team up a crowded aisle past the Illinois delegation, but he was having problems getting to whomever he was trying to reach. Now the smiling face of leathery old Harvey popped back into view, addressing the nation about the meaning of it all from his booth above the floor where delegates stamped and shouted and cheered. The view cut back to the podium now; Nixon, face aglow and arms raised high above his head, was acknowledging the cheers of the faithful.

"Ted, I'd better get back to work," Sarah said.

"Oh, sure."

He stepped aside and she fled past him, but not before he reached out and gently squeezed her buttock. She whirled on him and struck him hard across the mouth with the flat of her hand. "Don't you ever do that again!"

Some Scotch spilled over his wrist, and his upper lip had already begun to swell. His eyes seemed clouded, like those of a wounded animal, and he swayed slightly from side to side. "Bitch," he mumbled. "You're a coldhearted bitch, Sarah. Maybe not even that. Maybe you're not even a woman at all."

"I'm sorry for you, Ted," she said. "You're drunk and you don't know what you're doing."

She walked into the control room and did not speak to Ted Brennan for the rest of the night. Later she couldn't even remember whether she had seen him again. Perhaps he'd just passed out somewhere. Anyway, it was a relief to get back to work. This was where she felt most at home now, in this busy, crowded little room among the professionals, where history was being made and recorded, minute by minute. She watched the images on the screens, then decided to intervene with the way Harvey was handling things from his booth. The guy seemed to have lost his sense of timing in these past few days, or maybe he was just old and tired. Sarah pressed a button on the console in front of her position, then spoke into a microphone. Harvey heard the Telex in his ear come to life.

"Harvey," Sarah said, "let's go outside the hall for an on-the-spot interview. We've got Foster out there. Apparently the police are still having problems with demonstrators. . . ."

Am I really a cold bitch? Just because I don't want Ted Brennan's clammy hands on me? But is he right? Do I

141

want anyone's hands on me ever again? Have I substituted power for love?

At 11:07 P.M., the assembled Republican delegates arose as one to sing "God Bless America."

For a long time after the last gavel had fallen, the Nixons and the Agnews remained inside the convention hall, shaking hands with delegates, alternates, friends, onlookers, children, anyone who came forward to be close to them. In the aisles, the Nixon daughters mingled with guests on their own, smiling, laughing, and chatting as if it were one big Sunday picnic. Ray Bloch and his orchestra played tirelessly on, thumping away at every old tune ever written to enshrine the foxtrot. It was long after midnight when this spontaneous, truly unrehearsed event—the only one the convention hadn't scheduled—finally broke up. The Nixons left for Key Biscayne and, as they departed, the credits rolled on the great screen above the rostrum, much as they would have for any soap opera.

Alone inside his silent, darkened rooms, Ben Stryker sat and contemplated the future. Kathy had been calling him all night long, but he had ignored the steady rings. He hadn't stirred from the screen and the events in Miami except to relieve himself and, once, to make himself a sandwich. Now, at last, the long night had come to an end, but Ben wasn't tired. The Minolta sat on the table beside him and from time to time he would finger it lovingly. Yes, he knew what he had to do. Nothing less would satisfy him. Nothing else could matter. In this darkness, in this silence, he allowed the flow of cold, murderous hatred to congeal into an icy rage that consumed him now like a cancer. He had become what he had known for some time he *had* to become—the instrument of atonement, the enforcer of justice.

Without turning off the set, Ben sat in the darkness, alone with the flickering images on the video screen, until the first gray light began to seep through the shutters. Then his head sank slowly over his chest and at last he slept.

16

Cargill had been worrying about the situation for some time. There was nothing really specific, but it was troublesome just the same. He was certain others must have observed it as well, but nobody had mentioned it; once or twice Cargill had dropped hints, just to see if anybody picked up on them, but no one had. The man wasn't behaving normally, Cargill decided; rather he was behaving *too* normally. Even Bellucci had given up taunting him, since Ben never rose to the bait anymore, and the foul-mouthed assignment editor had turned his savage sarcasm on others in the news room. There had never been a lack of victims, and men like Bellucci needed them to keep themselves sane and functioning. But why should he have expected Bellucci to comment on Ben? He'd been naive, Cargill thought, to expect anything at all from that quarter. But only yesterday he'd encountered Campbell in the men's room and asked him if he'd noticed anything.

"About what, Derrick?" the cameraman had answered, drying his hands.

"I mean, about Ben."

"What about him?"

"Is he OK?"

"Sure he's OK. Why, is he screwing up?"

Cargill shook his head. "No, nothing like that."

"We've been shooting some pretty raunchy stuff recently and Ben's been terrific. What's wrong?"

"Nothing's wrong."

Campbell had turned toward him then. "I haven't seen Ben this happy in a long time. He seems to have adapted OK. The past couple of months have been really rough on him."

"I know."

"He's into photographing a lot of his own stuff, too," Campbell continued. "He likes taking his own pictures. I asked him the other day if he wanted to switch jobs and it was like he didn't hear me."

"No?"

"He was taking a lot of pictures from every angle. But he's not goofing off. I mean, it's on his own time. He's getting the stories, isn't he?"

Cargill nodded. "Oh, yeah. I didn't mean to imply he wasn't."

"He also told me he sold a couple of things. To magazines."

"So I heard."

"Well, that's good, isn't it? I mean, if his career is pretty well shot in TV news, maybe he can make it in magazines."

"Has he talked to you about it?"

"No, but that kid Kathy talks about it a lot. Maybe she's behind it. Anyway, Ben's pretty cool about everything these days."

That was when Cargill had decided to talk to Kathy. He knew that she and Ben were still seeing each other and he guessed she must have been encouraging Ben to branch out, but she was such an innocent and, anyway, he didn't want to pry. Still, he thought, there was something strange about Ben Stryker now, something he couldn't quite put his finger on, and Cargill had learned over the years to trust his instincts and to ask questions, even incautious or seemingly gratuitous ones.

"Mr. Cargill?"

"Oh, come in, Kathy," he said, smiling. She was a pretty thing; no wonder Ben was seeing her. "Sit down." He got up and closed the door.

"Anything wrong?"

"Probably not," he said, returning to his chair. "I wanted to speak to you about Ben."

She took that in stride. "Certainly. You know we're—dating. And I guess you don't approve, or something."

"Or nothing. I have no feelings about that, Kathy. Your private life is your own business. No, I—it's just that Ben seems, I don't know, distracted—"

"He's doing something about his life, Mr. Cargill."

146

"How do you mean, Kathy?"

"It's just terrible the way he's been treated here," she said indignantly. "I know it's not your fault. And I know you care, too. Ben thinks the world of you, Mr. Cargill."

"Does he?"

"Oh, yes. He says you're a real pro, probably the best in the business. He's never had anything but good things to say about you."

"I'm flattered."

"Ben's not distracted at all, Mr. Cargill," she continued eagerly. "He's very wrapped up in his photography now. And he's writing a lot on his own time. He sold a piece last week, you know, to *Tempo*. It was a story about that Bronx neighborhood action group. We did a feature here some weeks ago, but it never ran."

"Oh, yeah," Cargill remembered. "Good footage, but pretty special. I can see it would make a good magazine piece."

"Well, it did. Ben sold it right away. And he took all of his own pictures. Now he's got an assignment from *New York*. But it's all on his own time. I mean, there's no conflict, is there?"

Cargill shook his head. "No."

"I mean, they've asked Ben to write about the way he got fired from the Washington job and to do exposé stuff about the network and all, but he's refused to do that. Haven't you asked him about it? Hasn't he said anything to you?"

"No."

"Well, gee, you ought to talk to him. I mean, Ben's trying so hard. He wants to do something on his own. I mean, he doesn't just want to be a nightside reporter all his life. He's a really good journalist, you know. I guess Ben could be just about anything he wanted to be," she concluded

147

fiercely and a little defiantly. "I don't see why this bothers you."

"It doesn't bother me, Kathy," Cargill said gently. "I'm glad to hear he's doing so well. I was—curious, that's all."

She looked puzzled. "Curious?"

"Yes. Ben seems a little out of things. He walks around here and goes through the motions every day and he's doing a fair job and all that, but he seems pretty remote. I guess that's the word. You don't see that?"

She didn't answer right away and Cargill knew that he'd touched a nerve. "He's—he's very intense sometimes," she said, a little hesitantly. "I mean, I guess he's been through a lot."

"He's under a lot of pressure, Kathy? Is that it?"

She struggled to find the right words, but apparently it wasn't easy. He sighed and waited, leaning back in his chair. "Ben wants too much," she said finally. "He expects too much, maybe."

"Of you, Kathy?"

"No, of himself. It's like—it's like he gets really all caught up in something and then you just don't reach him. He—he doesn't want anybody around him then or close to him. I've—I've learned to stay away from him when he's like that."

"Would you say he's happy, Kathy?"

"Happy?" she echoed, astonished by the question.

"Yes," Cargill went on. "I've known Ben for a while now, long enough at least to know that I've suddenly lost touch with him. I worry about that, Kathy. I worry about it because I like Ben, too. And I like you and I don't want anything to happen."

"But—but what could happen, Mr. Cargill?"

148

"Ben's hiding something, Kathy. From us, from you, maybe even from himself. Don't you sense that?"

She did, of course; he could see it in her face, but she wouldn't admit it, perhaps not even to herself. "I—I love Ben, Mr. Cargill. He's been through so much—"

She began to cry and Cargill felt guilty. He came around from behind his desk and awkwardly began to pat her shoulder. What was the matter with him, anyway, prying into other people's lives like this? What right had he to meddle? And what if he was wrong?

But for some time after Kathy had gone, he sifted through his thoughts, turning over in his head everything he knew and felt about Ben Stryker. The feeling would not leave him that Ben was in some sort of deep trouble and that somehow it was connected to Kathy, himself, everyone at the station. *Something's going to happen, but I'll be goddamned if I know what. . . .*

"It's begun," Crawford said.

The Chairman nodded. He did not turn back immediately to probe further. There was no need to; he thought he could anticipate what the man had to tell him. Crawford appeared as cool and unruffled as ever. Below, in the streets of the city, people looked like so many fleas—tiny, hurrying specks obsessed by their own concerns. The Chairman liked to study them from this height; it soothed him and helped him to think clearly. He sighed.

"Brooks Alexander called me last night," Crawford continued.

The Chairman swiveled around. "Yes?"

"He's tapped into the White House taping system."

"Who is he? Somebody else on your team?"

Crawford smiled. "A part-time player, but a useful one."

"What about him?"

"Well, he helped install the recording system. He works partly out of Haldeman's office, sometimes directly for Colson. He's sort of a troubleshooter."

"He the one who tipped us off on the Watergate caper?"

"Yeah." Crawford laughed briefly. "I still can't believe he tried to talk the boys out of that one at first. He told me it seemed too amateurish. Brooks is an old pro who goes back a long way, but I'm afraid he has his prejudices." Crawford was warming to his subject now, enjoying his own dissection of that operation. "He was afraid the Cubans and Hunt wouldn't even get into the building, much less the Democratic headquarters itself."

"Good thing he didn't succeed."

"I made sure of that, Larry. Old Brooks just doesn't have your eye for opportunities. Sometimes it's hard to believe the people you work with can be so dumb."

"Actually, Crawford, Brooks was right. It was amateurish, and they did blow it."

"But not before they actually got into the place and were putting wires on the phones." Crawford leaned forward, looking directly into the Chairman's eyes. "And not without a little help and a little luck."

The Chairman shook his head sadly. "Luck, luck," he murmured. "I've never believed in luck."

"I don't believe in it either, Larry. I always have a fallback position. But every plan has to include the possible effect of luck, good or bad." Crawford launched into one of his favorite analogies. "Presume you decided to win a lot of money at craps. That's your goal. So you walk into a crap game with a pair of loaded dice in your pocket. Would you make the switch immediately?" Crawford

150

paused to let the Chairman answer, but he just flicked his wrist and said impatiently, "Go on. Go on."

"The answer is no. Your plan should allow for the possibility of good luck. You should roll the house dice a few times because there's a chance you could win without exposing yourself to the risks involved when you switch dice. But your plan should also allow for bad luck, like getting caught with loaded dice once you've switched."

"Crawford, you are nothing if not thorough. What have you got?"

Crawford opened his briefcase, producing a typed manuscript which he shoved across the desk. "It's a transcript. Just look at page two."

The Chairman picked up the slim sheaf of papers, turned to page two, and began reading:

Nixon: They are asking for it and they are going to get it. We have not used the power in this first four years, as you know. We have never used it. We have not used the FBI and we have not used the Justice Department, but things are going to change now. And they are either going to do it right or go.

Dean: What an exciting prospect.

Nixon: Thanks. It has to be done.

The Chairman lowered the paper and looked up at Crawford. "It's incredible they'd put this stuff on tape."

"Isn't it? They're so sure of themselves. It's our best guarantee the plan will work."

The Chairman swiveled back to the view from his window. "So they're on the way," he said quietly.

"Right. We found out today they're going to challenge WJXT, a CBS affiliate down in Jacksonville, Florida, that's

151

owned by *Post-Newsweek*. It's the station that unearthed that old segregationist speech by Carswell, Nixon's Supreme Court nominee, and it helped him get rejected by the Senate. That really pissed Nixon off."

"When and what are they up to?" the Chairman asked.

"They'll move right after the election. The station's license is up for renewal and there are three groups down there getting ready to challenge it. One of them is headed by a guy named George Champion, Jr."

"Anyone you know?"

"Sure. He's Nixon's Florida finance chairman."

"Who else?"

"Some guy named Powell, who works for Wallace, and another fellow named Mills, who used to be campaign treasurer for Gurney, the Republican senatorial candidate in sixty-eight."

The Chairman whistled softly. "They don't kid around."

"No. All three of these groups are hiring Washington law firms and they have a whole bunch of prominent business types lined up behind them. We also hear Chuck Colson may be involved. And, incidentally, they're going after the license of the *Post-Newsweek* station in Miami."

"No kidding? It's that far out in the open? Well, I called it a long time ago. It's the tip of the iceberg." The Chairman's voice was harsh with anger. "One part of the scheme is to attack individual stations. The other, and much more serious one, is the legislation they're drawing up to break up all the networks. They want to reduce us to regionally owned outfits, which would just about put all of us out of business in any significant way."

"Some prospect."

"See what I mean?" The Chairman spread his hands wide

and stared at Crawford with the intensity of a bird of prey. "Right after the election all this is going to hit the fan. And who's going to stop Nixon if we don't?"

Later, as Crawford rose to leave, the Chairman began his familiar finger drumming on the edge of his desk. "Crawford," he said, "this man Alexander, can he keep these transcripts coming? There's plenty of ammunition in them."

"Maybe. Some, anyway."

"Good. I want all the evidence we can gather on this administration. Our very survival depends on it."

"The *Post* contact is working out fine, by the way."

"And Stryker?"

"I'm in touch," Crawford said with satisfaction. "He's a time bomb, Larry. All we have to do now is set him."

"You make it sound easy."

"It isn't," Crawford observed dryly. "Nothing's easy."

"Anything we haven't anticipated?"

"There's that girl," Crawford mused. "I don't know . . ."

"What are you doing?" Kathy asked, coming to the kitchen doorway and glancing into the living room.

"Getting all this material together for the *New York* story," Ben answered without looking up from the coffee table where he had stacked his contact sheets and blow-ups. "I think I've got too much stuff."

"I love the shots of the black kids, the ones running away from the telephone company truck."

"Yeah, that's good stuff. I lucked into that one. They just about had the back door jimmied open when the cop car came around the corner." He smiled at the recollection. "Boy, did they take off in a hurry."

"You hungry?"

"Starved. How you coming along?"

"I'm heating the grill. In about five minutes you can put the steaks in."

"Great."

"And this hollandaise is super." She went back into the kitchen and turned up the gas burner under the steamer, checked the broccoli with a fork and then made a quick survey of everything else. The steaks were marinating, the salad waited, wrapped in a paper towel, in the refrigerator, and the dressing had been mixed; she'd toss the greens just before dinner. Ben would open the wine and cook the steaks. She dried her hands and began humming softly to herself. She loved cooking for him, even these simple dishes, and she thought she was becoming pretty good at it, too. "You want to get the wine?" she called out.

"Sure."

She heard him go into the front hallway, where he kept a small rack of bottles, mostly French and California vintages, in the coat closet, and then she headed for the bathroom off his bedroom. For some reason she decided to use the small john at the very end of the hall, just beyond the second bedroom that Ben now used as a writing room and studio. The door was locked, or perhaps it was just jammed. She wasn't sure where the light switch was and in the dark she couldn't tell what was wrong, so she jiggled the knob impatiently.

She'd just about given up when suddenly the door gave way. She opened it a crack and smelled something frightful, something so disgusting that it made her instantly nauseous. She felt her knees buckle and she had to steady herself with one hand against the wall.

"Kathy!"

She gasped, but couldn't answer him. She felt his hands on her, dragging her away even as he slammed the bathroom door shut again. "What the fuck do you think you're doing!" he shouted.

She stared dumbly up at him. She had never seen him this way before. His face was pale yellow in the half light and his eyes were different, dangerous. He shook her so hard that her bones seemed to crack.

"You dumb bitch!" He shook her more violently still. "I told you to stay out of there!"

"But—Ben—I—what?" she stuttered.

He flung her away and she staggered across the living room, coming up hard against the coffee table; she braced an arm against the back of the sofa to keep from falling. "I—told—you—to—stay—out of there!" he shouted again.

She turned, wide-eyed with terror. He was standing in the doorway, and she hardly recognized him. "Ben?"

As she watched, in fascinated horror, he made a tremendous effort to gain control of himself. She could almost see the machinery at work, all the gears grinding down to take the pressure off himself, as well as off her. "That room, Kathy," he said in a trembling voice. "You must never go in there again, do you understand?"

"Yes," she whispered, hardly able to speak.

He told her then, over the next half hour, what was in there—an improvised darkroom where he worked very hard to develop his pictures; by opening the door she had almost ruined a week's production. That was why he was so upset. The smell? A special acid solution, very expensive, that the Japanese had developed recently. It worked wonders. Couldn't she tell from the quality of the prints he was making now?

She nodded, but she didn't believe him. That was death she had smelled through the crack in the door, death or something even worse. In his bedroom later that night, Kathy lay on her back, cradling his head in her arms, and stared into the darkness. She was frightened now, more for him than for herself.

17

"We're not going to get any closer than this," Ben said. "Let's park it."

Jeff Campbell pulled the white Ford over to the curb at Forty-eighth and Seventh. They'd been sitting in a huge traffic jam for twenty minutes and over the blaring of the horns they could faintly hear the chanting.

"Nixon the dike bomber! Nixon the dike bomber!" Four blocks ahead, a mob of anti-Nixon protesters was swelling in front of the Seventh Avenue entrance to the Americana Hotel, spilling into the street. A double row of uniformed policemen, massed shoulder to shoulder behind wooden barricades along the sidewalk for two blocks north and south, kept the angry crowd at bay, but the traffic jam the demonstrators were causing in midtown was hopeless.

Ben switched on the microphone of the news car's two-way radio. "Seven-seven-one, local desk."

"This is the local desk. What's up, Stryker?"

"We're leaving the car a few blocks away from the hotel, Mario. It looks pretty lively up ahead, so you might tell Derrick to leave a couple of minutes open at the top of to-night's program."

"Roger. I'll tell him the star wants the lead story," Bellucci jabbed.

Ben slammed the microphone into its holder and said tersely, "Let's go."

Ben, Campbell, the sound man, and the light man got out of the Ford simultaneously, locking the doors behind them. Campbell opened the trunk, pulled out an extra camera battery which he shoved into his pocket, stuffed a loaded film magazine under his belt, and shouldered his camera. The sound man extricated his portable amplifier, along with a long, slender shotgun microphone, draped the amp's strap over his head, and adjusted it, with the amplifier dangling over his stomach, knobs and meters up. Using a short audio cord, he plugged one end into a socket in the front of the amp, the other end into the microphone.

"Hook up," Campbell said, handing the sound man another heavier wire that was already plugged into the back of Campbell's camera. The sound man slipped its heavy, silver jack into another socket on the amp and locked it into place. The two men were now one, connected by an umbilical through which all the sound picked up by the shotgun microphone would be recorded on a thin, magnetic stripe down the edge of the film in the news camera.

The light man took what looked like an ammunition bandolier out of the trunk and threw it over his left shoulder—the battery belt that would power his hand-held movie light for about half an hour.

"Everybody saddled up?" Ben asked.

"Yeah."

"Okay, let's go."

The four of them began to pick their way through the traffic jam toward the Americana. Inside the hotel, Richard Nixon was speaking to 1,500 fat-walleted supporters at a fund-raising dinner, the end of his first campaign day in New York City. "The power of the United States is not a threat to the peace of the world but the guardian of the peace," he said to the cheers of the faithful. Outside, the protest was growing, getting surlier.

"Stop the bombing! Stop the bombing!"

Ben could hear the chanting more clearly now and see the placards waving above the car roofs. Somebody unfurled a Viet Cong flag and began swinging it back and forth on a long pole.

Ben led his camera crew across the street to get behind the demonstrators. "Jeff, get me a couple of shots of the traffic jam and maybe one wide shot of the crowd, but save your film. I have a hunch this thing's going to break loose when Nixon leaves to go back to the Waldorf."

"You bet."

"I'm going to nose around a little. If I don't get back to you, meet me at the car at nine."

"At the car in one hour."

"Right."

Ben waved to Campbell and slipped behind the double row of policemen, heading for the hotel entrance. Two patrolmen cut him off. "Sorry, buddy, this entrance is closed."

"WACN News," Ben said, flashing his police working-press pass.

"Sorry," one of the officers said. "No one comes in or out this way right now. We've got enough trouble."

"Just guests in the hotel," the other policeman said.

Ben retreated, rounded the corner of the barricades, and rejoined his crew. Campbell was enjoying himself and wanted to sniff around down the cross streets. "Nixon will probably show up at one of those side entrances," he said. "That's his usual style in New York. The cops have both streets blocked off."

"I'll look around and try to let you know," Ben said. "I don't think we can all get through."

"OK," Jeff said. "I think the network guys got through earlier. They probably went up Fifty-third Street. Nixon must be coming out that way."

"Sure must be great to be a guest at this hotel," the light man cracked. "Christ, you can't even get in or out of the goddam lobby hardly. Some fun. And imagine having a room over this racket."

"The windows are sealed," the audio man said. "With the TV on, they probably can't even hear this."

"Get those shots," Ben told Jeff. "I'll see what I can find out."

Campbell's crew was now directly across the street from the Americana. He climbed on top of a concrete trash container, looked through the camera's viewfinder, and twisted the barrel of its zoom lens until the legend "Americana" above the hotel's entrance filled the picture. Campbell then reached forward to the focus ring, rolling it back and forth until the image was sharp. He was ready for his first shot, a zoom back from the close-up of the hotel's name to a wide shot revealing the sea of angry protesters in the street. He turned to his sound man. "Turn it on." The sound man flipped a toggle switch on the amplifier and the needle of one of the two meters started dancing in rhythm with the chanting. Campbell instructed his light man. "Keep it high on flood and don't light it until I tell you."

"Okay." The light man raised the battery-powered light over his head, finger on the switch.

Campbell set his exposure without a light check or meter reading. A hundred night protests had taught him what it would be. He pressed a red button on the front of the camera and it rolled silently. The second meter on the sound man's amplifier began bouncing parallel to the first, confirming that sound was being recorded on the film. The sound man looked up at Campbell and barked, "Speed!"

Without taking his eye from the viewfinder, Campbell yelled, "Light!"

The light man flipped the switch on the back of his movie light, flooding the scene with brightness. It was almost as if he had somehow wired that switch into the crowd. The instant the light went on, the protesters spun away from the hotel to face the camera crew, aware now of its presence. The placards leaped and the chants got louder. A frenzy set in, starting with those nearest the light and rippling back through the mob.

Campbell held his close-up of the word "Americana" for ten seconds, then zoomed back to capture the angry crowd scene on film.

"Nixon the dike bomber! Nixon the dike bomber! Stop

161

the bombing!" The chants were becoming hysterical, just mindless din. Suddenly, one of the younger demonstrators rushed at Campbell and thrust a placard in front of the lens, blocking the crowd shot. Campbell reached out and shoved it away with his left hand. "Fuck Nixon! Fuck you!" the protester screamed, covering Campbell's lens again. Without even looking down, Campbell kicked out violently with his right foot, catching the yelling protester in the chest, sending him and his sign flying back into the crowd. Campbell spun around and jumped down from the trash container, shouting, "Let's go!" to his crew.

They shifted instantly into combat stance. The sound man flipped his amp to automatic gain control—no time now to fuss manually with sound levels. Then he grabbed Campbell's belt with his left hand and thrust the shotgun microphone out in front of him like a sword. Campbell's vision was blocked to his right because the camera was on his right shoulder, so the sound man's job now was to protect the right flank and the cable that linked camera to amplifier. The light man closed in on Campbell's left, grabbing the cameraman's belt with his right hand and holding the switched-off light like a club. Campbell zoomed his lens back to its wide-angle setting, where everything from a foot away to infinity was in focus—no time to maneuver the focus ring or try for fancy shots. He racked the iris wide open. There'd be no more illumination from the light man. He had to make a picture with just the light available from the hotel and streetlamps. As soon as he felt both men hook up to his belt, Campbell shot his left hand out to stiff-arm people out of the way and, camera rolling, headed for the protection of the police lines. The wedge of cameraman, sound man, and light man cut through the enraged mob, knocking people out of the way, leaving a trail of fist fights and curses. *Amazing how easily it works,* Campbell thought; *half of them don't know what hit them and those who figure it out are swallowed up by the crowd and only antagonize others if they try to get back at us.*

Again Ben skirted the line of police, then cut across the avenue and ducked up along Fifty-third Street, keeping close to the buildings opposite the hotel. He walked east to Sixth Avenue, turned south and then right again at Fifty-second, where he encountered more barricades and a cluster of policemen. They looked cynical and bored, since the action was obviously down at the other end. Ben could see a line of dark limousines parked halfway down the block and he guessed that the presidential party would load there, if anywhere. The trick would be getting close enough.

After a moment or two, he decided to try to bluff his way in. Looking casual and confident, he ambled toward the police, smiled, nodded, and started down the street.

"Hey!" Ben turned. "Hey!" the big sergeant said, coming up to him. "You can't go this way."

Ben tried his credentials again. "WACN News," he said. "I've got to get back to my crew." He pointed down the street toward Seventh Avenue.

"Yeah? Well, you can't go this way."

"Why not? I came this way ten minutes ago," Ben lied. "The president isn't due for a while, is he? So what's the big deal? I have to cover the demonstration."

"Them punks," the cop said. "OK, go ahead. But you may run into some Secret Service guys. I can't promise they'll let you through."

"I'll take my chances," Ben said, smiling. "Thanks, Sergeant."

The big cop waved him on and Ben walked rapidly along

Fifty-second back toward Seventh Avenue. As he neared the row of limousines, two agents in civilian clothes cut him off, but before Ben could say anything one of them recognized him. "Stryker," the agent said. "You covering this?"

"Hello, Walters. Yeah. For local news. Look, I just want to get back to my crew without having to detour another block, OK? I'm in a hurry."

"Well, move it," Walters said. "We're not supposed to let anyone through."

"Yeah, I know, but we have some time."

"No telling," the agent said. "The chief may be out of there any minute. He's already late. Get going."

"Thanks."

Ben knew exactly what he had to do. He would marshal his crew at the corner of Fifty-second and Seventh, position them where they'd be able to film the presidential party emerging from the hotel, and instruct Jeff to turn his camera on the demonstrators, who would surely try to halt the progress of the government limousines as they hit the avenue. Meanwhile, somehow, he himself would have to get close enough to Nixon to use the Minolta. He might just be able to do it, he told himself, especially now that he'd been recognized by that Secret Service guy. That had been an unforeseen break, and he was determined to make use of it. God knew when he'd get a second chance at the bastard. He took the camera from his pocket, hung it around his neck, and then strode up the street. He could feel his pulse quickening, his gut tightening. He was driven as if possessed, in the grip of some terrible, inexorable force he could neither analyze nor resist. He was a hunter now and he moved like one—cautiously but swiftly—up the street toward the corner from which he could lie in wait.

Crawford had experienced his first moment of panic in the whole affair when Ben managed to get past the police at the corner and headed up the street, apparently able somehow to talk his way through the Secret Service checkpoint. If Ben could do that so easily, Crawford realized, it was conceivable he might even get close enough to Nixon to take a shot at him. Sweating, the big man broke into a loping run down Sixth, then turned up Fifty-first toward Seventh, and slowed to a quick walk in order not to seem too conspicuous.

By the time Crawford got back to the main body of demonstrators, Ben was nowhere to be seen. Campbell and the WACN crew were out in the middle of the street, filming the rhythmic, defiant chanting of the marchers. Across the way, New York's finest, equipped with helmets, shields, and tear-gas grenade launchers, eyed the mob in grim silence. Above them, silhouetted against the lighted windows, most of the hotel guests whose rooms fronted on the avenue stared down at the action. Crawford cursed softly to himself as he tried to spot Ben somewhere in the shadow of the buildings. Failing, he turned his attention toward the WACN crew; he reasoned and hoped fervently that Ben would soon rejoin them. *My God, what if he did get a shot at the president tonight? And what if he got lucky and hit him? It would blow away the whole scheme, to say nothing of Crawford himself.*

The sight of Kathy froze him. Just when Crawford had decided to try to get past the police lines himself, he saw the girl running across the avenue toward Campbell, who greeted her and also began looking around for Stryker. Crawford merged into the crowd of demonstrators, determined now to do what he could to speed the inevitable confrontation with the police. That, at least, might cause enough commotion to keep the presidential party inside the hotel and so safely out of range of Stryker. Unshaven, in his jeans, sneakers, ragged, black turtleneck, and army fatigue jacket, the agent blended well with this anti-war mob. *Goddammit,* he cursed to himself, *how could I have anticipated that this loony would try so soon. Shit, once we had him set up, we should have fixed it so he'd go for it at the right time and under the right conditions. This is turning out to be amateur night.*

"We don't want your bloody war!" a bearded youth brandishing a sign sang out behind him.

Crawford turned on him. "Let's get past these pigs!" he said fiercely. "The cocksucker's going to come out one of those side entrances and we can't get to him!" Shouting and waving, Crawford surged out into the avenue at the head of a small group of militants. It would grow, he knew; he could feel the intensity of the emotion in this crowd and he would tap into it, like the pro he was. . . .

As the demonstrators became noisier and more active, the WACN crew retreated down the avenue just below Fifty-second Street. Kathy, sticking close to Campbell and the others, peered around for Ben, but still she couldn't pick him out. Now she saw movement up Fifty-second Street and made out a cordon of men emerging from the side entrance of the hotel. At the same moment, a swarm of demonstrators, shouting slogans and waving placards, washed up to the police barricades. There was some pushing, a woman screamed, and the crowd fell back; then it surged forward again. The police lines bent and stiffened again, while knots of struggling people swirled and eddied up the avenue, the more timid taking refuge in doorways or fleeing west up the side streets. Crawford was in the middle of it, still straining to find Ben. Suddenly he saw Nixon, ringed by secret service agents, moving rapidly toward the presidential limousine. To his horror, he spotted Ben not ten feet from the car, in the front line of the roiling protest, camera to his eye.

"Shit!" Crawford yelled aloud and began plowing toward Stryker.

Ben was operating on instinct now. He could see Nixon's face bobbing in and out of the Minolta's viewfinder, about thirty feet away now. *The ass. The ass. Got to see his ass.* The protesters surged forward again, knocking Ben into a barricade. The camera flew from his hands and bounced around on the end of its strap. Nixon was near the car now. The door was open. Frantically, Ben grabbed the Minolta and focused. *Jesus.* He could hardly believe it. Just as Nixon bent over to dive into the limousine, two of his bodyguards shoved in different directions; there, in his viewfinder, Ben saw Nixon's butt. *Jesus.* His finger shot toward the shutter release. Suddenly the picture was a blur.

"Hey, what the fuck do you want to take the Mad Bomber's picture for, man?"

Ben jerked his head up. An enraged protester had jumped directly in front of him, ranting and gesturing.

"Why take a picture of that scum!"

Ben lunged around his tormentor just in time to see the door slam on the president's bulletproof limousine.

Jesus. I almost had him. If that bastard hadn't . . .

Crawford was panicked; he had no way of knowing if Ben had gotten a shot, and it was too late to do anything other than continue to help the drama play itself out.

Halfway down Fifty-second, the black limousines began to move away, escorted front and back by motorcycle police. A small group of protesters succeeded in breaking through the police lines, racing up the street after the departing convoy. Ben ran with them, his camera bouncing on its cord. Kathy couldn't imagine what he was up to, but she could see that they had no chance of catching up with the powerful cars. Besides, the police were moving in now, swinging billy clubs and trying with some success to fragment the mob and arrest some of the more aggressive demonstrators.

Again Kathy tried to reach Ben, and this time Campbell couldn't stop her. She ran up the street and into a doorway as the attackers were dispersed; some came running back toward the avenue. "Ben!" she screamed.

He might have heard her, because he stopped and ducked into an entrance. Screaming demonstrators and police ran past, caught up in their own drama. "Ben!" Kathy shouted again, but this time he did not appear to hear her.

Crawford stood deep in the doorway of an office building, monitoring the movements of his charge. He could see the back of Ben's head among the group of fugitives huddled in the recess. An angry, scraggly-bearded young man, still holding his sign, was arguing with Ben. Ben looked furious; it was the same protester who'd blocked Ben's shot at Nixon. "Hey, man, what's with the camera? I mean, you a reporter or something?" Ben must have answered, but Crawford couldn't make out the words. The bearded youth thrust his head forward. "So what do you want to photograph the Mad Bomber for? You want to put him on TV?"

Crawford could read most of the sign now—a standard anti-war slogan in which Nixon's name had been spelled

with a swastika in place of the x. The protester had chosen
to identify Stryker with the enemy and continued to badger
him. "You media freaks give me a pain, you know that?"
Crawford heard him say. "I mean, you glorify the bastard,
know what I mean? If you'd never photographed him, like
who would've known he was even alive, you dig?"

The big man pushed forward through the knot of chat-
tering demonstrators until he could be sure Ben could hear
him, even through the emotional diatribe of the hairy boy.

"Hey, man, you press?" he called out.

"Fuck off," Ben snarled. "I don't like the sonofabitch any
more than the rest of you."

"Yeah, I'll bet," the young man said. "You media whores
glorify the bastard, that's what you do! You put the Mad
Bomber on TV! Bunch of scumsuckers, all of you!"

"Hey," Crawford broke in, "you must be some lousy reporter. How do you expect to photograph the guy from
here? You need special passes, don't you? What do you
photograph from here in this light, limousines? Motorcycle
cops? Secret Service storm troopers?"

"Bunch of scumsuckers!" the young man bleated. Suddenly he leaped into the street brandishing his sign. "Fas-
cist pigs!" he screamed. "Goddam Nazis!"

Two running policemen turned back and went after him.
The boy dropped his sign and fled. In a second, Ben was in
the street, kneeling to steady himself as he snapped the
picture.

"Ben!" Kathy shouted, waving at him from another doorway up the block.

In the noise and the darkness, Ben apparently didn't
hear her. He stood up and watched as the boy stumbled
and the patrolmen caught up to him. The boy, overpow-

ered, began to struggle, but a third policeman arrived to club him to the ground. Ben turned and walked away calmly.

Kathy stepped out of the shadows. "Ben, darling, it's me!"

He walked past her like a stranger; she was struck by the oddity of his expression.

Ben turned at the corner of Seventh Avenue, heading downtown. He walked briskly back to the car and waited calmly for Campbell and the others. They were all very pleased with their footage. A minute and a half of it, with Ben's cool narration as a background, was seen on the local news that night. Unfortunately, no one had any film of the police arresting and clubbing a young bearded demonstrator. It was too bad, because the boy had died in the paddy wagon, ostensibly of a heart attack, on his way to be booked.

The next afternoon Kathy asked Ben about the still pictures he'd shot of the incident; he looked astonished. "I took a picture of him? Nothing came out."

"But I saw you photograph him."

"Yeah? The pictures didn't come out, I guess. I'm still finding out about this camera." He dismissed her brusquely; he had copy to write.

A little later, Kathy went in to discuss the whole episode with Cargill. She wasn't really scared, she told the older man, just confused and more than a little worried.

18

"Yes, now we know he can do it," Crawford said, "but that was a zoo out there, Larry. The whole thing got way out of control. Stryker damn near got him."

"But he didn't."

"He got a lot closer than I thought he would."

"It's your job to stay on top of this situation."

"He's resourceful and he moves fast." Crawford felt reproved. "You can't expect me to guarantee every move. He's not a puppet."

"He's as close to one as we can manage," the Chairman snapped. "And I do expect you to stay in control. That's what I pay you for."

Crawford exhaled heavily and slumped in his chair. He had expected the Chairman to be shaken by the account of the events at the Americana the night before, but Hoenig gave no sign of distress. On the contrary, to Crawford's surprise the Chairman actually seemed pleased by the way matters had turned out. Crawford had his own ideas about their course of action and he was determined to get them across to the Chairman. He couldn't risk a failure and that had been a near thing last night. "You know there's going to be an autopsy, don't you?"

"On the boy who was killed? Yes. And?"

"They'll find out he didn't die because the cops beat on him or manhandled him in the paddy wagon. They'll find that he was shot in the ass by some kind of pellet and that he died of poisoning. That doesn't bother you, Larry?"

"Some," the Chairman admitted, "but not much. It'll make an interesting news story, but no one will ever connect it to anything else, if you see what I mean."

"The girl might."

"You think so?"

"I always anticipate the worst," Crawford said. "It's a way of staying alive."

The Chairman thought this over for a minute or two; then he looked intently into Crawford's eyes. "You think we might have a problem there?"

Crawford nodded. "Not a major one. Not yet." He sighed, hunched his huge shoulders, and stretched; then he sat back again. "I have a suggestion."

"I'm listening."

"That we drop this whole scheme and shift gears. I can arrange the big job myself and see that it gets done by a couple of qualified professionals. Quickly and cleanly, with no loose ends. We minimize the risk and we accomplish the mission."

"We accomplish nothing," the Chairman snapped. "I don't care how efficient you think you may be, there's always a risk. If we do it your way, it could backfire. Christ, man, can't you see that?"

"No risk," the big man said evenly. "In these capers I see to it that the risk is eliminated. You know my track record; that's why you hired me. I can guarantee you success and no risk with a professional job. When you deal with amateurs and setups, there's always a risk. Stryker is an amateur."

"All the more reason to use him," the Chairman pointed out. "If something goes wrong with your professional operation, and something very often does go wrong—"

"Larry—"

"Let me finish." The Chairman leaned forward in his chair to drive every point home. "I'm not through."

"Sorry. Go ahead."

"The whole idea of using someone like Stryker *is* his amateur standing, as you might put it."

"Why?"

"You guys in the business think you're infallible," the Chairman said tightly, "but I know you're not. I can tick off a whole list of mistakes in our intelligence activities over the years."

"Not from me."

"Not from you, granted. But you're not infallible either, Crawford; I don't believe you can walk on water."

173

The big man smiled. "I haven't tried it yet, but I may get around to it."

"If you should screw up, you know what would happen? The trail would lead straight back to this office and the whole operation would blow sky-high—you, me, everybody along with it. Now what happens if something goes wrong and Stryker gets caught?"

"He's alone."

"Precisely. Just like Lee Harvey Oswald and Ruby and all the others. Amateurs. Loonies. Crazed citizens acting alone. Hell, Crawford, half the people in this country and the rest of the world are absolutely gut certain that none of these guys acted alone, but no one can prove anything. The trails lead nowhere except into fantasy land; it's all pure speculation. And pure speculation won't get you an indictment, while it could bring the whole house down around your ears. Look at Jim Garrison."

"I worry about Stryker, Larry, that's all. How sure are you about him?"

"As sure as I can be, Crawford," the Chairman said affably, relaxing a little now, pleased at having conveyed part of his message so eloquently. "As you know, we have psychological profiles of every employee of this network and we update our files every six months. I suspected Stryker might be our man from the very first time I met him, and I was sure of it after I had lunch with him."

"I believe you, Larry."

"All those hints about his unhappy childhood, his missing father, the moving, the hated other man in his life— my God, Crawford, he was handed to us on a tray. All we had to do was stick an apple in his mouth."

Crawford smiled. "I could still do it faster and more cleanly my way."

"Maybe," the Chairman said, not returning the smile, "but you never really understood one aspect of this operation."

"Me? What's that, Larry?"

"That the most difficult thing in this world to assassinate is an idea. Killing the man who espouses it doesn't work, especially once it's become a 'cause.' "

"I don't know about that."

"It doesn't work, Crawford. It never has. In fact, history has taught us that killing the apostle only martyrs him, accelerating his cause."

"So what does work?"

"Precisely what we've planned—and only what we've planned. You kill the idea by killing the credibility of its authors at the absolute peak of their power and influence. You destroy their character, reputation, ethics, even their minds—but they must survive."

"Sometimes that isn't always possible."

"No, but we're not going to make the obvious mistake. We're going to follow the plan, just as we outlined it from the beginning."

Crawford rose to go.

"Can you do anything about squashing the autopsy?" the Chairman asked.

"On the kid Stryker killed?"

"Yes."

The big man shook his head. "I don't think so. I have one possible contact, but it may be too touchy to explore."

"Then don't."

"And the girl?"

The Chairman paused for several minutes to chew on that nagging problem.

Crawford picked up his briefcase and waited for a decision. He thought he knew what it would be, and he had begun to relish the prospect in store for him. He smiled; it had been a long time since he'd been able to indulge fully his more insistent and demanding fantasies. The girl had a good body, he knew that, and he would play it as delicately as a finely tuned instrument. "Well?"

The Chairman looked up at him. "Do you really think we're running a risk here?"

"She's already talked to Cargill about him."

The Chairman nodded. "Do what you must do," he said.

Crawford turned without another word and walked softly out of the room.

Ben had begun to dream again. His nights were full of clearly remembered childhood scenes, most of them painful, and he would wake up night after night drenched in sweat. One particular dream recurred more often than any of the others. In this one, he'd be standing in the middle of the living room, the long, bulky package clutched tightly in his arms, while the sarcastic voice of his stepfather rang in his ears.

"What you got there, boy? Something from your daddy? Don't tell me he actually remembered your birthday. We thought, your mother and I, yeah, we thought he'd just about given you up, boy."

Ben would not answer. He'd unwrap the package, tearing at the stiff brown paper with eager fingers. Finally he'd manage to open it and inside he'd always find the long, shiny rifle his father had sent him on his twelfth birthday. It lay there in its box and he'd hardly dare to touch it, it would seem so beautiful. How had his father guessed? Had he written him to say what he wanted? Ben couldn't remember that part of it too well. For months he'd been shooting at birds and squirrels with his pellet gun, though once his mother had caught him and scolded him angrily and he'd had to hide the gun away. But how had his father known? More than anything else in the world, at that time of his life, Ben had wanted a .22; somehow his father had divined the wish and miraculously fulfilled it. The boy had stood there for what had seemed like hours but what could only have been a minute or two, gently stroking the smooth, brown stock of the gleaming weapon.

"Well, look at that," his stepfather would say, "won't you just look at that? That s.o.b. don't even pay his child support and don't never come to see you, boy, but he sends you a rifle so's you can go out and shoot birds just for the hell of it. Don't that beat all?"

"Now, Harry," his mother would say, though Ben couldn't be sure she was actually in the room with them, she'd sound so far away, "now, Harry, I wrote Burton about Ben. This is what he wants for his birthday, I told him, just so long as he doesn't shoot at animals or any living thing. You won't, will you, Ben?"

"No, Mom, I won't," Ben would hear himself say. "I promise."

"Aw, you always promise, boy," his stepfather would say. "He's always promising things, Ellen. He don't never do what he promises. You know he don't deserve to have that gun."

"Now, Harry, it's his birthday—"

The man would seem so huge in the dream and, as he'd move to take the gun away from the boy, he'd become enormous, menacing, indestructible.

Ben would scream, "Don't you touch that!"

The man would reach out for the weapon and here,

very often, Ben would wake up crying. Even awake, he could remember so clearly how much he had wanted that gun and how he'd suffered when his stepfather had taken it away from him. He'd weep with rage and anguish at his loss, because his whole childhood had been made up of such losses, and through his tears he'd nurture the cold hatred that grew in him hour by hour, day by day, until it all but obsessed him.

Sometimes in his dream Ben would not wake up at the moment his stepfather took the gun away from him. Sometimes he'd dream on and see himself creeping along a darkened hallway. He'd enter the room where a man lay sleeping and in the darkness he would kneel, prop the loaded rifle against one knee, and take dead aim at the huddled, snoring form on the bed. Slowly, with infinite care, he'd squeeze the trigger—and a huge explosion would rock the whole house. In his fantasy, the very walls of the room would run rivulets of blood, as the massive form toppled with a dull crashing sound to the floor.

He'd hear his mother screaming. "No, Ben, no! For God's sake, son . . ."

He'd see the gaping, dazed expression on the blue-white face of his stepfather. He'd revel in the mouth opening and closing, unable to speak. And he'd hear the gun go off, again and again and again. . . .

If the dream took him this far, he'd remember on waking that he never had actually managed to shoot his stepfather. He had sneaked downstairs that one night, retrieved the gun from the closet where the man had flung it, loaded it, and gone silently back upstairs. He'd meant to kill him, yes, but his mother had sat up in bed and stopped him soundlessly—not by anything she said or did, but by her very helplessness and look of terror.

178

Harry had snored on, oblivious to the fate Ben had prepared for him. "I will kill him someday, Mom. I swear I will," Ben had told her later.

Was that why they'd sent him away to school that year? Was that why he'd never been allowed to stay at home for more than a few days after that? Was that why his mother had begun to cry to herself in the soft, cool hours of early dawn, when he'd awaken and hear her sobbing through the paper-thin walls of the bedrooms?

Dear Dad, he'd written to his father sometime later, *it's a neat gun. Harry won't let me use it, but Mom lets me shoot it when he's out of the house. I'm pretty good now, Dad. I can hit the tin cans we set up along the fence from about fifty yards, and I'm a sharpshooter at the target range the Legion runs out on Post Road. When are you coming to see me, Dad? I sure do miss you. . . .*

"Kathy, what's wrong?" Cargill said pleasantly.

"I'm sorry to bother you."

"It's OK. You didn't wake me. Are you crying?"

"I'm all right." Kathy's voice was tremulous. "It's Ben."

"What is it?"

"He doesn't want to see me anymore." She began to sob. "He just threw me out."

"Why?"

"I don't know. It's his nightmares."

"What nightmares?"

"He thinks he's shooting somebody. But he's still a child in the dreams—I'm sure. I'm so worried about him, Mr. Cargill."

"Kathy, how can I help?"

"I don't know," she said desperately. "I just felt I *had* to talk to somebody."

179

"I understand. Do you want me to speak to Ben?"

"I don't know." She was calmer now. "I guess so. I don't know. I'm sorry I sound so dumb."

"I'll speak to him, Kathy."

"Thanks. You're really nice. I'm—I'm sorry. I won't call you again."

After the girl had hung up, Cargill got out of bed and went into his kitchen. He fished out a tea bag, put some water on to boil, and lit a cigarette. He would speak to Ben, he decided, if only to keep Kathy from calling him at home in the middle of the night. She was just a child, but he was too old now to become a father again. *I wish I'd never gotten into this one,* he told himself, *but I can't back out now. Maybe Ben is heading for some kind of breakdown, or this girl is hysterical. One way or the other, I'm going to put an end to it, or at least find out what's going on. . . .*

19

She had been expecting to hear from him for some time, but when the phone call finally came it surprised her. It had been a long, tiring day, punctuated by an irritating conversation with Farwell over domestic matters that now seemed as remote to her as the social doings of mice, and she'd been about to leave her office for a nice hot tub. At the first ring she'd groaned, afraid it might be Brennan again; the man had been absolute hell to deal with ever since she'd resisted his clumsy overtures in Miami. She recognized the caller's voice at once. "Ben?"

"Yes, it's me."

"God, I've been meaning to call you. How are you?"

"OK, I guess. You did a hell of a job in Miami, I hear."

"Ben, it was a mess. It was also an education. My God, haven't we seen each other since then?"

"I'm afraid not."

"Isn't it silly? Here we are, in the same building, even if we're on different floors."

"It's a little tough on me to visit the network offices these days."

"I understand, Ben. I should have called you, but it's been hectic."

"I can imagine."

"And I've been away a lot. I'm still trying to get settled. I've got an apartment but no furniture and Farwell's being difficult as hell about everything—"

"You don't have to explain. I would like to see you, though."

"Ben, it's been a rough day. I've had the painters in my office most of the afternoon and Brennan on my back all morning—"

"Sarah," Ben interrupted, his voice urgent and pleading, "you're the only person I can trust here. We spent too much time together in Washington to play games with each other. I need to talk to you."

"Well, sure. When?"

"Tonight."

Sarah didn't answer for a few seconds. When she did speak, the starchy formality was gone, blown away by a long sigh that Ben interpreted correctly; the sound of it narrowed his eyes and made him smile, more out of relief and satisfaction than of pure pleasure. He knew that what happened to him was still important to her. He'd make use of that if he could. He had to.

"Ben—no, we don't need to play games with each other. You know I like you. We've been friends; we *are* friends. I feel so funny about all this. I mean, here I am, just promoted, and you—well, I mean, you're . . ." She paused again, uncomfortable. "God, this is difficult to say."

"Don't say it, then," Ben told her placatingly. "I know. I'm persona non grata now, the condemned one, and you don't want any of my failure rubbing off on you. Believe it or not, I've gotten used to that reaction from most people."

"I'm being awful," Sarah said contritely. "Just awful. And I was about to say it, too. Ben, I'm so sorry. You get caught up in this career thing and you begin to lose perspective. Will you forgive me?"

"I'll do it over dinner tonight."

"All right. Where?"

"As I recall, you're a sucker for Chinese food. How about Pearl's? My favorite New York restaurant."

"Sounds wonderful."

"Pearl's it is, then. See you there about eight?"

"Fine."

Pearl's doesn't have to advertise for clients and makes no effort to lure them in from the street. Nor will the visitor be made to feel immediately at home. Pearl herself, the matronly but slender Chinese lady whose almond-shaped eyes miss nothing, will treat you like a naughty child if you've neglected to make a reservation. A prompt confession of oversight and a promise to do better the next time will persuade the lady to admit the possibility of an empty table and enough food to feed you.

The choice of tables is limited. Pearl's is small, occupying the ground floor of an old brownstone about fifteen feet wide and ninety feet long, with a twenty-foot ceiling. The decor is cleanly contemporary; shallow booths line the left side of the room and tables are strung along on the right, accented by Stendig chairs of bentwood and cane in their natural state. The left side of the room is completely mirrored, an illusion which doubles its size and seems to pack it with people. The net effect of space and subdued elegance, to say nothing of the splendid food, has made the place a favorite with show-biz and media people.

"Do you mind if I order for you?" Ben asked Sarah, as they sat down across from each other at a corner table.

"Please do. I've only been here once before."

Ben consulted with the waiter, then lowered the menu. "How about a drink?"

"I could use one," she said. "It's been a day to remember. A Tanqueray martini, straight up with a twist."

"Make it two," Ben added, grinning. A couple of those gin bullets, he figured, wouldn't hurt his cause a bit. The waiter took the menus and departed. "Sarah—my God, it's good to see you."

"Same here, Ben."

"How have you been?"

"Just fine. I love the job."

"You said you were having a rough time."

"Logistics." She grimaced wryly. "Everything I own is still in Washington and right now I'm sitting under a canvas tarpaulin in my office. Otherwise it's great." She hesitated and reached across the table to take Ben's hand. "I almost asked how you are, but I think I know."

Ben's smile faded briefly, but he forced himself to remain cheerful. "I'm OK," he lied. "I sure as hell am not overjoyed about everything, but I'm not ready to dive off the Empire State Building either." He decided he liked the touch of her hand and he pressed her fingers before she withdrew them. "What about your husband? He's still in Washington?"

"Of course. Virginia, actually. I have weekend visiting privileges, which I may choose to exercise from time to time."

"I don't want to sound as if I'm prying—"

"You're not."

"We never really talked about your marriage, but I suspected you had problems."

They lapsed into silence briefly as the waiter served their drinks and departed. "Ben, it's no secret," she resumed. "Farwell and I don't have 'problems.' We have an accommodation. We share a house and certain possessions, but we aren't in love. I don't know that we ever were."

This frank confession so early in the evening surprised Ben, but pleased him as well. It seemed to augur well for any future relationship he might wish to develop with her, though that part of his plan remained somewhat hazy. "So why did you marry him?"

"Do you remember an old Western movie a few years back with Steve McQueen? And some Mexican bandit asked him why he decided to take on a whole gang of bandits singlehandedly?"

"Not offhand."

185

"Well, anyway, Steve said he did it for the same reason a fellow once took off all his clothes and jumped into a cactus patch. It seemed like a good idea at the time."

Ben laughed and raised his glass. "Here's to the good old days."

Sarah touched his glass with the rim of her own. "Yes, to the good old days. May we have more of them."

"Well, I don't know about the days," he said, staring over the top of his drink into Sarah's large green eyes, glowing in the soft light of the room, "but there may be some hope for the nights."

Sarah blushed slightly. They sipped their drinks in silence. Idly, she fingered the stem of her glass, gazing at the image of her fingertips distorted by the liquid within. "Speaking of cactus patches," she mused, "it looks as if we're in for another four years of Nixon."

A rush of adrenalin halted Ben's glass halfway to his mouth. He felt his abdominal muscles tighten; a dizzying wave of anger blinded him so that he had to fight for control. His heart hammered and his armpits grew wet, but he compelled himself, with slightly trembling fingers, to bring the drink to his lips and take a sip. *How wrong you are, Sarah. Not four years. Not even four months.*

"Ben, you look strange. You OK?"

"I'm fine." He forced a small grin. "Just remembered something I forgot to do." *If she only knew. You, my darling, you are going to open the final door for me. Sincere, beautiful Sarah, the unwitting conspirator. Together we'll eliminate this scum from the earth.* The thought suddenly amused Ben. He took a big swallow of gin, reveling in the heat that coursed through him, making him feel powerful and in supreme control. "I suppose you're right about

Nixon," he said calmly. "McGovern's certainly tripping all over himself. But it really doesn't matter, does it?"

"Of course it matters," she said sharply. "And you know that, Ben. We can't have four more years of this man. He has no morality. He thinks of himself as a pragmatist, but he has no ethical sense whatsoever. He's like a tone-deaf person trying to analyze a musical phrase. He doesn't *hear* it, Ben. That's what makes him so dangerous. Pragmatism is all right as a way of governing. But Nixon's the kind of pragmatist who'd like to do away with the inconvenience of Congress and the Constitution of the United States. Of course it matters."

"I didn't mean it that way." Ben held up a hand. "What I mean is, it doesn't matter how you and I feel, or what McGovern does. Nixon's going to be reelected. And I suspect the country will somehow muddle through the next four years. Care for another drink?"

"Sure. We could toast King Richard."

Ben hailed the waiter and ordered another round, tossing off the last drops of his first drink. He turned his attention back to Sarah and began to maneuver toward the real point of the evening, always keeping the tone of his conversation deliberately casual, comfortable, relaxed. *This isn't easy, damn it.* "You know, I did what I could to expose the real Nixon, when you and I worked together," he said. "Right now I wish I hadn't tried quite so hard. But that's a dead issue, isn't it?" He paused reflectively, and then added, in an afterthought, "Well, how's the old bureau doing without me?"

"Miserably," she answered. "I'm haunted by the suspicion that if I still had you pounding the White House beat we'd have an election on our hands. But, as you say, it's

187

a dead issue." She studied Ben for a moment. "You do seem to be taking it well. I got the impression from your phone call this afternoon that you were pretty down."

The waiter arrived with fresh drinks and Ben took a healthy gulp of his. "I suppose I am a little down, but what I really needed was to spend some time with someone I know and trust. And you're the only person in New York who qualifies."

"Thanks, Ben. I'm flattered."

"Of course, I do have an ulterior motive."

"Oh?"

"You know I've been doing some free-lance magazine stuff, don't you?"

"Yes, so I'd heard."

"I'm taking my own pictures, too. It seems to be working out pretty well. At least I'm getting assignments."

"That's wonderful, Ben."

"And Cargill's been terrific about letting me do this. He could be hairy about it, if he wanted to."

"I gather he's a fine man."

"The best. He's the reason I'm still around. But I may need your help, Sarah."

"Really? What can I do, Ben?"

"Well," he began, picking his words carefully now, desperately anxious not to give too much away too soon, "I— I sometimes need entrée into places network types have access to and the rest of us mere mortals don't."

"Such as?"

"Oh, Sarah, this is a little premature." Ben sat back, smiling amiably. "I'm up for a story I may need some help with, that's all. If it does come through, can I call on you?"

"Of course," she said. "If I can do it, you know I will."

"Terrific," he said. "When and if . . ." He raised his glass to her and took another deep swallow.

He was becoming more and more relaxed as the gin did its work, and he found himself enjoying the evening. He also realized he was aroused by the possibility of making love to this woman, who was obviously as alone in life as he was. Their relationship in Washington had been so professional that he'd forgotten how attractive she was. He'd had occasional sexual fantasies about her, as he had about most of the beautiful women he'd met, but they'd been fleeting, never really serious. Now, as she sat, smooth-skinned and elegantly feminine, across the table from him, he realized that the seduction of Sarah would bring its own rewards, quite apart from the practical benefits. As the waiter arrived with their food, Ben began to plan his next move carefully. He shifted uneasily in his chair; after the waiter had gone, he looked up and gazed directly into her eyes. "Sarah, it's wonderful to be here with you. It's been lonely, you know. That's been the worst part of all this, I think. I've never felt quite so alone."

They looked into each other's eyes for a long moment, Ben waiting for a reaction from her and Sarah groping for the right words. Finally, she smiled, keeping the tone light. "When were you ever alone before, Ben?"

"Most of my life."

"Now, now, Ben," she chided. "You weren't exactly alone when we worked together. Half the women in Washington must be pining away right now. Somehow I just can't picture Ben Stryker all alone."

"The Ben Stryker you knew was a big network star," he said calmly. "It's amazing what failure will do to your sex life."

"You don't have *that* problem, do you, Ben?" she asked

189

teasingly, as she stared at a limp piece of lemon chicken dangling from her fork.

He laughed. "No. All I meant was that women aren't particularly wild about has-beens."

"What are you talking about, Ben? Media groupies?"

"Most women."

"Oh, come on. Some men rely on their positions in life and their wealth to attract women. Some just attract them naturally. I wouldn't have guessed you were in the fame-and-power category."

Ben looked pensive and toyed with the food on his plate. "I have to be honest with you, Sarah," he said. "I did seduce a lot of women, but it wasn't a conscious, calculated use of so-called fame. Maybe that isn't even the right word. Let's say it just happened. I went through a period when I needed all that, I guess. And it came so easily."

"I know," she said. "But I suspect a lot of women just find Ben Stryker attractive. Not the TV Ben, the video Ben. The *real* Ben Stryker." She looked at him searchingly and her own feelings must have betrayed her, because suddenly she blushed slightly and looked away. "You're an extraordinarily handsome man who also happens to be bright and charming a lot of the time. If you think you need to be a TV star in order to succeed with women, well, maybe it's just because it was too easy for you and you've gotten a little lazy." She looked up at him again and found him staring into his empty glass. His right hand was locked around the stem so tightly that the knuckles were white.

"Thank you, Sarah," he said, in a strange, tight voice. "But what I don't think you understand is that whatever charm or self-confidence I ever had, I feel I got it from that damn network news operation . . . and I'm absolutely lost without it. Lost. Sometimes I actually hurt physically

190

when I think about the life I had." Ben made himself stop. The discussion was getting out of hand; genuine feelings were beginning to surface. "But I'll get over it, Sarah," he said more calmly.

She extended her left hand across the table, gently pried his fingers away from the glass, and took them in hers. She gazed again into his eyes. "Ben, of course you will. It takes time. Everything worth doing or having in life takes time. Don't you know that?"

20

"Ben, I'm frightened," Kathy said over the phone. "There's something strange going on."

"Really? Like what?"

"I don't know. I get phone calls."

"From whom?"

"From nobody. I mean, nobody answers. The phone rings and I pick it up and nobody's there."

"Kathy, this sort of thing happens all the time in New

York. A lot of people get a charge out of making anonymous phone calls."

"But it's never happened to me before. And—and there are other things."

Ben sat up and looked at his bedside clock. It was barely nine and he could have used at least another hour of sleep. It had been a heavy night, laced with Bellucci's renewed sarcasm. Kathy's early call—she was probably using it as an excuse to resume their relationship—was close to being the last straw. Nevertheless, he felt oddly calm and detached, as if the voice at the other end of the line were that of some dimly remembered acquaintance from the past, and not that of someone he'd been making love to only a few days before. He rubbed a hand over his eyes, yawned, and shifted the receiver from one ear to the other.

"Ben, are you there?"

"Yes, Kathy, I'm listening."

She began to cry. "Darling, can you come over?"

"Now?"

"Please. Please, Ben. I'm frightened. And I miss you."

He shut his eyes as she pleaded, trying to remember her more accurately. Yes, she'd had a miraculous body, long-limbed, with smooth, fragrant skin and high, firm breasts; as he recalled the feel of her in his arms and the way she would arch beneath him as she climaxed, he became aroused. He opened his eyes, fully awake now, and swung his legs out of bed. "Kathy, you sound terrible. I'm coming over."

"Oh, please, Ben. I miss you so. This place is so empty without you. At the office you look past me now as if I don't exist. I can't take it."

"I know. I'm sorry, Kathy. I'll be right over."

After hanging up, he got out of bed and went into the

bathroom to shave. Moving calmly and deliberately, he picked out his wardrobe for the day. He'd see her once more and it would be all right. Because what if Sarah refused him? Their dinner had been a success, but he'd only been with her twice since then, both times briefly for a drink, and he'd had no opportunity to spend enough time with her. With their different schedules, he'd have to conduct a weekend courtship, but last weekend she'd gone home to Virginia. He'd try to pin her down to this coming Saturday night, but she'd mentioned something about the Chairman's invitation to a network function and also that she might have to go out of town again. It wasn't certain. Ben intended to keep the pressure on; he knew Sarah liked him and he liked her. Besides, time was becoming a factor now if the plan regarding Nixon was going to work out. Meanwhile, there was Kathy, who loved him and wanted him and was wonderful in bed. . . .

On his way out, Ben made certain, as usual, that the door to the guest bathroom was securely locked; he must never make that mistake again.

It was after ten when he arrived at Kathy's place. Her face was tearstained and she was naked under her robe. He kissed her lightly; she trembled as she responded to him, her mouth open to receive his tongue. He disengaged himself gently; there'd be plenty of time for lovemaking. "Kathy, are you OK?"

"Not really. I phoned in sick. Oh, Ben, I'm a wreck."

"You don't look *that* bad, honey."

She tried to smile. "Maybe you're prejudiced."

"Yeah, maybe I am."

She made a visible effort at control. "Want some coffee?"

"Love some."

"You know, since I telephoned you"—she led the way into her kitchenette—"I've had another one of those calls."

"You'd better change your number."

"I'm planning to, but it's—Ben, I keep having the feeling I'm being followed or watched."

"It's your imagination, Kathy."

"Maybe. Anyway," she said, squeezing his hand, "you're here now and everything's fine."

"Yes, Kathy, of course it is."

Why did he feel so far away from her? How could he be so detached about her, as if she'd never been anything more to him than a casual score? Was he really such a bastard about women? Didn't he care for her at all, he wondered, even as he marveled at the beauty of her body? No, all he could think about was Sarah. This would have to be the last time with Kathy. He'd speak to Cargill about her; he would know what to do—get her transferred, maybe to an out-of-town affiliate. Cargill liked her, and it would look like a promotion to Kathy.

As soon as they finished making love, Ben realized it had been a mistake to yield to her again; it could only make the final break so much more difficult. She had cried and clung to him for a long time and he'd done his best to be patient. He was ashamed of himself for having used her. The office gave him an excuse to get away from her, but it had not improved his state of mind or eased his guilt.

He kissed her and promised to stop by later that night. She was so weepy he'd have to make himself do that, but somehow he'd also have to begin, gently but firmly, to disentangle himself from her finally. She'd gone off the deep end, he thought, with this obsession about being watched and followed and harassed. It wasn't quite sane, really.

195

Then she said something that startled him. He had been lying there, listening to her ramble on, when she asked, "What did you mean about the plans?"

"Plans? What plans? When?"

She giggled and ran her fingers through his hair. "When you dozed off just now. You were mumbling about the camera and some plans. You still talk in your sleep, you know."

"I have no idea what I meant."

"Does it have something to do with the plans I found?"

He propped himself up on one elbow and turned to look at her. "What do you mean, Kathy?"

"You know, that outline for some kind of camera gun. I found some papers on the kitchen table one day and I was so worried. I thought they were yours, and then I remembered you telling me, a long time ago, about some CIA contact you had back in Washington."

"Oh, yeah. I'd forgotten," he said slowly. "I was going to do a special report."

She had been snooping around his apartment again. He'd caught her once and that had been nearly disastrous; he'd realized then that he'd have to break with her. God, he should have gotten the apartment key back from her, or had he? His memory was becoming hazy. Why? Anyway, now he would have to find out exactly how much she knew. Suppose she went to Cargill with this kind of information; she was just naive enough to do that. He'd have to see her again, perhaps later that evening, and find out how much she had discovered. But he must never, never spend the night with her again.

"Kathy," he told her, "I'll be back tonight. You stay home and get some rest; I'll call you right after the six-o'clock news, OK? Don't worry about anything. It's all going to come out all right in the end, believe me."

Later he couldn't remember what she'd answered after he kissed her good-bye. In fact, he couldn't even remember leaving.

He tried to call her just after seven, but the line was busy. He kept on trying, fruitlessly, and shortly after eight he went in to see Cargill. "Derrick, I'm worried about Kathy," he said and outlined her fears about being watched, the strange phone calls, her agitated condition. "Things are slow around here, but we've got two usable stories already. I'd like to run up and see her, make sure she's all right," he concluded.

"Sure, Ben, go ahead," Cargill answered. "I've been worried about her myself. We know where to get you. Just check out with the desk and let Bellucci know."

"Of course."

"When did you last speak to her, Ben?"

"This morning. She called me at home and she sounded like hell."

He took a taxi to her place and rang the downstairs bell. There was no answer. He went to a corner phone booth and called; the line was still busy. He returned to the tiny lobby of her building and rang the doorbell more insistently; after a minute or two, he let himself in and took the stairs two at a time. At her front door, he inserted his key into her lock and paused. What if something really was wrong? What if an intruder were still on the premises? He turned the key and cautiously opened the door. "Kathy?" he called.

There was no answer. The apartment was dark, except

197

for a soft orange glow from the bedroom. Ben groped for a light switch, found it, and shut the front door behind him. The apartment seemed to be empty. "Kathy?" he called again.

There was still no answer. He walked slowly to the bedroom door, pushed it open all the way, and looked in. "My God," he heard himself say. "Oh, my God—!"

21

"Ben," Cargill told him over the phone, "I'll put some-body else on this story."

"No, Derrick, it's all right," Ben said grimly. "I'm OK. The police are on their way and Steinman wants to question me."

"You sure?"

"Sure."

"I've dispatched Campbell and a crew. What about when everybody else shows up?"

"I'm OK, Derrick. I can handle it."

"Jesus, the poor kid." Cargill's voice was uneven. "Look, if it gets too rough, call me, or have Jeff do it and I'll put somebody else on it."

"Yeah. But I told you I can handle it."

Ben hung up; the door burst open and police officers swarmed in. Steinman, looking as bedraggled and exhausted as ever, the inevitable cigar stub clamped between his teeth, sauntered in a few minutes later. He took Ben into a corner for a rundown of events.

"And you hadn't seen her for several days?" he asked at one point.

"No," Ben lied. "But I spoke to her this morning."

"Anything between you two?"

"Yeah," Ben said. "We dated for a while. But nothing too serious." He told Steinman of Kathy's highly nervous state and her obsession about being watched and followed.

"And what do you think of that?" Steinman asked.

"I didn't take it too seriously." Ben stared at the floor. "Everybody gets crank calls in this town, especially women living alone. I told her to change her phone number."

"Good advice," Steinman rumbled. "By the way, how'd you get in?"

"I still had a key."

The detective grunted and went to examine the scene in the bedroom.

Stryker, numbed but able to function, waited for Campbell and the crew to appear; then, professionally and calmly, he began to put his story together. Campbell, who had liked Kathy, was distraught; he asked Ben how he could go through the motions. "Jeff, she's dead," Ben said quietly. "There's nothing we can do about that. But maybe we can help by getting the story." Campbell simply looked at him; then quietly, grimly, he went to work.

When Steinman finally emerged from the bedroom, where investigators were still at work gathering evidence, Ben thrust his mike under his nose. The first to interview the detective, he asked succinct, pertinent questions, after which he guided his crew into the small, overcrowded room in which the body of Kathy Lewis still lay on the bed, exactly as Ben had first seen it. Jeff Campbell nearly vomited at the sight; Ben moved through the scene as if armored in ice.

It was after ten o'clock when Ben, with Mapes's help, finished cutting his story. Cargill, who had been standing silently in the back of the room for some time, approached now. "Ben?"

Stryker turned. "Yeah?"

"Go home."

"But—"

"I'm telling you to go home, Ben."

"Yeah. OK."

On his way out, Ben ignored the assignment desk and Bellucci let him pass in silence. My God, Ben thought to himself, the cynical sonofabitch is close to tears.

Ben did not remember how he got home that night. It was as if he'd gone into a deep sleep and awakened standing in front of his door, groping for the keys to his apartment. He must have walked all the way home, but he couldn't remember a step of it. He let himself in and wandered absently through the apartment. Eventually, he sat down on the edge of his bed and began to put together in his head the pieces of the long, ugly day.

201

He recalled, first of all, the surgical precision with which Dick Mapes matched the scenes and counted the frames detailing the circumstances of Kathy's grisly death. He remembered how he himself had cut the narration track, speaking precisely and carefully into a microphone inside a tiny, sound-proof booth, recording on 16-millimeter full-coat under the careful ministrations of the audio engineer.

"You ran a couple of words together, Ben. Give it to me again."

"OK—Kathy Lewis murder, take two—"

It didn't seem incongruous at the time. When TV professionals went to work, all events—great and small, poignant or merely piquant—could be reduced to abstract, mechanical exercises.

Ben forced himself to think back to the murder scene. He saw it through a haze of Steinman's cigar smoke, which made it seem somehow otherworldly. Turning his head slightly, he found himself gazing at the blank screen of his twelve-inch Sony Trinitron TV set.

It was almost eleven o'clock, and soon the results of his labors would be viewed by the estimated two million people who turned on WACN's late-evening news. Automatically, he punched the on-off button.

The picture blossomed fuzzily at first, then focused and sorted itself out into the proper flesh tones and colors of the network's latest announcement of its prime-time fare, a final urging designed to coax an audience back to the ACN channel the following night.

Ben turned up the sound just in time to pick up the booth announcer's voice saying, "—tomorrow, on ACN!" That was the cue for the local station to take over; now Bill James's face appeared on screen, just as the faces of hundreds of local anchormen and women were doing all across the country, each one gravely spouting in ten seconds just enough doom, irony, and promise to keep those TV watchers from going to bed until after the late news.

"This is Bill James. A murder that saddens WACN! The latest on the presidential hustings! Sports and weather! Next!"

Bill James's half-smiling face vanished, and for the ensuing minute and ten seconds Ben found himself being exhorted to fly Eastern, the wings of man; to buy a stereo from Crazy Eddie, whose prices can't be beat; and to have his transmission fixed by Lee Miles. The commercials were followed by a still photograph of Bill James, his beaming face flanked by the channel number and call letters, while the booth announcer's voice boomed, "The news is next on WACN, your community-minded station!"

Suddenly Ben had an urge to put some distance between himself and his TV set. Was it apprehension he felt? Or was it just a desire to shore up the emotional and mental detachment he'd maintained all day? He wasn't sure, but he settled himself back against the headboard, propping himself into a half-sitting position against the pillows.

On screen came a wide shot of the WACN news set, with animated letters marching jerkily across the foreground, the opening "super." The white letters spelled out THE LATE EVENING NEWS, while the recorded, hammering sound of teletype machines blended with a staccato musical rendition of the WACN theme. When the music faded, the booth announcer trumpeted, "This is the WACN late evening news, brought to you by Barney's!" The opening super vanished, to be replaced by one advertising New York's biggest men's clothing store.

"Good evening." Bill James was back on screen. "I'm Bill James. Our top story tonight is particularly sad for us here in the WACN news room." The camera shot zoomed back to include a rear-projection screen behind the anchorman. On it was a picture of Kathy, reproduced from a college yearbook photograph. "Kathy Lewis was one of us," James intoned. "A bright, attractive twenty-two-year-old woman who worked here, helping us get our early-evening news broadcast on the air each night. She had a bright future."

Look at that bastard, Ben thought, look at him sitting there, allowing just the right amount of sorrow to seep through that professional anchorman delivery. And they're eating that up out there in TV-land!

"But that future ended brutally today," James was saying. "Ben Stryker reports."

Ben's filmed report filled the screen. It opened with a wide shot of the exterior of Kathy's apartment building framed between a police car and ambulance pulled up at the curb, their rotating beacons flashing rhythmically. Ben heard his narration begin.

"Kathy Lewis was murdered here today," he said. "Murdered in her own apartment on the fifth floor of this building."

A new shot revealed the hallway leading into Kathy's apartment; the camera moved through the front door, the living room, and then into the bedroom itself.

"Police say there was no sign of forced entry," Ben's dispassionate narration continued. "The body was found nude, face down on the bed."

The film cut to a shot of the bed, the shape of Kathy's body clearly visible under a sheet.

"Police think she was smothered."

The next shot was a close-up of Steinman holding a plastic bag by means of a pair of tweezers.

"This plastic bag was found over her head—taped around her neck."

After a pause for dramatic effect, the film cut to a medium shot of the body that concentrated on a single, slightly blue hand hanging limply below the edge of the sheet. Ben remembered that he and Mapes had agonized over that shot, and then concluded that neither would have questioned using it for a moment had the corpse been that of a stranger.

"And police say that there is evidence of rape."

As the camera zoomed in on Kathy's hand, Ben's questioning voice flowed out of the Sony's speaker: "Chief, is it possible the victim was being raped as she was suffocating?"

Steinman's cynical, worn face bloomed on the screen. "As I said before," he answered, "there's a possibility—"

The first sentence of the chief's "sound bite" had drawn groans from everyone in the editing room. Both Ben and Mapes had lamented the fact that Steinman had never understood that anything said while the cameras weren't rolling didn't exist for TV viewers, that an answer to a reporter's on-camera question should never begin with, "As I said before . . ." This time Steinman had compounded his error by starting to answer before Ben had managed to complete his question. The overlap had made it impossible for Mapes to edit out the offending phrase.

"The medical examiner," Steinman continued, "will have to determine the exact time and cause of death, and whether she was actually molested, as it appears. But it looks like a pretty vicious crime."

205

The shot widened and pulled back to include the death-bed. "Vicious," Ben's voice resumed, "and frightening for those who live in this building."

The film cut to a talking-head shot of a woman obviously excited by the presence of TV crews. She said dramatically, "Am I scared? You bet I'm scared. You read about these things happening all the time, but you never think they'll happen right next door. Right next door! Horrible! And she seemed like such a sweet girl. Always a smile. Never bothered anyone. I'm just shocked! I mean, it could have been me!"

Next came an exterior shot of the building, a medium close-up of the front door as it swung open and ambulance attendants wheeled the stretcher out, Kathy's body covered and strapped securely to it. Ben had handled this last scene particularly well, hurrying his crew out to the sidewalk just before the body was removed and positioning himself beside the open ambulance doors for his closing "stand-upper." It was the one time he'd be seen on camera during his report. Ben had instructed Jeff to follow the stretcher as it was whisked out of the building, and then to widen the shot to include him just as the body was being loaded into the ambulance and driven away. It had been a gamble. The removal of the body was a crucial shot; if Ben blew his lines, it would have to be scrapped with no hope of a retake. But it had worked.

As Kathy's remains were wheeled toward the ambulance, Ben began speaking into his microphone. "It could have been any woman in this city," he said somberly. "No woman is safe now because somewhere a madman is loose. Police speculate that this killing may be linked to a series of similar rape-murders over the past year, attributed to the so-called City Stalker. But that's only speculation. Clues are scarce. And the police need your help."

By now the camera had followed the body to the ambulance and the shot widened to include Ben. As the doors were swung shut, Ben stared into the camera lens, adding, "If you have any information that might help solve this crime, the police ask you to call this special number: 555-1111. That's 555-1111. All calls will be held in strict confidence. Ben Stryker, WACN News."

As if on cue, the ambulance siren wailed, and the car sped away into the night behind Ben's impassive countenance.

That's funny, Ben thought, Bill James is back on screen introducing his next report, but—I can't—hear him. The ambulance siren is drowning him out. And the picture's fading—

Ben felt a wetness on his cheeks. Suddenly he realized he was crying and the high, mournful wail that filled the room was coming from him—a moan that had boiled up from his depths and was now overwhelming him with a sense of dread and loss. He drew his knees up to his chest and wrapped his arms around his folded legs. He was on his side now, in the middle of the bed, his sobs mingling with the television sound track.

Here, Tony, he said aloud. *Here, boy. It's all right.* The words were tender and heavy with pity. *Poor Tony. Poor Tony. Poor Tony*— He sobbed again and again. It was over twenty years ago and once more they were moving, only this time his stepfather had said that Ben's ten-year-old collie, the only living creature Ben had ever truly loved, couldn't come along. They had driven to a farm and given

Tony to some strangers. Ben and Tony had had to be dragged apart.

Ben could still see the last few moments vividly—the determination in the collie's eyes as he raced behind the car, his gold-and-white hair streaming along his lean flanks, his long nose cutting the wind. Ben had shouted, "Stop! Stop!" at his stepfather, but the man only drove faster. Thirty, forty miles an hour down that winding country road, and still the dog was there, his feet a blur, pouring every ounce of strength into his desperate run.

After ten miles of Ben's tearful pleas, while white foam streamed from the anguished animal's mouth, his mother intervened and finally his stepfather stopped the car. Ben opened the door; Tony hurled himself into the boy's lap, heaving and whining and licking Ben's face, his paws staining Ben's clothes and the car seat with blood.

"I'm sorry, Tony. I'm sorry. It's all right. Poor Tony. Poor Tony." His stepfather would change his mind now. Tony would surely be allowed to come along.

But the car turned around and drove back ten miles of betrayal. At the farm, Ben's stepfather told the strangers to hold the dog more tightly—and they did. Ben never saw Tony again.

Now, alone in his room in a fetal embrace, Ben's sobs slowly ebbed.

22

"Ben, I'm so sorry," Sarah said. "It must have been awful for you."

"It's odd," Ben told her, "but it didn't seem so bad at the time. It really didn't hit me until afterwards. I can't even remember a lot of it."

"You were traumatized." Her voice was soft with compassion. "You must have gone into a kind of shock."

"Something like that, I guess."

"She was a nice girl, I hear."

"A kid, really. A nice kid."

"I gather you and she—"

"Yes," Ben said quickly, "but it didn't mean that much to me. It sounds callous, I know, but it's the truth. I should have been more careful with her, but she sort of threw herself at me."

Sarah smiled knowingly. "Like a lot of other women have?"

"You make me sound like some kind of heartless Don Juan. I'm not. At least, I don't like to think of myself as one."

"I don't think of you that way, Ben. Really I don't. I meant the remark as a compliment. You know you're an attractive man."

He looked directly at her. "Am I, Sarah?"

She blushed slightly and smiled. "You know you are. Come on now, don't fish for compliments. Want to freshen that drink or are you ready to eat?"

"A short one," Ben said. "Our reservation's for eight."

"Good. I could use a dividend myself."

She picked up their glasses and went over to the bar. Ben sank back into a corner of her new sofa, almost the only piece of furniture in the huge room, watching her with admiration. She was an extraordinarily beautiful woman, and he felt proud to be in her company. She was also bright and elegant, the quintessential sophisticated urbanite despite her relatively humble background. They had that in common, too, Ben thought, and they were both committed and ambitious. Only her real career was just beginning, while his own was practically over. *Unless . . . unless . . .*

"What are you thinking about?" She handed him his drink. "You looked so lost there for a moment."

He sighed. "It's how I feel a lot of the time."

"Oh, come on, Ben," she scolded. "We promised each other for tonight—no shop talk, remember?"

He saluted her with the glass; then he stood up and walked over to the window. From this height, the seventeenth floor, he could look down at most of Central Park and south to where luxury hotels and apartment houses lined Fifty-ninth Street, their lighted windows suspended in the twilit haze like lanterns over a dream city. It was a perfect early-fall evening, Ben thought, and it suited his decisive mood. He wanted Sarah, and tonight he'd find out if she cared for him at all, beyond the demands of friendship and good will. He needed her, too, but above all he wanted her in his arms, in his life. Something had to change for him; he had to regain control of his destiny, his entire future, which hinged now on a single act of violence, dangerous, and unthinkable perhaps, but essential to him and his peace of mind. Sarah would help him accomplish it. He'd convinced himself of that and he clung to that conviction. It was his only chance. He couldn't, he mustn't bungle it, nor could she let him down. *She couldn't . . .*

"Ben, you *are* in a mood tonight."

"I've got a lot on my mind. I'm sorry, Sarah." He forced a smile and turned away from the window. "You've got an incredible view here."

"Isn't it something?" She laughed. "If only the rest of my things would arrive I could begin to enjoy this place. Right now I feel as if I'm living in an abandoned skating rink. And I've had to buy so much stuff, you can't imagine. That sofa alone cost me a fortune. And someday, any time now, I promise to hang some pictures."

"Sarah . . ."

"What is it?"

He stood at the window and looked at her in the gathering dusk. She met his eyes and, drink in hand, came to him, touching him softly on the shoulder. "Ben, I'm so glad you're here with me." She stood close to him and, as if on cue, his free arm went around her and they kissed. It was an affectionate rather than a passionate kiss, but he could feel her tremble under his touch. She broke away from him. "I thought so," she said.

"You thought what?"

"That I'd enjoy kissing you."

"And you do?"

"Very much."

He grinned at her. "Want to try again?"

"I think, my darling," she said, patting his cheek, "I think we'd better eat first, or we may never get out of here at all."

Ben had chosen Barbetta's, an elegant Italian restaurant on West Forty-sixth Street specializing in *risotto* dishes. Their table was outside in a corner of the garden, where they could eat by candlelight under the stars. Again Ben ordered for both of them and, as they sipped a cool Venetian wine, they began to talk with an intimacy and a daring Ben had not imagined possible. As if reading his thoughts, Sarah impulsively reached across the table to take his hand. "Good Lord, Ben, I haven't spoken this openly about my checkered past in years." She laughed a little nervously.

"We both had the same sort of childhood in a way," Ben mused, keeping her hand. "It's strange, isn't it? I mean, I feel we know each other so well. Why didn't we talk like this in Washington when I was working for you?"

"Probably *because* you were working for me," she said. "And we were both so driven to succeed."

"Yeah . . . Tell me about your marriage."

"What marriage, Ben? I told you, it's hardly even one of convenience now. Farwell's come out of the closet these past few years. He's discreet about his young men, for both our sakes, but there it is. A little humiliating for me, I suppose, but then I married Farwell for security, not love, and I've no one to blame but myself. I suppose we'll get a divorce eventually."

"No one else in your life?"

"No, not recently." She blushed slightly and gently extricated her hand from his. "I had a couple of minor affairs, but I'm not good at the casual lay. I guess I just buried myself in my career."

"I can understand that. And now?"

"And now, Ben Stryker, what?"

Without another word, he raised his glass. She picked up hers, gently touched it to his, and they drank, eyeing each other tenderly in the gathering darkness. Ben felt a great sense of relief, as if this evening fulfilled some long-felt, desperate need within him. He knew that with Sarah's help he could succeed in rebuilding his shattered career, even his whole life. *Once this is over, once I've accomplished my mission* . . .

"Sarah?"

"Yes, Ben?"

"I know we agreed not to talk shop, but I've got to ask you for a favor."

"Oh?"

"This isn't why I wanted to see you tonight, you must know that," he said very seriously. "I'd have asked you in the office, but you haven't been around much this week."

"True. What is it, Ben?"

He told her again about his new career as a photographer-writer for various magazines and how he hoped that

213

way to repair his ruined network image. "You see, a few solid credits with the right publications, a couple of really important stories, and surely they can't go on ignoring me much longer."

"Maybe not, Ben. But if they do, you'll be building another career for yourself, won't you?"

"Exactly," he agreed, "though television is still what I want. Anyway, you see my point."

"Sure. How can I help?"

"I've got another *New York* magazine assignment. They want me to cover Nixon's Westchester and Long Island campaign stops. That's in about two weeks."

"October twenty-third," she said. "I'm going to have a crew there myself."

"I figured. My basic story angle is that this one-day swing of Nixon's will be the high point of his campaign locally. Last month in the city, he had all those protesters and a small riot on his hands. In Westchester, Nassau, and Suffolk counties, he'll be completely at home—in the very heart of suburbia, among the faithful. He should be at his most relaxed and accessible, right?"

"I would think so."

"So if I can get close enough to him, I could get a very revealing picture story, do you see? Nixon looking happy and relaxed, for a change."

"I get the idea, Ben, but what can I do?"

"Sarah, with just a magazine reporter's credentials I can't get close enough to the guy for a good picture without using a zoom lens."

"Ben, I can't include you on my own staff, if that's what you have in mind. Good God, if the Nixon people spotted you, it would get back to the Chairman, and Christ knows what kind of heat they'd put on us. Larry would have to fire you, for sure." She looked at him intently. "You do know, don't you, that the Chairman has your best interests at heart? He feels rotten about what's happened; I know he does."

"I believe you. No, Sarah, I'm not asking you to take that kind of risk. All I want is a network press pass and Secret Service credentials."

She thought it over for a minute, doodling aimlessly on the tablecloth. "I might be able to put your name on the credential list we'll submit to the Secret Service."

"Swell," Ben said. "I promise to stay as far away from the ACN crew as I can. I'll keep pretty much in the background. After all, I don't want the Nixon people to see me, either. After the story comes out, I won't care. But I've got to get close enough to get really good pictures. Out there in Siberia, with the rest of the local reporters, I might as well forget it. Do you see what I'm driving at?"

She didn't answer immediately; head bent, she was weighing the risks. Finally, just as he'd begun to think that he'd demanded too much of her too soon in their relationship, she smiled and again reached across the table for his hand. "All right, Ben," she said. "But if I'm caught, it's both our behinds."

"Sarah, you're wonderful." Filled with a wild elation, an exultation he could not completely conceal, Ben leaned across the table to kiss her.

She responded to him in a way that startled him. "My God," he whispered, "let's get out of here."

"Yes," she answered, with a smile, "or we'll behave so disgracefully they won't ever let us back in."

Making love to Sarah was unimagined delight. She had a wonderful body, not as perfect or as freshly beautiful as

Kathy's, but full-breasted and strongly curved, a lush body that would have delighted Cézanne. To make love to her was to be in touch with a miracle of womanhood. Beyond the merely physical joy of her, was Sarah herself. She made love with the uninhibited abandon of a happy courtesan, with all of the refinements and intimacies that such a word implied. She hurled herself into the act of lovemaking with an abandon and a commitment that startled Ben and made him feel like a neophyte at love. When at last it was over and Sarah lay on her back in the darkened bedroom, her body gleaming in the light that filtered into the room from the hallway, Ben propped himself up on one elbow and stared down at her. "Sarah?"

"What?" she whispered.

"You're incredible. I had no idea—"

"I've wanted you for a long time," she said softly.

"And you weren't disappointed?"

"No. Were you?"

"No. I—I—" Suddenly, for no reason that he could fathom, his eyes were wet. "Jesus," he said brokenly, "I don't know what's wrong with me."

"I'm surprised it took so long," she whispered. "Come here." She took Ben in her arms and cradled his head on her naked breasts. He clung to her with desperate strength for what seemed like hours until he fell asleep. Afraid to wake him, Sarah went on holding him until the first, faint streaks of dawn tinted the walls of her room. She smiled, feeling, at last, an expectant joy in her life; then she closed her eyes and slept.

23

At about one o'clock on the afternoon of October 23, Air Force One, the Boeing 707 bearing Mr. and Mrs. Richard Nixon and the rest of the presidential party, landed at the Westchester County Airport and taxied slowly to a halt not far from where the local reception committee waited to welcome it. Present were Governor and Mrs. Nelson D. Rockefeller of New York and other state officials, including two Westchester Republicans, Representative Peter A. Peyser and District Attorney Carl A. Vergari, who were involved in hard campaigns for congressional seats. The president seemed to be in a very good mood when he disembarked, waving and warmly exchanging greetings with the assembled notables.

From where he stood, Ben could see the whole party, but, like the other photographers, he was forced to use a long lens to get his pictures. Security at the airport was tight; the press had been isolated and kept at a considerable distance. The general public had not been admitted at all to the area, and Ben was worried. With these restrictions, he'd never be able to get close enough to Nixon.

After the welcoming ceremonies, Ben and the rest of the press had to scramble for seats on the seven buses and five open trucks provided for the occasion. Because he carried less equipment than most of his competitors, Ben was able to swing up into the first truck and nail down a position near the tailgate, from where he could jump off at the stop and get as close to the president as possible.

Everything now depended on how accessible Nixon chose to make himself during the motorcade. Obviously, the whole visit had been very carefully orchestrated, as were all of Nixon's public appearances, and Ben had already begun to sweat it out. From the advance press briefing, he knew that the presidential motorcade was scheduled to pass through twelve towns, making brief stops here and there before proceeding to Governor Rockefeller's Pocantico Hills estate. There Nixon would address some two hundred party leaders from the Northeast, before pushing on by helicopter, after dinner, into Nassau and Suffolk counties on Long Island.

Ben had carefully studied the route and the timing; he'd have to get to Nixon before 2:50 P.M., when the motorcade was scheduled to reach Hastings-on-Hudson. Ben had already informed the station that he might be an hour or so late, but he'd have to get to his office by four, no matter what, which meant he had to leave the motorcade at Tuckahoe. Now, as the long line of cars, buses, and trucks slowly wound out of the airport, Ben was grinding his teeth. The first anti-war demonstrators had already appeared along the route with their signs and shouted slogans, and Nixon might—even here in the very heart of friendly territory—chose to keep a safe distance between himself, the press, and the people.

The first indication that Ben might be in luck came fifteen minutes later, as the long procession wound its way through White Plains. The knots of demonstrators were pretty well isolated, and the vast majority of people who turned out to see their president were friendly. The crowds were surprisingly large, Ben thought, and Nixon seemed to respond very favorably to them—a good sign. Then, at the cross section of two principal avenues in Mamaroneck, Nixon suddenly got out of the limousine and began shaking hands with rows of beaming onlookers.

The move took Ben by surprise. He bolted from the truck and raced toward the presidential limousine. An exuberant crowd was closing in around Nixon, thrusting eager hands over and around the grim-faced Secret Service agents who were trying to maintain some semblance of order and security. Ben elbowed quickly through the crowd. *Twenty feet to go. Don't get back in the car.* He saw a baby hoisted into the air and pushed forward. Nixon took the screaming infant and kissed it, and the crowd roared with approval. *Ten feet to go.* Ben shoved and lunged and suddenly found himself just behind the front row of the jostling crowd. *The ass. The ass. Gotta see the ass.* He

219

dropped to his knees and forced his camera between the thighs of two people. There, not five feet away, was Richard Nixon, smiling and nodding and making inaudible comments. *Jesus.* Ben focused. Nixon waved and turned to get into the limousine, his back to Ben's camera. *Jesus.* Ben cocked the shutter, instinctively feeling for the end of the tiny gun barrel beside the Minolta's lens to make sure his hand was out of the way.

Horror swept him. *The cap nut. Christ. I've forgotten to remove the cap nut.* Frantically, he unscrewed the nut that concealed the true purpose of the camera and rendered it harmless. He jerked the Minolta back up to his eye—just in time to see Nixon's limousine pull away. The blood drained from Ben's face. *The perfect shot and I blew it.*

The motorcade was moving. *Got to pull myself together,* he thought as he ran to board the press truck. *No more mistakes. But it was a good sign. If the bastard makes a move like that this early in the day, he'll do it again. And I'll be ready.*

"No more war" and "Stop the bombing," chanted clusters of protesters, brandishing red-splashed signs along the way, but they no longer seemed to trouble Nixon. He stood up, waving and smiling, on his home grounds at last, among true believers. He made a few other forays out of his car to shake hands and bask in the admiration of his followers, but he cut them much shorter, and there wasn't enough time for Ben to set up another shot. At the Eastchester War Memorial, Nixon paused; Ben maneuvered his way to the front ranks of jostling photographers and cameramen, but the Secret Service agents suddenly became agitated. They had just learned that at the last stop—in New Rochelle—the police had arrested a young man carrying a sawed-off shotgun in his car; the Secret Service detail closed in around the president like a vise, shielding him from any approach —from the press or the public.

By the time the procession reached Tuckahoe, Ben was nearly frantic. Sweating hard, the Minolta dangling around his neck, he clung to the side of the truck, determined not to be pushed away from the exit by the restless crowd of newsmen. He was hard put a couple of times to defend his territory. "You step on my foot one more time, buddy," he heard himself snarl at a fat AP still photographer festooned with expensive equipment, "and I'll kick you in the shins."

"Jesus, buddy, we're all in this mess together." The AP man was still good-humored. "Have a little compassion."

"Go fuck yourself," Ben snapped.

"I've tried that," his amiable antagonist answered. "It hurts like hell."

Ben did not join in the laughter around him. From where he stood, he saw the presidential motorcade pull up to the steps of the Tuckahoe village hall, where still another reception committee had gathered, surrounded by a large, friendly crowd of cheering locals.

Now, Ben told himself, *now, or never again. I'll stop him here and now. It's my best chance, my only chance, and I will not fail.*

He was the first one out of the truck; he ran across open pavement and up to the steps where Nixon, arms raised high and face aglow, was acknowledging the cheers of his supporters. Within seconds, Ben was only one of a swarm of cameramen, all angling for shots of the president, who, indifferent for once to the intrusion of the media, seemed amenable to allowing himself to be photographed in close-up. In vain, his Secret Service men struggled to keep a distance between the president and this assault of admirers

221

and ruthless professionals. For once, neither the press nor the public would be denied intimate contact with the leader. It was a wild melee of shouting, gesturing newsmen, and Ben was thrown off balance. He concentrated on keeping his place in the front ranks; then quietly he edged up along the steps until he closed in on the network TV crews.

"Hello, Ben," an NBC reporter whispered, as Stryker wormed his way up beside him. "What the hell are you doing here?"

"Just working, Charlie, like all of us."

Ben didn't hear the NBC man's answer; it was drowned out by cheers and applause. Mayor Robert D'Agostino of Tuckahoe had just presented Nixon with the key to the village.

Smiling, the president quieted the crowd. He was going to speak now; he began by informing everyone how impressed he was by the warmth of this reception.

There were more cheers and applause.

Then the sound died away, except for the whirring and popping of television and flash cameras.

Ben dropped to one knee and brought the Minolta into focus. Nixon was still too far away, but he would have to walk down the hall steps and pass within fifteen to twenty feet of Ben to get back to the limousine. Cool, absolutely collected, and suddenly confident, Ben waited.

The president launched into an attack on the Democratic-controlled Congress, which, he informed his listeners, had recessed last week without enacting the $250 billion debt limit he had requested. This Congress, Nixon said, was embarked on "a spending spree in which the federal budget was ballooned dangerously by big spenders oblivious to higher prices and higher taxes."

Come on, you sonofabitch, come down here now where

I can put you out of your misery. Come on, you bastard, for all the dead and dying men in Vietnam, for all the victims of your paranoia and your scheming; come to me, Richard Nixon. . . .

"I am going to use every weapon at my command," Nixon said, "to hold spending this fiscal year as close as possible to two hundred and fifty billion dollars, so that we will not have a new wave of crippling inflation and there will be no need for higher taxes."

No, no need for higher anything, you blood-sucking maniac. No need for war. No need for punishment. No need for the grinding down of the poor and oppressed. No need for you, Richard Nixon . . .

A stirring among the press of bodies around him suddenly sent Ben pitching forward. *Shit!* Quickly he righted himself and scrambled back to his firing position. Checking the Minolta, he turned to look at his target.

Nixon was shaking hands now—with Mayor D'Agostino, with various local officials, with everyone around him or within reach.

The Secret Service men pushed forward, a hollow square with the president within their watchful guard, as the party began to move toward the limousines.

Here he comes. Steady now . . .

He's within range!

Ben sighted the camera, focusing just below Nixon's waist, and waited for him to pass.

The president moved away, turning this way and that to wave to his supporters.

Now!

"Mr. President, Mr. President!" someone behind Ben called out—a cameraman or a photographer wanting one last, good angle.

Nixon began to turn.

Ben fired!

Someone jostled him from behind and he plunged forward; he kept himself from falling by steadying himself with both hands against the pavement. The Minolta dangled uselessly from his neck.

Nixon smiled and waved, raising his arms in the triumphant V before he turned back toward his limousine, scratching his left leg as he did.

I shot him, I know I did, but did I hit him? What happened? Goddam the sonofabitch behind me! Goddam him!

The photographers and reporters streamed after the president, heading for the buses and trucks behind the motorcade. Ben did not move from his spot. He glanced at his watch. It was 2:05 P.M. Within ten minutes he would know; the whole world would know.

Ben stood alone now on the steps of the village hall. Around him the crowd of notables and well-wishers had begun to disperse. He watched the motorcade pull away from the curb and the street gradually empty; then, the Minolta still dangling from his neck, he turned and began walking briskly toward the railroad station.

"I don't know," Crawford said, shaking his head.

"What do you mean, you don't know?" the Chairman snapped.

"Just what I said."

"Did he take the picture or didn't he?"

"At the time he took it," Crawford explained, "I was behind the NBC crew and I couldn't see him clearly. He was crouching on one knee. Then the subject and his people came down the steps and passed between me and the photographer's position."

224

"So you didn't actually *see* him snap the picture."

"No, but I'd be willing to bet he did."

"Not good enough."

"The only thing is," Crawford continued, "I caught one glimpse of him as the subject passed. Somebody must have jostled him or knocked him forward. I saw him prop himself up on both hands."

"When?"

"Either just before or just after."

"Great."

"Yeah. I'm coming in now."

The Chairman hung up. Crawford stepped out of the phone booth and walked back to his car. Before getting in, he ripped off his press badge and thrust it into his pocket. As he drove back into town, he began to whistle softly and tunelessly to himself. *They'd soon find out, maybe by that very evening. And then again maybe not . . .*

Even on the station platform, waiting for the next train into Grand Central, Ben fully expected to hear the news. Somebody would hear it on a car radio and stop long enough to shout it out to passersby, who would in turn spread it to others within earshot. That was how Ben had first heard about both the Kennedys, as well as Martin Luther King. People had to share that sort of event immediately, even with strangers. The sudden death of an American president, or of any major world figure, was not to be accepted in silence; a disaster of that magnitude brought out the herding instinct in people, sent them clustering together for reassurance and warmth.

Ben kept his eye on the station parking lot where cars came and went, disgorging travelers, picking up earlier arrivals. About twenty minutes must have passed since the shooting, Ben told himself, and the deadly toxin must have done its work. Any second now, a car window would be rolled down or a door would open and some distraught messenger would shout out the news. But of what? *Of the death of kings.* Or, at the very least, the sudden, mysterious illness, the inexplicable collapse of an American chief executive on the campaign trail, ironically while in the very heart of friendly territory.

By the time forty minutes had passed and Ben had boarded the commuter train into New York, no news of any sort of catastrophe had reached him or anyone in his vicinity. Unable to sit still, he got up and began walking through the half-empty cars, expecting at some point to run into someone with an ear glued to a transistor, who would look up, stricken by the enormity of the event, to inform him of the tragedy.

In the last car Ben came upon two plump teenage girls tuned into a rock station. He paused and forced himself to smile at them. "Hi," he said. "What's happening?"

One of the girls shrugged; the other smiled back. "Nothing."

"I was wondering if you heard any news?"

"News? Like what, man?"

"Oh, I don't know. News."

"Nah," the heavier of the two answered. "Just music. You wanna sit and listen? This is the Top Forty."

"No, thanks. I was just . . . uh, killing time, you know?"

"Yeah, sure."

He turned and walked away from them. His mind was in a complete whirl and he sat down in the nearest empty seat. He was alone and he needed time to think. *Christ, I missed him. I must have missed him. But in that crush of*

people all around him, I must have hit somebody. Who?
Who's dead today instead of Richard Nixon?

His hands clenched tightly in his lap, Ben sat and stared straight ahead as the train rattled on into Manhattan. He'd failed. He knew that now, and he would have to make his peace with that reality and learn to live with it. But it was all so confusing suddenly and so unreal. He'd have to pull himself together, as if nothing had happened, go back to work and wait for another chance. Questions, wild speculations, morbid fantasies crowded in on him; unexpectedly he had a brief, horrifying vision of Kathy's naked body pinioned to her bed, her mouth open, screaming soundlessly inside a plastic sack.

Ben moaned. He shook his head and fought to master himself.

I mustn't crack now. It's too late for that. It's over and it's too late. Somehow I'm going to put all these pieces back together and I'll know the reason why. There must be an answer here, there must be. . . .

24

Cargill moved from behind his desk and put his head out the door. Almost the first person he spotted was Dick Mapes on his way back from the fast-food machines at the end of the corridor. He was balancing an open container of hot soup and seemed to be in no particular hurry. "Hey, Dick, is it in the house yet?" Cargill called.

Mapes nodded. "They just got here about twenty minutes ago and we're processing it now. We'll be ready to run the raw footage in about ten minutes."

Cargill glanced up at the wall clock. "It's nearly four-thirty, Dick. If we're going to make the six-o'clock show, we'd better get with it."

"I know, Derrick," Mapes said soothingly, "but it shouldn't be too complicated. You want to tell network we're about ready to go?"

"OK."

Mapes disappeared into the cutting room with his soup; Cargill was heading for his phone when he spotted Ben. Stryker was standing in the entrance to his cubicle, a sheaf of wire copy in his hands. "Ben?"

At first, Stryker seemed not have heard him, but eventually his gaze focused and he made an attempt to smile. "Derrick."

"You all right, Ben? You look like death warmed over."

"I'm—I'm all right, Derrick," Stryker said distantly. "I'm all right."

"What's up?"

"What?" Ben looked down at the wire copy in his hand. "Oh, this? Nothing, Derrick. Just checking out some material." He faded back into his cubicle.

Cargill looked puzzled. Returning to his desk, he picked up his telephone and dialed an extension number. "Sarah?"

"Yes, Derrick."

"You wanted to know when the local film on the Nixon motorcade came in."

"Yes, I did."

"We'll be looking at the footage in a few minutes."

"Oh, thanks. I've got to finish up something, but I'll be down. I haven't seen what the network crews brought in,

229

so it'll be doubly good to know what you've got. I appreciate it."

"All in the trade, Sarah. See you." Derrick hung up, then sat behind his desk for a few minutes, thinking hard. These last few days, something about Stryker really bothered him, and he couldn't quite put his finger on the source of his uneasiness. Over the years, Cargill had learned to trust his reporter's instincts, and he would continue to gnaw at this one until he could make the connection in his head. There had to be an answer, and all Cargill needed now was a solid clue. He found himself wondering where Ben had been earlier that day and why his nightside reporter suddenly had become so obsessed with covering presidential affairs, especially on his own time. Cargill had already checked with the various magazines Ben had mentioned; Ben had indeed been assigned stories, but always at his own request. Was Ben really trying to build a new career for himself, Cargill wondered, or were there other motives in all this literary maneuvering? Kathy Lewis had worried about it, too, and now Kathy was dead. Suddenly Cargill leafed quickly through his address book, found the number he wanted, and dialed it. "Winters, please," he said into the receiver.

"Hello? Winters here."

"Max, it's Derrick Cargill."

"Hello, Derrick, what's happening?"

"I want you to do me a favor."

"Anything I can, Derrick, you know that." The voice was gruff but good-humored, that of a professional cop who had heard everything. "What is it?"

"You remember that demonstration at the Americana last month, when Nixon was in town?"

"Sure."

230

"That boy who was killed?"

"Yeah. What about him?"

"Do you think you could get me a copy of the autopsy report?"

"I could try."

"You're a scholar and a gentleman, Max."

The rumbling male voice chuckled. "Knock it off, Cargill; I don't need your phony compliments."

"I try to be nice, Max."

After he hung up, Cargill, lost in thought again, hunched over his desk, propping his head on his hands. What was it about Ben Stryker these days that filled him with such foreboding and such quiet dread?

"Hey, look at that crazy bastard," Mapes sang out. "Isn't that Ben, right there behind Nixon?"

"You're right," Campbell said. "What the hell is he doing?"

"Beats me. Let's run that again."

Mapes rewound part of the film and ran it through the Moviola a second time. When Ben reappeared on the small screen, the editor slowed down the film, then still-framed it. There was no mistaking it. That *was* Ben Stryker up there, crouching in the front ranks of the assembled photographers. But while all the others seemed to be shooting up at the president's face, Ben's small camera was trained on the chief executive's backside. Apparently Ben had snapped a picture just as the president, attracted by someone's call, turned back toward him; then Ben had tripped forward, breaking his fall with the flats of both hands, the camera dangling uselessly from around his neck, along with his press credentials.

"What kind of a shot was that?" Mapes asked, laughing.

231

"Beats me." Campbell shook his head and opened the door of the cutting room. "Stryker!" he called.

Looking pale but controlled, Ben emerged from his cubicle and stared across the long room at the cameraman. "What is it, Jeff?"

"Come here. I want you to see this."

Ben stepped into the cutting room and shut the door behind him. Grinning, Mapes ran the film. Both he and Jeff were laughing by the time the on-screen Ben was down on his hands. "What the hell were you doing, Ben?" Mapes asked curiously.

"I didn't even see you there," Campbell put in. "What kind of mag assignment were you on? Shots of famous men's asses?"

"What were you trying to do, Ben?"

"Ben's coming out of the closet, Dick," Jeff said, feigning seriousness. "He has this irresistible penchant for presidential backsides."

"Have you spoken to your psychiatrist recently, Ben?" Mapes asked. "I mean, is this a major breakthrough or are we still facing more years of in-depth therapy?"

Ben felt paralyzed, unable to move. He was afraid that a single step in any direction might break him apart. *They actually had his assassination attempt on film! God, if they only knew, if they weren't so entranced by their own wit! Couldn't they see? Were they really so blind, so stupid?*

"Ben, is Dickie Nixon such a cheeky little fellow that you'd want to immortalize that remarkable *ass*et on film?" Mapes chortled.

"You sure this *ass*ignment was for *New York*, Ben?" Jeff chimed in. "I'll bet it was for *Men's Wear Daily*. Come on, own up, Mr. Stryker."

As if from an enormous distance, Ben heard himself

laugh. "How else *can* you take a picture of an asshole?" he said. His voice sounded remote to him, as if heard from the other end of a long tunnel, but apparently nothing in the way he sounded or looked struck Mapes or Campbell as unusual. They laughed heartily at his riposte. "Listen, you guys," Ben continued, "I'd never been in the front lines with those ghouls before, and never again. Did you see that guy knock me on my face just to get his own picture? Whew, you're in a rough racket, Jeff. I think I'll stick to the word game." As he turned to go, there was a knock on the door of the cutting room.

"Welcome one, welcome all," Mapes called cheerfully.

Sarah looked in. "Hello. I came down to see what the local's got on the Nixon motorcade."

"We're running it off now," Mapes said. "Come in."

"And you're going to love it, Sarah." Jeff grinned. "We got some really unusual footage of your fair-haired boy here."

"Sarah, I'll—" Ben began.

"Oh, don't go, Ben," Mapes said, with mock concern. "Don't you want your old boss to see you in all your reportorial glory?"

"I think not," Ben said. "I've paid my dues for today in this nuthouse."

"Honestly, Ben, what *have* you been up to?" Sarah raised a quizzical eyebrow.

He forced a grin. "They won't let you out of here until you've seen it, Sarah," he said, heading for the door. He paused and looked back. "One thing, you wiseapples. You show it to Bellucci and I'll have *your* asses." He shut the door behind him.

Sarah looked down at the amused editor who was still seated at his pale green machine, his hands over the controls, while on-screen, frozen into a ludicrously awkward position on all fours, handsome Ben Stryker stared furiously out at the whole world. "Dick, let me see what you've got," she said quietly. "Not just the comedy parts. All of it."

"It was a good hit," Crawford said. "Absolutely."

"Run it again," the Chairman said tightly. "Run it one more time."

"Sure."

The phone in the study rang and the Chairman impatiently picked up the receiver. "Yes, what is it?"

"You've been up there for a long time, dear," Louise said pleasantly. "Would you like me to send up some supper or a sandwich?"

"No, Louise. We're busy."

"I'm so sorry, dear. I was just asking."

"Louise, please don't disturb us again." He hung up.

"Look," Crawford said, still-framing the film in the Chairman's Moviola. "See that?" He pointed to the wisp of smoke just above the camera Ben was pointing toward the president. Crawford clicked off three more frames. "Now look at this."

The Chairman hunched over the machine for closer scrutiny. Crawford pointed to Nixon's left pants leg. "See that dimple in the cloth, right there?" The Chairman nodded. "That's where it went in," Crawford said. "Now look." He clicked off twelve more frames; then he froze the picture in place again. "See what he does?"

Nixon's hand had moved down to scratch his leg at the point where the dart from Ben's camera gun must have penetrated. "What did he feel?" the Chairman asked.

"A momentary prick, maybe a little sting there, that's all. The anesthetic coating on the capsule will have gone

234

into immediate action. I'm telling you it was a hit and a good one."

"Yeah, but will it work there, in the calf of the leg?" The Chairman looked up from the film. "Is there enough fatty tissue? You told me this pellet was structured for a hit in the buttocks."

"Don't worry, it'll work," Crawford said with confidence. "I've already checked it out. It'll take the same amount of time to react in the leg as anywhere else in the body. The stuff will travel through his system in exactly the same way. The capsules are coated to dissolve in body heat at precisely calculated intervals over a period of about three years."

"How accurate is that estimate? The three years, I mean?"

"As I told you, Larry, we can't pin that down to the hour or the minute or even the day. But we *can* predict it to within a week or two. The substance will begin working on his nervous system within hours, and we should begin to see some results in a matter of weeks."

"And no aftereffects?"

"Absolutely none. He'll be the same old Nixon by the time all this is over."

The Chairman nodded grimly; he rose and went to the window, pulling aside the drapes to peer down into his empty, darkened garden. "Big stakes," he said softly. "A long throw of the dice."

"There's no risk in it, Larry," Crawford said, turning off the machine.

"You have one glaring weakness, Crawford," the Chairman said, without turning around.

Crawford looked up. "What's that?"

"Like all people from the intelligence community, you think you're infallible. I know you're not. Mistakes can always happen. The shot should have penetrated a buttock, but it didn't. That was a mistake." The Chairman turned slowly and fixed his eyes on Crawford. "What guarantee can you give me that this device will work just as well in the leg? None, really. It's all sophisticated guesswork. When I make plans, I plan for mistakes, for procedures to work despite mistakes and not on the assumption that no mistakes will be made. We've already made several."

Crawford smiled indulgently. "No major ones."

"I have a feeling, Crawford, that you're holding something back from me. What is it?"

Crawford's smile faded slowly as he leaned back in his chair. "There *is* one very small hazard about the pellet dissolving in his calf. It could cause irritation which might then trigger internal blood-clotting. It'll be diagnosed as phlebitis, though. They won't find the pellet."

"What about X rays?"

"It won't show."

"How serious could this phlebitis become?"

Crawford shrugged and paused before answering. "Possibly very serious," he said at last.

The Chairman allowed the drapes to fall back into place; he returned to his chair and began drumming his fingers on the arms. After a minute or two, he looked back at Crawford, who seemed unperturbed by the implications of what he had said.

"Too late to worry about that now." The Chairman's face was granite. "You were right to tell me. Don't ever hold anything back, Crawford. I always want to know the worst."

"Yeah."

"Now, there's another matter we haven't discussed at all."

"Which is?"

"The matter of Stryker."

236

Crawford grimaced impatiently and shifted his huge bulk in the chair. "I've thought of that."

"We've got to keep him under very strict surveillance night and day," the Chairman continued. "Under no circumstances must he be allowed near Nixon again. You'll take conclusive measures if that happens. Do I make myself clear?"

"Very. But I'm ahead of you, Larry. I've got a tail on Stryker already. I've had one on him since this morning."

"And I've come to the conclusion that Ben's career will now take a dramatic step forward."

"I thought it might."

"We'll provide a ray of sunshine in his life and ease all that psychological pressure he's been under."

Crawford smiled. "I like the way you handle things, Larry. You'd have made a great spy."

"You think so? I only play for big stakes, Crawford. I don't play for the fun of playing." The Chairman reached for the telephone and quickly dialed a number. He waited through several rings before the receiver was picked up. "It's Larry," he said calmly. "Sorry to call you so late. Are you alone? Good. OK, we have what we need. Now it's up to you."

25

"You know something, Ben?"

"What?" he said sleepily.

"Last night was the first night since we've been together that you didn't have nightmares or cry out in your sleep."

He opened his eyes and looked up at her. He had never seen a more beautiful woman, he thought; the sight of her voluptuous nakedness beneath the thin silk of her night-

238

gown almost took his breath away. "I didn't?" he said huskily.

"No," she said, sitting down on the edge of the big bed. "Want some coffee?"

"Yes," he said, pushing himself up into a sitting position and smiling at her. "What time is it?"

"Nearly nine. I've got to go. Here." She handed him a cup of very hot coffee, strong and laced with just the right amount of cream and sugar. He sipped it gratefully.

"You'd have made somebody a wonderful wife," he said.

"I did. It wasn't appreciated."

He set the coffee down on the bedside table and reached for her. "Come here."

"Listen, I've got to go." She rose. "I'm late. Ben, please."

He ignored her protests and pulled her down beside him. Gently, firmly, he undid the laces of her gown and pushed it off her shoulders. He leaned over to kiss her breasts, delighting in the way her large, brown nipples stiffened even before his lips touched them.

"Ben, please . . ."

He finished undressing her and paused above her to admire the spectacle of her nudity. "You're very beautiful, Sarah."

She did not answer or protest this time. He kissed her hard and passionately; then he caressed her with consummate care and tenderness until he could feel her wetness, feel her flesh tremble in its desire to yield to him and return his passion. "Sarah, you're wonderful," he whispered.

"Take me, Ben."

"Do you like this?"

"I love it."

"And this?"

"Yes—oh, yes—"

"This?"

"Ben—oh, God, Ben—oh, God—"

She opened to him with an ecstatic abandon that thrilled him. They came together, Ben beneath her this time, penetrating her from behind, his hands over her breasts, her ribs, her belly, along the insides of her thighs, until she moaned and went taut, shuddering from the force of her orgasm. "My God," she said as she rolled away from him, "it's lucky I can't have children."

"Why?"

"Because we'd make them together every nine months, like an assembly line."

He laughed. "I love you, Sarah."

She reached out a hand to stroke his face. "It's such a big word, Ben—love."

"The biggest. I don't use it lightly. In fact, I've never used it before."

"Really?"

"Really."

She groaned. "Christ, look at the time."

"It's still early."

"Not for me, you dummy." She scrambled out of bed, dragging her nightgown after her. "Ask not for whom the bell tolls—"

"Just like a woman," Ben called out from the refuge of his pillows, "love 'em and leave 'em."

She laughed and ran into the dressing room, shutting the door behind her.

Ben lay in bed and stared through the windows at the clouds scurrying across a clear blue sky. Not for many months had he felt such peace, and now, even after all his pain, he had begun to hope again. The name, the thought of

240

Nixon, the sight of that jowly, hated face had lost the power to stir him any longer to the blind, instant hatred of before, and he knew it was Sarah's doing. Her presence in his life was slowly restoring his sanity. He could even ask himself now how he could have acted as he did. He had been in a dark place, which he was now defensively shutting out; one day he would have to face that reality. He'd have to recall everything he had done during these past weeks and months, look at it all unflinchingly, and then deal with it. That day would come, but Sarah would help him through it. He was healing inside in the love and warmth of this shared time, and together, he knew, they would exorcise and forever banish all his ghosts and demons. He would be a whole man again, stronger for all that he had been through. Sarah had done that for him and he loved her for it, and for herself.

When she emerged, twenty minutes later, sleekly dressed and made-up, the glamorous New York career woman, Ben was still in bed where she had left him. "More coffee?"

"No, thanks."

"I've got to go."

"So go, you heartless creature."

She sat down on the edge of the bed again, this time at a safe distance. "Ben, now don't do anything, but I have to tell you something."

"What, my love?"

"The Chairman has plans for you."

Ben's eyes widened. "Are you serious?"

"Very. He's been dropping hints all week. I didn't want to say anything to you until I could be sure."

"And are you?"

"I have a meeting with him today."

"Does he—does he know we're seeing each other?"

"I don't know. It's no secret, is it? But I haven't said anything about it to him. Why would I? But he knows I've been on your side. He may want to sound me out."

"You mean I'd work for you again?"

"Now, wait a minute, let's not rush things." She stood up and smoothed her skirt. "I've told you all I know. I'll call you later."

Long after Sarah had gone, Ben lay immobile in the bed, watching the sky. He had not been this happy for a very long time, since the day, so incredibly long ago, when he heard he'd gotten the Washington job.

Cargill spent most of the afternoon alone in his office behind a closed door. Those who sought him were informed that he was working on a yearly operations report, and that he was not to be disturbed except for an emergency or a major crisis over the assembling of that evening's news show. Staff members who saw him during occasional appearances noticed that he seemed more than usually preoccupied. Shortly after four o'clock, he called Jeff Campbell into his office. "Please shut the door, Jeff," he said wearily.

The cameraman slouched into a chair. "What's up, Derrick?"

Again Cargill asked whether Ben Stryker had been acting oddly of late, whether Campbell had noticed any aberrational behavior.

The query surprised Campbell; it was not the first time Cargill had put it, and now he seemed visibly agitated. In fact, Campbell realized that he'd never before seen Cargill show such tangible signs of pressure. "No, Derrick," the cameraman answered at last, "unless it's for the better."

"What do you mean?"

"I mean that he seems more normal lately."

"Normal?"

"Yeah. More relaxed. Happier about things. You know the rumor, don't you?"

Cargill shook his head.

"He and Sarah Anderson are having a thing."

"You sure?"

"They've been spotted together a couple of times."

"I see," Cargill said slowly. "Thanks, Jeff. I've got a call to make."

Sarah was surprised at the urgent tone of Cargill's request for an immediate meeting. She had just emerged from a long planning session with the Chairman and Brennan, and she'd been hoping—for a few minutes, at least—to unwind and get her notes and thoughts in order. Cargill would not be denied; he appeared in her office a few minutes after his call. His worried expression sobered her quickly and she choked off her annoyance at his insistence on seeing her. "What is it, Derrick?" she asked quietly. "You look pretty upset."

"It's about Ben."

"Oh?" She felt herself pale. "Has something happened? Is he all right?"

"I'm sorry," Cargill assured her. "Yes, he's all right. Nothing's happened to him."

"I thought an accident—"

"Nothing like that."

"Then what is it, Derrick? Has he done or said something?"

"You're going to find this hard to believe, Sarah."

"Try me, Derrick."

Cargill took a deep breath, looked into Sarah's eyes, and said, "I think Ben may be trying to harm the president."

Sarah's jaw dropped. "What? Who?—Nixon?"

Cargill nodded. "I have good reason to think so, Sarah."

"Derrick, you can't be serious! What is this, a joke or something? Whatever it is, it's in very poor taste."

"I'm not joking, Sarah."

She didn't answer; she stared at him in silent disbelief. Undeterred, Cargill, speaking urgently and with conviction, explained how he had arrived at his conclusion. "I think he's trying to get close to Nixon, close enough maybe to kill him," he concluded. "I believe he's got some sort of weapon. And I don't know whether he's acting alone or not; the weapon may have been supplied to him. Someone may be using him, taking advantage of the way he feels about Nixon. And I also think he may already have killed somebody."

"Who?"

"Remember the boy who died after being arrested during the Americana demonstration a couple of months ago?"

She nodded. She was white now, but determined to hear Cargill out.

"The kid didn't die of police brutality or anything like it. He was shot."

"That's conjecture, isn't it?"

"No, it's fact. He was shot with some kind of pellet gun. He died from the effect of a poisonous substance, a toxin of some kind. I've seen the autopsy report. He was murdered, Sarah."

"And you think *Ben* did it?"

"I think he may have."

"What else?"

"Kathy."

Sarah's eyes widened in amazement. "You think he killed her, too?" She laughed abruptly. "Derrick, you're way off base on this. Good God, Ben's not a pervert. You know we've been seeing each other, don't you?"

"Yes, I heard."

"And that's why you came to me."

"That's one reason."

"Do you really expect me to believe Ben is a maniac who murders girls and boys and now wants to kill the president of the United States? Derrick, you've gone round the bend yourself!"

"Maybe. Look, Sarah, I'll accept the fact that you know Ben as a woman who cares about him and therefore you know him better than any of us. I'll also grant you that he almost certainly didn't kill Kathy Lewis. But I can tell you that she came to me several times and she was worried as hell about him. He seemed to be two people, she told me. He had these violent, inexplicable rages, which would be followed by periods of coldness, of total alienation, if you like. She made him sound like a schizoid personality with paranoid tendencies."

"I can't believe this, Derrick."

"I'm not asking you to believe all of it." Cargill ran his hands through his hair. "I'm only asking you to consider the possibility."

"Why should I?"

"Because you may be in danger. Because people like Ben go through incredible transformations. They may seem to be one sort of person one minute and be completely different the next. How well do you know him, really?"

Her eyes met his squarely and she said with the utmost

sincerity, "I *know* him, Derrick, I know him better than you do. I've worked with him, and I know him as a man, as a friend, as a lover."

"And you think I'm the one who's nuts."

"No. I don't know what to think. I have enormous respect for you, Derrick. I know you're not an hysteric. But I can't buy this. I—I want to think about it."

"I've been considering going to the police," Cargill said tonelessly.

"Oh, my God, but you mustn't!"

"I have to, Sarah. For Ben's sake, too. If he's done what I think he has, I know it's not because he's a cold-blooded assassin or a hired killer. It's because he's disturbed, deeply disturbed, and we've got to prevent him from doing anything that would destroy his whole life, if he hasn't already. If I'm right and he did kill that boy, then he's capable of anything, and he's certainly clever enough to succeed with any scheme he's cooked up. We know he hates Nixon, and Nixon would be a logical target for Ben, assuming that Ben is psychologically out of control."

Sarah, ashen now and overpowered by Cargill's outburst, rose from behind her desk and began to pace the room. Cargill knew that she was trying to make her decision and he waited to hear it.

"Derrick," she said finally, "you've got to give us some time."

"Us, Sarah?"

"Ben and me. I love Ben, Derrick. And I think he loves me. I *can* tell you that I agree with you on one point—that Ben is a highly volatile and very disturbed man. But I can also tell you that he's coming out of it. We're good for each other, Derrick. He makes me feel like a woman again. And

246

I haven't felt that way for a very long time. I know I can help him. I want you to let me talk to him."

"What if he harms you, Sarah?"

"He won't, Derrick. You don't know that, but I do. Will you accept that much, at least?"

Cargill nodded. "But I *will* have to go to the police."

"Give me a chance to talk to him first."

"When?"

"Tonight. After work. I'll talk to him here, in my office."

"All right."

"I want at least until tomorrow, Derrick."

"Call me at home." Cargill's voice was heavy. "Either late tonight—I don't care what time—or early tomorrow. I want to hear what you have to say. I want to know what he says when you confront him."

"All right."

"But for God's sake, Sarah, don't take any chances."

"I'm not afraid of Ben," she said, with defiance in her voice. "I love him."

"I know you do." Cargill stood up to go, looking old and tired, his craggy face more heavily lined than usual, his eyes bloodshot with fatigue and anxiety.

"Derrick," she asked as he reached the door, "who else knows anything about this?"

"No one, really. I spoke to Campbell and Mapes. And once to Bellucci. They have the most contact with Ben on a daily basis. And this morning I called Brennan."

"Oh, God. What did you tell Ted?"

"I told him I was worried about Ben, that's all." He rumpled his hair again absently. "I told him I thought Ben was under too much pressure and that I was looking into it."

"Why Ted Brennan?"

"Because he's an old pal and colleague and I needed to talk to somebody, Sarah," Cargill said patiently. "I knew I'd have to come to you, even before I heard you and Ben were more than just friends. I'm sorry about this. But you understand that I will have to act on my conclusions, whatever you may tell me later?"

"Yes," she said, shaken, her voice hardly audible. "Yes, Derrick, I understand."

26

She ran the film through the Moviola several times, slowing it up at the crucial sections, then examining it carefully, frame by frame. She, too, spotted the faint puff of smoke wisping from Ben's camera, the dimpling of President Nixon's pants leg, Nixon's involuntary move to scratch himself, as if he'd been stung by an insect. For a long time, she sat alone in the network editing room; rousing herself, she unthreaded the film, returned it to its can, and quietly returned to her own office. When she was sure she had steadied herself, she called the local station and left a message for Ben to come by her office as soon as he was through for the night.

She didn't have long to wait. It had been a slow day, and Ben got his good-night from the assignment desk early. Just before midnight he knocked on her door. "Hi," he said, "what are you doing here so late?"

"Waiting for you," she answered.

"In the dark?"

"I was thinking." She switched on her desk lamp, but her face was still in shadow.

"Sarah, is anything wrong?" he asked with sudden concern.

"Please come in," she said quietly. "And close the door behind you."

"Sure." He stood with his back to the wall, his face full of concern for her.

"I think you'd better sit down," she said.

He sank into a small leather armchair opposite her and looked intently into her face. "Sarah, what's wrong? The Chairman isn't going to do anything for me, is that it?"

She shook her head. "Ben, you're on your way back to network news eventually, if Larry has anything to say about it. He's talking now about your anchoring the local news at eleven, as a beginning. A sort of test for you."

"My God, darling, that's wonderful."

"Ben, Derrick came to see me today."

"To see you? What about?"

"You." Unable to face him so cold-bloodedly, she got up and pretended to fiddle with the window drapes. "Damn, this thing is stuck," she said, tugging at the cords. "And I had them especially made for me. The sun beats in here in the morning—"

"Sarah, for God's sake . . ."

She turned to look at him; he saw the tension in her face. "I've seen the film, Ben."

"What film?"

"Of the Nixon motorcade through Westchester."

"You saw it the day it was shot, didn't you?"

"I didn't look at it that closely. I have now. I ran it in slow motion, Ben, and then I still-framed it."

Feeling suddenly as if a giant hand had closed on his insides and was slowly, inexorably twisting, twisting, Ben went white. "And . . ." he whispered.

"I know what you tried to do, Ben," she said gently. "I know."

He didn't answer her. The hand inside him was tightening the grasp; the pain was more than he could bear.

"Thank God you didn't succeed, Ben." She looked at him with compassion. "Nobody knows about this except the two of us. But if anything happens to Nixon on this campaign, or anytime at all, the FBI will study all the film available of every crowd shot and they'll catch up with you."

"I wanted to kill him," Ben heard himself say in a flat monotone, as if he'd prerecorded the statement in his head. "I hated him so much I wanted to kill him. He took away everything that meant anything to me, my whole life—"

"I know. I know how bad it's been for you. I'm not surprised, Ben."

"You're not?"

"No. And I love you, you must know that."

He began to weep then. He sat frozen in the chair and wept silently in great, wracking sobs that shook him from head to toe. She came to him and cradled him in her arms until it passed. She held his head to her breasts and stroked his hair and kissed him. Gradually, his grief wore itself out and he was able to stand, even to return her embrace. Then he broke away from her and began pacing the room. "My God, what'll we do?" he said frantically.

"Nothing, Ben," she said calmly. "There's nothing to do."

He stopped abruptly and looked at her. "But you said that Derrick—"

"He only suspects," she said. "He doesn't know anything for certain."

"But won't he tell someone else? He told you."

"I made him promise to wait." She hesitated. How much could Ben absorb at once? He was being forced to confront his own madness, in a sense; she couldn't push him too far. She put aside the other questions Cargill had raised—the boy, and Kathy.

Ben fell back into his chair. "Will he? What can we do? My God, Sarah, I can't believe I did these things. I was out of my mind, I know—"

She came around behind him and gently began massaging his shoulders, softly kissing the top of his head. "I'll speak to Derrick tomorrow," she said. "I know who and what you are, Ben, and I know you're going to be all right. I'll make Derrick understand."

"What made him come to you, Sarah?"

"He knew we'd been seeing each other; he's been worried about you for a long time. And that girl spoke to him about you."

"What girl?"

"Kathy—was that her name?"

He felt his head spin; if he'd been standing, he would surely have fallen. *Kathy? Kathy Lewis? How could I*

*have forgotten her? What happened to Kathy Lewis? She
knew, but then—then—*

"Ben, it's all right. Really. It's all right."

She kissed him and he clung to her like a drowning man. "Sarah—help me," he whispered, "please help me—"

"Ben. Ben, darling. I love you. It will be all right, Ben. Trust in me, my darling."

The stalker was hunting again. He sat in a corner of the building doorway, his head slumped on his chest as if he were asleep, but he was listening and watching the empty subway entrance. It was very late and the autumn air was crisp and chilly. Few people were out at this hour, in this weather, and in this seedy area; that suited the stalker perfectly. He needed such empty, silent streets. Motionless, hardly visible in the dim light cast by the single street-lamp halfway down the block, he waited.

He heard the rumble of the night trains beneath him, the screech of the brakes that signaled doors opening to disgorge the homeward-bound—his prey. Already, his hand had closed over the handle of the knife; he felt the icy anticipation rise inside him.

A middle-aged woman appeared at the head of the subway stairs. She had one hand in her pocket, probably around a weapon of some sort; she moved warily and alertly down the street, keeping at the edge of the sidewalk, her eyes evaluating the darkness. A practiced veteran of these streets, the stalker concluded. His eyes followed as she scuttled rapidly away from him, crossed the avenue, and disappeared into a well-lighted entrance. His excitement fell, and he resumed his vigil.

About twenty minutes later, an older man emerged from the subway entrance, alone and looking tired. His head was hunched into the collar of his overcoat; he walked unevenly, as if weighted down by the large black brief-case he carried. The stalker knew him well and knew exactly where he lived—in one of the older, remodeled brownstones along the heights overlooking New York harbor. The man had money; the stalker knew that no one lived in that part of Brooklyn who couldn't afford high rentals. That could have been the inducement compelling the stalker to move, though this old man was not the stalker's usual victim. There were other nights; the stalker's needs were varied and each had to be fulfilled.

He closed in on his victim around the corner, between two tall apartment houses that shadowed a small rubble-strewn lot. The older man had not heard the stalker creep up behind him until instinct made him turn gray with fear, swinging up the briefcase in front of him like a shield. "What do you want?"

The stalker's hand tightened on the wooden handle of the long knife thrust into his belt; he grinned at the man. "Give me the case," he whispered. "And your money."

The man reached into the inside pocket of his jacket and threw his wallet on the sidewalk. "Here," he said, backing away.

"Don't move," the stalker whispered. "Now put the case down, turn around, and walk away very slowly."

"There's nothing in the case but—"

"Do what I tell you." The stalker flashed the knife.

Staring at the long blade, the man dropped the briefcase, turned, and took two steps—and the stalker's left arm was around his neck. The knife plunged into the man's back, puncturing the aorta as it thrust and gouged between the ribs. The man tried to cry out as he fell, but his voice died to a gurgle as the stalker's blade sliced the flesh beneath his chin and a geyser of blood spurted crimson down his white shirtfront.

The stalker picked up the wallet but left the briefcase where the man had dropped it. Moving swiftly through the shadows of buildings, he found the battered Ford sedan parked down the block and drove away into the night.

Derrick Cargill, gasping his last breath of life away on the sidewalk two blocks from his home, died full of fury at his own stupidity.

The Ford sedan, bought in New Jersey two weeks before, was abandoned on West Seventy-ninth Street near the river. Afterwards, satisfied he was unobserved, the stalker walked north to Eighty-first Street, then east for two blocks, and let himself into a small basement apartment halfway down the street. Without turning on the lights, he moved across the sparsely furnished single room and into the bathroom. Shutting the door, he flicked the light switch and grinned at himself in the mirror. "Say, baby, what's happenin'?" he said aloud.

Jesus, what a lot of blood that old bastard had in him! The stalker stripped off his clothes, rolled them into a ball, and dropped them into a wicker hamper. His body was startlingly white in contrast to his darkened face and hands. From the medicine cabinet he took a large jar of cold cream, ripped off the Afro wig, and vigorously cleaned the black makeup from his face. In ten minutes, he looked back into the mirror and grinned again; then he washed the knife carefully and returned it to the rack over the kitchen sink.

Relaxed now, he sat down on the edge of the bed and

reached for the telephone on the floor. He dialed a number and waited. "Reynolds here," he said when the female voice at the other end answered. "One-one-two—"

Yes, this would be a very special night, Crawford told himself as he stretched out on the cot to wait for the girl the Service would send him. *This would be one of the more elaborate scenarios he would work out with his simulated prisoner.* Gazing at the knife on the wall, he felt himself harden in anticipation of pleasure to come.

27

On election evening, the Hoenigs gave a large dinner party for thirty couples, representatives of the power structure in the arts and the communications media. The drinks were strong and plentiful, the food exquisite, and the conversation of a consistently high level of wit and sophistication. Louise Hoenig looked radiant; lavish dinners of this kind, to which only the most powerful figures in the arts, business, and politics came, were her special forte. Her parties were always the talk of gossip columns from coast to coast; people fought for invitations—not an easy task since Louise always checked her guest lists with her husband and both were known to be ruthless about eliminating arrivistes. To be invited to the Hoenigs on any major occasion was equivalent to being officially authenticated as an established force in one's chosen arena.

After dinner, the guests filled the huge downstairs living room, where servants dispensed coffee and liqueurs. Nationwide election returns were flashed on the two large television screens installed for the night at either end of the long room. From his chair near the fireplace, quietly dominating the proceedings by the force of his personality, the Chairman foresaw, from the very first figures, an electoral landslide of major proportions. Only one or two states had an outside chance of stopping the Nixon steamroller.

It was not quite midnight when the Chairman rose, made excuses, smiling and chatting, and took the elevator up to his den. He shut the door carefully behind him and dialed the outside line. Crawford answered on the second ring. "Been watching your screen?" the Chairman asked.

"What else would I have to do tonight?"

"Don't be facetious, Crawford. Then you know it's a Nixon-Agnew landslide."

"It looks that way. That's no surprise, is it?"

"No. I had hoped it wouldn't be quite so devastating."

"Wishful thinking."

"Apparently. They'll be sure to go after us immediately with this sizeable a mandate."

"It's a phony, you know."

"What do you mean?"

"Half the country isn't voting. A lot of people stayed home rather than vote for either of those clowns."

"Half the country doesn't count, Crawford. It never has. Nixon will see this election as a complete confirmation of his administration. He's likely to stop at nothing now."

"I agree."

"How long do you think we'll have to wait before we see any tangible evidence of our experiment?"

"Some weeks, maybe, but very soon. It's a cumulative process that affects the whole nervous system. You know that."

"We must have our alternative ready, in case it fails."

"It won't fail, Larry."

"Now, about the Agnew matter—"

"We have him nailed to a cross. We have a complete dossier, with enough evidence to leave him hanging forever."

"Let's not be extreme, Crawford. This nailing and hanging are metaphors you're employing primarily to impress me. Don't bother."

Crawford chuckled. "A little Nixon phraseology I threw in there."

"When do you propose to act?"

"I'm primed to move right now. All you have to do is push the button."

The Chairman thought for a few seconds. "These investigations always take time and there will be some obstructionism," he mused. "After all, we're trying to get the vice president of the United States indicted. My guess, though, is that Nixon will want to unload him immediately, the minute it becomes clear they have the goods on him. Loyalty is not Nixon's long suit."

"We've got too much on Agnew for anyone to ignore," Crawford said firmly. "And we could always make an end run around the authorities to the press."

"I'd rather not have to do that, as I told you. I don't want that sort of distraction. We're saving the press for the Watergate affair."

"I mentioned it as an alternative, that's all."

"I understand." The Chairman sighed. "Those two *Post* reporters—"

"They're not quite as bright as I thought they were and as *they* think they are," Crawford enlarged. "I keep having to pick them up and repoint them in the right direction. It's tiring. But that's coming along, too. They especially enjoy the conspiratorial aspects. They think they're onto a single inside informer." Crawford chuckled again. "I don't disillusion them."

The Chairman's fingers began to drum on the edge of his desk. "I have to rejoin my guests. Look, I think it's time to move on Agnew. Feed all the information to Justice and keep on top of it. I want regular reports, as usual."

"Sure thing. I'll get on it in the morning."

"Oh, you can wait till everyone stops celebrating."

The Chairman hung up and sat without moving for a few minutes, exploring all the possibilities and ramifications over and over in his mind. Could anything go wrong now? Had he prepared for every eventuality? Was the timing too delicate to succeed? Could he count this heavily on Crawford and his team? Had he, for once, overreached himself, by going after the elected officials of his own nation? For the first time in his long and successful career, the Chairman was experiencing serious doubts and anxieties. It was another half hour before he rejoined his guests, most of whom, by the time he reentered the festive room, were toasting—genuinely or cynically—the Republican victory.

There would be four more years of freedom and license for the corporate magnates of America and their political creatures to do with the country whatever they willed. Only the television networks, with their awesome power to mold and influence public opinion, now stood between the Nixon gang and the continued viability of the nation's most cherished democratic institutions and traditions. How ironic, the Chairman thought, as he watched his distinguished guests enjoy themselves in his living room, how truly ironic that the preservation of what everyone liked to think of as the American way of life depended now on the success of an operation that was every bit as illegal, as thuggish, as the most devious machinations of Nixon's own administration.

The Chairman had never pictured himself as a hero, nor as anything more dramatic, really, than a successful businessman building himself an empire in the highest traditions of free enterprise. Whatever he did now, everything he had already done, arose from one basic need—self-preservation. Would history, if it ever uncovered the facts, regard him as a savior? The Chairman did not know nor, fundamentally, did he care. That sort of thinking was merely idle speculation. What counted most, as always, were the realities, as they applied to the maintenance and increase of his power.

It was after 3:00 A.M. on election night when Ben finally got back to his apartment. The place seemed emptier and colder than usual. From his office, he'd tried repeatedly to get through to Washington, to Sarah, without success. He'd been busy himself, covering local citywide reactions to Nixon's sweeping triumph at the polls. Ben had wanted merely to hear the comforting sound of Sarah's voice; he had come to rely on it heavily, and tonight his nerves were drawn unbearably tight.

The whole staff was still deeply shocked at Cargill's death, and the atmosphere at the station had become all but intolerable. Even Bellucci was quiet these days. Ben had fled with relief from this oppressive miasma into the city streets, welcoming the temporary oblivion of work. He had kept his crew out long after there was anything left to film and report, until Jeff, in exasperation, had finally turned on him and said they were going in, with or without him. "We got enough on film to make a documentary, for Christ's sake!" the cameraman had shouted. "What the fuck are we doing, Ben? How many interviews with disgruntled citizens who hate Nixon do you think we can get on the air? This new guy Hartwick's too dumb to know what he's doing, but Derrick would have had your ass." Ben had to give up and follow his crew back into the station.

He sat down in the darkness now and switched on his TV set. The beaming face of Richard Nixon, both arms aloft in triumph, loomed into view. Ben began to tremble. The night closed in around him. He could not will himself out of his chair to banish, by the twist of a dial, the triumphant features of the man he hated. Tears flowed freely down his face.

Why did he sometimes hear Kathy's voice now, calling to him longingly, as if from a tremendous distance? He opened his eyes. The room was still cold and empty, but a pale gray predawn light threw objects and pieces of furniture into clear relief. The TV was still on, but the screen displayed the abstract design of the WACN station test pattern. He looked at his watch. It was not quite five o'clock. Had Kathy called him? No, the phone was ringing now. He got up and stumbled into the bedroom.

"Hello?"

"Ben, it's Sarah."

"Oh. Sarah. Yes."

"Ben, are you asleep?"

"I guess—I guess I was."

"Are you OK? You sound so strange."

"I'm all right."

"I wanted to hear your voice."

"Where are you?"

"In Washington, at the bureau. We just wrapped up. I'm going back to the hotel now. I'm absolutely wiped out. I'll be home tonight. Ben, are you sure you're all right? Have you been having the nightmares again?"

"Yeah. But I'm fine now. I need you, Sarah. Please come home."

"I will. You heard the final results?"

"No."

"Nixon carried every state but Massachusetts."

"God—"

"Ben, don't think about it. It has nothing to do with you now. Hang on to that and trust me. We're going to be fine. I love you, Ben."

After she hung up, he thought he heard Kathy's voice again. Why Kathy? He wandered around the bedroom and stood, puzzled, in the doorway. The room was empty, the bed still made. He went over to his bureau and stared at the closed drawers. There was something he had to re-move, to get rid of, but what was it?

Yes, he remembered now. Slowly, he opened the top drawer and looked inside. It was empty. He had left his camera in there, but now it was gone. Had he given it to someone? Why couldn't he remember that? Had Sarah asked him for it? Maybe she had. He tried hard to think back now, but he couldn't.

"Ben? Ben, darling, is that you? Come in . . ."

He looked around, but the room was still empty. That had sounded like Kathy again. Or was it his mother's voice he was hearing, calling to him? Perhaps it was time he went home to do his homework, or to eat. What time was it, anyway? What time—time—time—

He began to tremble again. He lay down on his bed, pulled the blankets up over his head, and tried to sleep. He fell into an exhausted doze. When he awakened, it was well after ten and he was soaking wet. A pale sunlight filtered into the room. He sat up. *God, what a night! But Sarah's coming home today. Hang on to that, Ben Stryker, hang on to that and shut the voices of the night out of your mind—*

28

It was very hot in Washington on the morning of Friday, July 13, 1973, when Alexander Butterfield appeared in Room G-334 in the new Senate Office Building to be questioned by the Watergate Committee staff. Butterfield, pleasant and clean-cut, made a favorable impression on most of those present. A former Air Force colonel who had resigned his commission to work for H. R. Haldeman, he had enjoyed his stint in the White House as a deputy assistant to the president, and he was perfectly willing to tell what he knew. At first, that didn't seem to be significant. When asked whether he had any reason to believe that Nixon himself might have been involved in efforts to keep the facts from the public, Butterfield explained that at the time he was "phasing out" of his job and getting ready to go to work for the Federal Aviation Administration. "I can't document anything or prove anything," he said. "I don't remember Watergate being anything."

When Butterfield was handed a typed transcript containing Nixon's version of several conversations the president had had with John Dean, the ex-colonel seemed puzzled. He commented a number of times on the substantial detail of these accounts of conversations. He was particularly struck by a record of a meeting held on March 21, 1973, in which Dean had told Nixon that Howard Hunt apparently was trying to blackmail John Ehrlichman. Butterfield observed that one of the sentences in the transcript contained an actual quote. Nixon had asked Dean how any sum of money could possibly be paid to Hunt. "What makes you think he would be satisfied with that?" the president had said.

"Where did you get this?" Butterfield asked his interrogators. It had been provided to the committee, he was told, by J. Fred Buzhardt, special White House counsel on Watergate. Could the direct quote have come from someone's notes of the meeting? "No, it seems too detailed," Butterfield answered.

"Was the president's recollection of meetings good?"

"Yes, when I came I was impressed," Butterfield replied. "He is a great and fast learner. He does recall things very well. He tends to overexplain things."

"Was he as precise as the summary?"

"Well, no, but he would sometimes dictate his thoughts after a meeting."

"How often did he do so?"

"Very rarely."

"Were his memos this detailed?"

"I don't think so."

"Where else could this have come from?"

Butterfield paused before answering. He inspected the transcript closely as minutes went by. "I don't know. Well, let me think about that a while," he said at last, pushing the papers away from him toward the center of the table.

The little gray man in the gray raincoat was very nervous. He had been waiting in his car in the basement garage of the huge apartment complex for nearly an hour, and he had begun to wonder whether anything had gone wrong. He was about to drive away to locate a pay phone when a blue Chevrolet sedan wheeled down a ramp from the street side, easing into the vacant space beside him. Crawford got out, opened the door on the passenger side of the man's car, and slid onto the seat beside him. "I was about to call," the man said. "I thought something had happened."

"The plane was late," Crawford said easily. "I told you to wait and not to move from here."

"I was getting worried."

"What about?"

The little man glanced nervously around the subterranean, dimly lit cavern. "I don't know why we always have to meet here. This place gives me the creeps."

Crawford smiled. "It's one of our better information posts. We feed the *Post* reporters regularly down here. I thought you'd like to see it."

"Thanks, but no thanks. I could use a drink."

"OK, Brooks." Crawford became brisk. "Let's get to it. Do you have any word on today's hearing?"

"Nothing specific. I'm not sure Butterfield knows."

"He knows about the taping system."

"Sure, if they ask him about it."

"They will. The Chairman gave the word on that procedure last week. We want that information out now. The timing is right."

Brooks Alexander nodded thoughtfully. "Then I imagine we'll find out in a couple of days when the hearings go public."

"If anything breaks before then, get on the phone. Nothing must go wrong. This operation is timed like a precision watch. What about inside the White House? What have you got for me?"

"Nothing too unusual yet," the little man said. "Nixon's basic character is what it is, but there's some evidence that he's cracking."

"Details, please."

"Well, everything seems accentuated now." Alexander became expansive. "The paranoia, his capacity for hatred, his obsession with revenge—they're all stronger now. That and his fear that everyone's out to get him. His strongest allies have been peeled away from him. He really began to go downhill after Haldeman and Ehrlichman left. He talks to himself a lot now. And to the machines. You get the impression he'd rather talk to his microphones than to anyone around him. A lot of people have noticed that, including his son-in-law."

"Cox?"

"Yeah. According to Cox, Nixon's up and down. He's having trouble sleeping. He calls people at all hours of the night. He's drinking a lot. He comes back from meetings and he's not making sense—there's a lot of irrational babbling. I even heard a rumor that he walks the corridors at night, talking to the pictures."

"Just any pictures?"

"The ones of former presidents. He makes speeches to them, talks to them as if he expected them to answer him."

"What else?"

"Well, he's still spouting all that stuff about the Jewish cabal being out to get him, and he raves about the so-called fucking academics and goddam Ivy Leaguers. But he says vile things about everybody, now. He's even turned on Ziegler a couple of times, and there are occasions when nobody can get near him. I hear the family is pretty worried."

"Sounds good."

"And, of course, he's obsessed with Watergate. He can't get it out of his mind. He keeps shouting that we've got to put it behind us and get on with the business of running the country, but it's all bravado, as if he's got some kind of monster sitting on his shoulder and whispering into his ear all the time. It's weird. People who talk to him have the feeling he's not listening, that he's hearing some other voice instead. And, naturally, nothing gets done. The man can't seem to make a decision about anything."

"That's good. What about his health?"

"I just told you."

"His physical health, Brooks."

"That seems OK. Nothing out of the ordinary, except fatigue. I don't think he sleeps much."

"All this sounds very good," Crawford said. "It's working. The only thing we have to worry about now is his physical health. I want you to keep on top of that. Report to me at the first sign of trouble. Colds, fatigue, a cough— anything. If he gets too tired or rundown, it could lower his resistance and trigger an attack of the kind we *don't* want."

"You think there's a real danger?"

"I do."

"Does the Chairman know?"

"He does." Crawford shifted in his seat and reached out for the door handle. "I've got to catch the last shuttle back to New York."

"Listen, Crawford," the little man said urgently, "is it true what I hear?"

Crawford turned and fixed Alexander with a hard, impassive stare. "What do you hear, Brooks?"

"You know, about Stryker and the Anderson woman . . ."

"But what do you hear?"

"That there's some trouble—"

"No trouble."

"But if he talks—"

"No trouble." Crawford was emphatic. "I guarantee it, Brooks. They're as happy as two teenage kids in love for the first time. We have the whole thing monitored and under complete control. And let me tell you something else."

"Yes?"

"I don't like rumors. I don't like the feeling there's talk going around, because I know who it comes from and I have a pretty good idea what it's really about. You tell your sources to clam up. And you, too, Brooks. I value you very highly, you know."

The little man went white and withdrew as far as he could toward the window. Crawford grinned, reached over, and patted his knee; then he opened the door of the car and got out. "Keep the faith, baby," he said and drove quickly up the exit ramp toward the airport.

Alexander waited ten minutes before turning on the ignition. He noticed that his hands were shaking.

During the afternoon of the 13th, Alexander Butterfield, in reply to a question from Don Sanders, deputy counsel to the Republican minority of the Watergate Committee, revealed the existence of a taping system within the White House. "No, Dean didn't know about it," Butterfield said. "But that is where this must have come from. There is a tape machine in each of the president's offices. It is kept by the Secret Service, and only four other men know about it. Dean had no way of knowing about it. He was just guessing."

It took Butterfield about forty-five minutes to explain to the committee exactly how the taping system worked. His testimony did not become public knowledge until the following Monday, when he repeated it before television cameras in an open session. "I believe, of course, that the president is innocent of any crime or wrongdoing," he concluded, "that he is innocent likewise of any complicity."

Many on the White House staff who watched Butterfield's testimony could not believe that this revelation had not been carefully orchestrated. When Leonard Garment, a counsel to the president, discovered the existence of the taping system and how Nixon used it, he expressed the opinion that to record the evidence and then to preserve the tapes was an act of transcendental lunacy.

29

Ben switched off the television set just as Sarah, holding two chilled glasses, reappeared from the kitchen. "I don't understand," he said. "What are we celebrating?"

"I'll tell you, all in good time," she answered, smiling. "Come on out. The champagne's in the bucket and the only thing you have to do is open it. That's your department."

"Sure thing." Ben got out of bed and into his bathrobe and sandals. In the living room, Sarah, beautiful as ever in her nightgown, was waiting for him. "Mystery woman," Ben teased and smilingly began to ease the cork up out of the neck of the bottle.

"Don't you know what day this is?" Sarah asked.

"June twenty-first, 1974," Ben intoned, as if beginning one of his nightly broadcasts as the eleven-o'clock anchorman, "and of what significance is that, pray?"

"Why, it's Mr. and Mrs. Richard Nixon's thirty-fourth wedding anniversary," Sarah said.

"And that's what we're celebrating?" Ben asked, astonished. Before she could answer, the cork popped and wine rose over his hands. "Hey, come over here!"

Quickly she thrust the empty glasses under the foaming champagne, then waited for him to return the bottle to the ice bucket before handing him his glass. "Drink up," she said.

Ben took a long swallow. "Fuck you, Richard Nixon," he said, raising his glass.

"And poor Pat."

Ben laughed. "Well, somebody should."

They drank in silence. Ben sat down on his sofa and looked around. "I'm going to move out of here," he said. "This place depresses me. Why did you want to come here, anyway? I practically live at your place. Why don't we move in together? Better still, why don't you marry me?"

"Easy, darling, easy," she said and sat down opposite him in the smaller of his two armchairs. "One thing at a time. I can't marry you until I get a divorce, and I'm not sure I want one or that Farwell will give me one. We had an agreement. And, anyway, I'm too old to have children. Why should we get married?"

"Well, we just about live together, as it is."

"How old-fashioned you are, Ben Stryker."

"I'm just a barefoot country boy, basically," Ben said. "The old virtues and the old ways appeal to me. Why did you want to come here tonight? Answer me that. Your bed is bigger than mine."

"We did all right, didn't we?"

Ben shut his eyes, enjoying a vision of Sarah's naked body beneath his own. He opened his eyes and smiled at her with love. "Yes, we did all right. Now—"

"All in good time. More champagne?"

"Why not?"

She refilled their glasses and sank back into her chair. "What did you make of the news tonight?" she asked softly.

"Well, I do think Bill James is a little boring—"

"Not that, silly. The item about the president."

"About his phlebitis?"

She nodded.

Ben put his glass down and rubbed a hand over his mouth. "I don't know what to make of it, quite," he said. "I feel a little guilt about it, I suppose."

"Why?"

"Because it could have had something to do with my shooting him. I'm pretty sure I hit him, you know."

"You did. And it's the same leg."

"Thank God it's only a mild attack."

"It wasn't."

"What wasn't?"

"Mild," Sarah said quietly. "It was a very serious attack."

"How do you know?"

"We got news of it ten days ago, but we were asked to sit on the information."

"You were? By whom?"

"It came right from the top."

"The Chairman?"

"Yes."

"Exactly how serious was it?"

She told him. On the morning of June 10th, on his way to Cairo, on the second day of a trip that was to take him a total of 15,000 miles on a five-nation visit, Nixon had been examined by his personal physician, Walter Tkach. The president's left leg was badly inflamed and swollen. A blood clot had formed—phlebitis. Tkach had been alarmed; the clot could, conceivably, break loose and be carried to the heart or the lungs, where it could prove fatal. He had advised the president to give up his trip and return home.

"Nixon refused?" Ben asked.

"Apparently," Sarah said. "He thought the trip was too important to be abandoned. Of course, it was designed to divert attention from the Watergate investigations and the moves to remove him from office. We were told that he referred to his decision to go on with the trip as a calculated risk."

"Who else knew about it?"

"Most of the aides on the flight, but Nixon gave orders it was to be kept absolutely secret."

"I gather he's out of danger now."

"Not really. We hear that Tkach is frantic. He's supposed to have told one of the Secret Service men that it's useless to try and protect a president who wants to kill himself."

Ben was shaken. He gripped his knees and hunched forward on the couch. "You know, I still don't understand why my shot didn't kill him. I'm glad now it didn't, but it should have."

"You look ill, Ben," Sarah said. "Why don't you stretch out? I'll get you an icepack. Is it one of your headaches?"

"No," Ben said slowly, "I—I feel a little sick . . ."

"Don't, darling," she said, "it's all over. Lie down now."

275

He stretched out on the sofa, his head against the arm. The overhead light in the room seemed very bright, for some reason, and he asked Sarah to turn it off. In the semi-darkness, she put a cool hand on his brow. "You don't have a fever," she said.

"I'll be all right," he whispered.

She sat down again in her chair, watching him. "The reason you didn't kill him, Ben, was that the lethal pellet was removed from your camera and replaced by another one. You shot Nixon with a very complicated and sophisticated little capsule containing a compound periodically discharging a mind-bending drug into Nixon's system. The drug is one of the many derivatives and variations of PCP, better known on the streets as Angel Dust. This particular version runs for a three-year cycle. It temporarily breaks down the nervous system and feeds whatever weaknesses the psyche may already have. Nixon was a perfect subject, you see. The drug is feeding his basic paranoia and has all but destroyed his ability to reason and to make rational decisions."

Ben lay on the sofa with one arm over his eyes, breathing in short, shallow gasps.

"Ben? Are you listening?" Sarah asked softly.

"Yes," he managed.

"You were supposed to shoot Nixon in the buttocks, where the fatty tissue could absorb the capsule better. By hitting him in the calf of the leg, you risked detection, also the sort of irritation that causes phlebitis. That annoyed the Chairman."

With a moan, Ben struggled into a sitting position, but he was overcome by nausea and leaned forward, his head on his hands. He could feel the sweat running down his back and trickling down his ribs from under his arms. He moaned again.

"I know all this, Ben," Sarah continued calmly, "because it was I who replaced the original pellet with the one you actually used on Nixon. The other times you fired the camera gun, of course, you were using the poison in its original specifications. You did a good job, you know."

Speechless, too stunned to articulate his thoughts, Ben looked up at Sarah over his folded hands.

She smiled at him and got up, moving easily around the room as she continued to speak. "We had to do it, Ben," she explained, touching the backs of chairs, rearranging her hair, caressing small objects in her path as she drifted casually. He followed her with his eyes, fighting off a recurring desire to vomit. "My only regret is that you had to be the instrument."

"Why—" he gasped, unable to go on.

Sarah paused and smiled at him. "Why?" she echoed. "Why? What else was the Chairman to do? Even with the Watergate revelations and all of Nixon's other misdeeds, he couldn't expect impeachment to follow. In fact, history and Nixon's extraordinary instincts for political survival argued strongly against impeachment. So the Chairman reasoned that he had to find a way to aid the process by driving Nixon into a sort of temporary insanity. He had the means and the apparatus to do it. You see, it isn't Watergate that's going to do Nixon in; it's his increasingly irrational responses to the problems he faces. His behavior has been growing more and more bizarre every day. Almost everyone around him has noticed it, even members of his own family. The Chairman had to kill Nixon's plans to destroy the networks, and this was the only way to do it. An assassination wouldn't have worked, and it could have wrecked the entire political system that all big corporations have learned to exploit so skillfully. The Chairman doesn't want to destroy the system, Ben, only the man at the head of it today. Nixon, like Agnew, has to be driven from office and disgraced."

Ben staggered to his feet and lurched out of the room. He barely made it to the kitchen, where he put his head down over the sink and heaved until his ribs ached. Gasping, his face drenched in sweat, he grabbed a towel, jammed it against his lips, and returned to the living room, where Sarah sat calmly waiting for him. She had turned on another table lamp and retrieved her handbag, in which she was rummaging about, as if searching for something. She looked up and smiled at him as he stood in the doorway. "Feeling better, darling?"

"Why—me?" he said with difficulty.

"The Chairman had a psychological profile done on you, Ben," she said, "as he has for everyone who works for him. Unfortunately, you turned out to be the perfect instrument. You see, if you'd been caught, Ben, you'd have been caught acting alone. Nothing in any of your irrational actions could have been traced back to the Chairman or any of his operatives."

"Like—you."

She sighed. "Yes, like me. Sit down, Ben. You really do look awful."

He sank into the other chair, dry-heaved again, and struggled to speak. Sarah dabbed lightly at her lips with a tissue, then put it back into her open bag beside her. "Take your time, darling," she said. "I know this is very hard for you and I'm sorry I had to tell you."

Ben's mind was reeling. He was overwhelmed by this incredible revelation of the way he had been manipulated and then rewarded for a far more sinister act than he had ever imagined. The most crushing blow had been the disclosure that Sarah herself, his one pillar of hope and salvation, had been deeply implicated in the entire plot. His defenses were crumbling; he struggled now to keep some shred of his sanity intact. She seemed so cool, so unfeeling, so collected about what she had just told him. When at last he thought he had some control over himself, he forced himself to look into her eyes. "Sarah," he heard himself say, as if from an enormous distance, "Sarah, why did you? Did I—did I have to know?"

She sighed. "Oh, Ben, my poor darling, we didn't want to tell you. I pleaded with the Chairman not to. But you left us no choice."

"I—left you—no choice?" he managed to say.

"No," she said, shaking her beautiful head sadly. "Your dreams, Ben. They haven't stopped, have they?"

He couldn't answer; he stared at her.

"You talk when you have your dreams, Ben. I hear you at all hours of the night. We're afraid you won't be able to shut them out forever."

"What—"

"The boy you shot, Ben. And then, of course, there's the girl."

"Girl?"

"Kathy—wasn't that her name? Don't you remember, Ben?"

It began as another moan, from deep inside him, but this time it became a scream. He clutched his head with both hands and rocked back and forth in his chair, holding himself rigid as if to keep from breaking apart. He saw Kathy's face now. He heard her voice again: "Ben? Ben, darling, is that you?" He moved through her apartment as he had that day, heard her glad cry, felt the weight of her in his arms again—

He tried to get up now, but he couldn't. Pressing his hands to his head, he began to sob. He saw Kathy now as he had seen her last, at the height of his frenzy, struggling to free herself from his grasp, her mouth open, her eyes staring in terror as she struggled for life, gasping for air inside the plastic sack he had tied around her neck. *Oh, God—*

Sarah sat quietly across from him now, watching him with pity in her eyes. She reached into her bag and softly spoke his name. Her voice cut through the madness he fought with his last remaining strength to control. Like a man drowning in quicksand, he stared up at her.

She sat directly opposite him with the Minolta trained on his neck, the cap nut removed from the tiny gun barrel that pointed just below the line of his gaping jaw. "Wha—"

"Smile, Ben."